Purchased from
Multnomah County Library
Title Wave Used Bookstore
216 NE Knott St, Portland, OR
503-988-5021

THE CHILD GARDEN

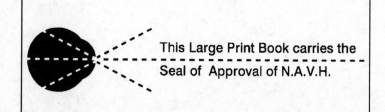

This Large Print Book carries the
Seal of Approval of N.A.V.H.

THE CHILD GARDEN

CATRIONA MCPHERSON

THORNDIKE PRESS
A part of Gale, Cengage Learning

GALE
CENGAGE Learning

Farmington Hills, Mich • San Francisco • New York • Waterville, Maine
Meriden, Conn • Mason, Ohio • Chicago

GALE
CENGAGE Learning®

Copyright © 2015 by Catriona McPherson.
Thorndike Press, a part of Gale, Cengage Learning.

ALL RIGHTS RESERVED
This is a work of fiction. Names, characters, places, and incidents are either the product of the author's imagination or are used fictitiously, and any resemblance to actual persons, living or dead, business establishments, events, or locales is entirely coincidental.
Thorndike Press® Large Print Mystery.
The text of this Large Print edition is unabridged.
Other aspects of the book may vary from the original edition.
Set in 16 pt. Plantin.

LIBRARY OF CONGRESS CATALOGING-IN-PUBLICATION DATA

Names: McPherson, Catriona, 1965–
Title: The child garden / by Catriona McPherson.
Description: Large print edition. | Waterville, Maine : Thorndike Press, 2016. | ©2015 | Series: Thorndike Press large print mystery
Identifiers: LCCN 2015037226 | ISBN 9781410484253 (hardcover) | ISBN 1410484254 (hardcover)
Subjects: LCSH: Alternative schools—Fiction. | Suicide—Fiction. | Large type books.
Classification: LCC PR6113.C586 C48 2016 | DDC 823/.92—dc23
LC record available at http://lccn.loc.gov/2015037226

Published in 2016 by arrangement with Midnight Ink, an imprint of Llewellyn Publications, Woodbury, MN 55125-2989 USA

Printed in Mexico
1 2 3 4 5 6 7 20 19 18 17 16

For Jessie Lourey and Jessie Chandler,
with love and thanks.

Children, you are very little,
And your bones are very brittle;
If you would grow great and stately,
You must try to walk sedately.

You must still be bright and quiet,
And content with simple diet;
And remain through all bewilderin',
Innocent and honest children.

Happy hearts and happy faces,
Happy play in grassy places;
That was how in ancient ages,
Children grew to kings and sages.

"Good and Bad Children,"
A Child's Garden of Verses
— Robert Louis Stevenson —

PROLOGUE

1985

It was far from silent in the dark wood. There were mice, rats too maybe, scuffling in the undergrowth, and the heavier tread of a hedgehog as it moved along the line of trees and later made its way back again. An owl's wings beat softly, rustling the leaves in the canopy, and just once a fox barked, setting all the nesting birds peeping their alarm.

Underneath these living sounds, the river glugged and churned, sucking at stuck logs and nudging at pebbles. Further downstream the waterfall fizzed over the rocks at the edge of the drop and crashed into the pool below.

So it can't have been quiet enough to hear all those sounds when the end came. It was imagination filling them in, nothing more. No one could have picked out a soft creak, a sigh, the sound of cloth rubbing on cloth as his arms and legs clutched at nothing while he pin-wheeled down. Even the splash as he entered the water was a quiet one. It could have been a rock dislodged or a piece of the bank collapsing.

Afterwards, the noises of the wood at night must have carried on — nothing to frighten the birds, nothing to stop the rats in their endless scurrying. Now it was only fear making the silence grow until it boomed. Now it was the very act of listening that blotted away all the sound. Now the clamourous thoughts themselves hushed every other thing besides them.

Those same thoughts were still racing around chasing their tails when the car engine started, roaring like a fairy tale monster, bringing real life and all the trouble in the world back into focus with a *snap!*

Time to think fast and get it right. Time to make sure only one life ended here tonight. He was gone — no getting him back again, no point going with him.

ONE

I've never thought my life was a tragedy. Not mine, not Nicky's, certainly not Miss Drumm's. I know other people don't agree. I can tell what they think from the looks on their faces when they think it, with their heads tilted and their mouths dimpled in at the corners. But as far as I'm concerned, I'm lucky. I've got the best kind of job — important yet easy — and a son who lets me hug him and a good friend. I wish I didn't have to shave her neck, but it's a small price to pay. I've got a beautiful house and an ancient monument to tend to. How many people get that?

But when the knock came on the door that night and turned my life into an adventure, I wasn't sorry. And if I'd known what was coming, I'd still have answered. If I'd had a crystal ball and seen the whole of my

11

future sitting there inside it, sharp and tiny, I wouldn't change a thing.

Work had been fine, two new bookings for offsite and no distress calls. Things went okay at the home too. Miss Drumm let me read the Margaret Atwood to her without arguing about whether it could really happen. She didn't ask about Walter Scott, hardly mentioned the election at all, and didn't make me go and complain to the nurses about the plug-in air fresheners, or ask me to tell them again about using a waxed jam-pot cover to stop the cocoa getting a skin on top when they came round with the supper trolley.

Quite a good visit. I like the home at that time of year, when it's dark outside and the lamps are lit, the fire crackling. It feels like a nest; warm and dry with good things on the telly. Later in the winter when the windows have been shut for months and no one's been out and someone's died — because somewhere around January time, someone always dies — it starts to feel more like what it is.

"A warehouse for damaged goods," Miss Drumm would say when she was in one of her black moods. "No good for Oxfam, no takers on eBay."

"I've a good mind to list you," I'd tell her. "See if you're right."

Sometimes she'd just glare at me out of her blind eyes, but sometimes she'd bark that laugh of hers. One time she asked me what I would say.

" 'Old lady. Good conversationalist but somewhat grumpy. No reserve.' "

That night, though, she was docile. When I got to the end of the second chapter, she waved a hand at me, telling me to stop.

"Are you rocking the stone?" she said.

"Every day."

"Twelve times?"

"You really don't have to ask every night, you know."

"If you're not rocking the stone, you'd be better off not living there at all," she told me.

"What about Walter?"

She nodded, her lip trembling, then she told me to ring for the nurse and be on my way.

It was Iveta who came to answer the call bell; I passed her in the passageway.

"What's the weather like, Glo?" she said, tipping her head towards Miss Drumm's door.

"Light cloud with a chance of politics," I said.

Iveta shook her head, laughing. "She's the only one in here who still votes," she said. "And she nags all the staff to vote. If they get in again, I don't know if it'll keep her alive out of pure rage or finish her off completely."

I tried to smile but Iveta must have seen the look that flashed over my face, because she put out a hand and shook my arm, her glittery-tipped acrylics flashing in the lamplight.

"She'll outlive us all," she said. "Now get along there and see that angel boy."

Nicky was in good form too. Carole had been in during the day to cut his hair, using a picture he and I had found in a music magazine. The new look suited him. He could have been in a boy band, could have had girls screaming every time he flicked the long front piece out of his eyes.

"Heartbreaker," I told him. "That's what your granny used to call you when you were a baby. Those big eyes and the lashes that could knock you over. 'You're going to break some hearts, Nicholas,' she used to say." He didn't answer. "Just the one so far, eh?"

I traced the line of dark hair on his lip, making him twitch. He'd be shaving soon.

14

"Right," I said. "Where were we up to? 'My Bed Is A Boat'. 'My bed is like a little boat, Nurse helps me in when I embark'." Then I broke off. "Nicky?" I said. "You would tell me if you were sick of this book, wouldn't you?"

But he was fine with it, so I carried on.

" 'She girds me in my sailor's coat and starts me in the dark'."

It's always been one of my favourites, that little boy in the boat-bed, steering across the darkness with his eyes closed until morning comes again. He's as safe and cosy as Nicky and Miss Drumm and all the other residents, tucked up with the curtains drawn and the doors locked, while the wind whips around the house and howls across the hills.

At eight o'clock, I pulled my anorak hood down close around my head with the toggles — no use even thinking of an umbrella that night — and scuttled across the gravel to my car.

It's a single-track road to my place from the home, twisting for ten miles between nowhere and nowhere else, cattle grids every hundred yards, and unless the care workers are changing shift, you never meet a soul. I started to unwind on the way.

Tonight though, the puddles on the road were deep enough to float a car, so I stayed in the middle, clear of the worst bits, trying to look past the hypnotising wipers (Iveta was only kidding around), trying to see through the sheets of rain coming in waves (what if Miss Drumm died first?) like a tide of water washing over me, again and again (how could I even *think* "first"?), and the windscreen wipers ticked back and forth, shoving the water like snow in front of a plough but making no difference and —

Nicky!

Blinded by headlights, I felt the wheels go out as I stamped on the brake, felt that sudden weightlessness as I drifted on the skim of surface water. I braced myself, arms locked, released the brakes, then slammed them on again and felt the jolt as they bit just in time. I stopped dead and peered out of the side window at the guy's face in the other car. It was pure white with wide eyes, just like mine must be. We stared at each other for maybe ten seconds, but neither one of us opened a door or even rolled down a window. Then I turned away. The car had stalled. I shifted to neutral, checked the hand-brake, turned the key, and crawled off in second gear, shaking.

Only, in the mirror, I thought I saw him doing a turn, as if to follow me, so I shifted up to third and chanced another skid to get away. Would anyone really chase down a near-miss and start kicking off tonight? In this? It wasn't as if I had scraped him.

I could see his headlights getting closer, starry and blurred through the rain on the back window. He really was coming after me. Well, maybe he was lost or wanted to apologise. But if he was lost, he must be a stranger and yet he was gaining on me; me who knows this road. And that was a lot of determination for an apology. I got my phone out of my bag and put it in my lap.

At the top of the hill, I paused. If I went down the track, there was no way out and no one for miles around. That was usually a good thing — the main reason I agreed to come here. Looking round on a summer's afternoon, with the swifts wheeling and a warm breeze wafting the coconut scent of the gorse blossom in at the windows, the silence was the best bit. Like I could have been the last person alive in the world. I could scream until my eyes turned bloody and no one would try to stop me.

Tonight, though . . . One bar on my phone and the black night filthy and wild, and a man in a car behind me and gaining. The clever thing to do was keep driving, bump all the way to the main road and go where people were.

But I wanted to be home, to have my feet in slippers, a whisky in one hand, a book in the other, and something whirling in the microwave. So I swung onto the track and rattled over the grid, told myself I was imagining things and why shouldn't someone else be driving this road as well as me?

I'd always been glad it was a grid instead of a gate, especially on nights like this when the wind blatted gouts of rain in every direction and the trees along the track thrashed and groaned. Sometimes the gales got so fierce they battered rocks right out of the dry stone wall, rolling them into the wheel ruts. They lay there like trolls on the track, waiting for me.

Tonight, though . . . I'd have taken a drenching to open a gate and shut it behind me. He was still there, but I could see the red of his taillights as well as the white of his headlights. He must be sitting right across the mouth of the lane. I trundled on, watching. Just before I turned the last bend, where the track gets narrow and rough, suddenly the lights were gone.

I blinked. They hadn't moved off; they'd gone out. He had switched off his engine, but he was still sitting there. Or was I wrong about where the view of the road-end disappeared? That must be it. I had never

18

driven along watching in the mirror before, had I? I was always looking forward to the sight of the house or minding out for animals. I had just driven out of sight of him — that was it — and the trees had cut off the view.

Thinking of the animals, I speeded up again, bumping and splashing in the potholes. I'd have to do something about the track this winter. Ask someone or go to the builders' yard myself and get sacks of gravel to empty into the dips. I could drive the car over and back and tamp it down. Only, that seemed like the kind of job that would be easy with a tractor, even a little one, but hours of toil for a woman with a hatchback and a snow shovel.

It was strange to arrive with no one to greet me: the byre cats trotting through the long grass, lifting their feet like dressage ponies, tails high and waving at the tips; Walter Scott with his paws on the windowsill and his snout against the glass at the sound of the car.

No cat would be out tonight, and it had been a few weeks since Walter last smudged the window. He wasn't in pain, the vet assured me, but if this was the final slide, it was a steep one.

Even without the animals, I felt welcomed

home. Rough House was well named, but I only loved it the more. It was long and lower than it should be at the front, the ground level too high and the downstairs walls showing it with a creeping line of damp. Round the back, the hill dropped away and from here the house was gaunt and dreary. Rough indeed. It never bothered me because I knew what was inside and what the views were, but sometimes visitors' faces would fall when they saw the tumble-down sheds and looked up at the windows, set so high that I had to stand a ladder on the concrete apron to wash even the downstairs ones. I had never washed the upstairs back windows at all, just the two of them in the guest bedrooms, slim as arrow slits. They were dappled with years of dust and rain now, bolls of insect eggs lined up along the transoms and spiders' webs clogging every corner. I had hung lace curtains to hide the grime, and I never had guests anyway.

The noise of water teeming out of clogged gutters and pouring down the walls drowned out all other sound but, when I turned the key in the back door and opened it, both house cats were there, weaving and purring, Dorothy collapsing on her back on the doormat and looking up at me, paws waving. I stepped over them and up into the kitchen, into the oily smell of the old Rayburn cooker and the sharper stink of the old dog who lay in front of it, in his basket under the oven door, thumping his tail. He didn't stand, and I hurried over.

"Walter?" I said, crouching down beside him. "You okay?" The tail picked up speed and he pushed his head under my hand as the cats came coiling around, trampling on his legs and nosing at me. I stood, pulled the kettle forward, and went to feed them.

Walter Scott didn't follow me at first. I rinsed bowls and opened tins, listening, and then at last, with a rush of warmth in my chest, I heard him get to his feet and the sound of his nails on the lino as he plodded out to the scullery sink to see about his dinner.

"Don't you dare give up on me," I said, setting the bowl of mush down on his mat. "You're third in the queue, and I told you that months ago."

I put the double dish of cat food on top of the chest freezer and watched Dorothy and William spring soundlessly up and start to eat in dainty bites. Walter Scott had driven his bowl hard against the loft stairs like he always did and was slobbering and grunting at it, as though he was devouring some beast he had slain instead of a packet of the soft

21

little nodules chosen to spare his teeth and keep his diabetes and his ancient bladder from turning on him.

Back in the kitchen, I kicked off my boots and stood in my damp socks in Walter's basket in front of the stove, warming my hands on the kettle, waiting for it to boil. I sometimes worried about the water, drawn from a well, sitting tepid at the back of the Rayburn all day, since I couldn't afford to let myself get ill. When the kettle was too hot to touch, I went to get the milk from the fridge down in the scullery. The cats were on the freezer top beside their clean dish, knowing I would splash some in there for them.

"Pretty things," I said, smiling at the way they were sitting there, paws pursed in front of them, still licking their lips with that little flag of pink tongue so startling against the black of their fur. They waited as I tipped the carton, just a puddle of milk in each side — enough for a treat but not enough to upset them — and I smiled again at the way they stretched up, arching their backs, and settled dow—

Nicky!

My arm jolted and a spout of milk doused the freezer top. The cats scattered, streaking away, leaving the dish rattling. I caught it and held it still. Had I imagined that noise or had someone just knocked on the front door?

At the pictures, every single person in the audience, every single time, asks why that idiot woman is going to see what the noise was, why that moron is going to answer the door. And every one of them, if the same thing happened for real, would do it too. I barely paused to think, certainly didn't pick up my phone or a poker on the way. I crept back through the kitchen and into the passageway, edged opened the glass door, and sidled out into the porch, listening.

There was no mistaking it the second time; that was a quiet but definite knock. I flicked the switch to turn the outside light on and heard the quick sound of his feet shifting. I had startled him. *Him? His* feet? Was I sure?

I opened the door anyway, on the chain, and put my face to the gap.

"Hello?"

He was soaked through to the skin, standing there with his shirt plastered to him and his suit trousers clinging round his legs. His face was red now, stung ruddy by the needles of rain, but it was the same face.

"Look, I'm sorry about that up there on the road," I said. He didn't *look* angry. But if he had followed me all the way down here and splashed through the garden from wherever he'd left his car, he must be fairly bothered one way or another. "But we're both okay, aren't we?" I went on. "Unless you've got whiplash or you banged your knee. I can give you a bag of peas to put on it."

"It *is* you, isn't it?" he said. "Knicker-bocker Gloria."

It took my breath away to hear that name after all these years. When I got it back again I was laughing.

"How do you know that?"

"You don't recognise me," he said. So I looked closer, past the bald head and the beer belly, past the dress shirt and the suit trousers, past the glasses covered in rain-drops. I looked right into his eyes.

"Stig of the Dump!" I said and closed the door to undo the chain, let him in out of the rain.

TWO

Stig of the Dump, Stephen Tarrant, came from Castle Douglas like me, but his family went to Saudi Arabia when he was six and so when they came home again, five years later, rich and different, he was a new boy. He joined Mrs. Hill's primary seven class and thanks to her theories, he sat next to me. Mrs. Hill reckoned the boys would fling fewer spit balls and the girls would giggle a bit less and in a lower key. Of course, what actually happened was that the girls giggled even more, flirting, and the boys threw monster spit balls, showing off, but Mrs. Hill hated admitting she was wrong and so I had spent a year close enough to Stig Tarrant to know that he sneezed in sunlight and that he washed his hair on a Sunday night and a Wednesday. It felt like yesterday.

"What are you doing here?" I asked him once we were in the kitchen. I meant why was he driving the back roads on a night like this, but a bit of me sort of meant *How can you be here, in this room, where no one ever comes?* And another bit of me sort of meant *How can Stig of the Dump be a man with stubbly jowls and a bad crown that's getting black along the gumline? How can Stig Tarrant be rubbing his bald head dry on that warm tea towel from the Rayburn rail, the tea towel I ironed on Sunday, because I like ironing and I ran out of clothes before the end of the good stuff on the radio?*

"Aw, that feels good," he said. "What am I doing here? I'm having the worst night of my life."

"Did you come to see me?" I said. "How did you know where I lived?"

"I didn't," he said. "It was like a . . . I mean, seeing your face through all that rain? You've still got the same hairstyle, Gloria. It's thirty years later, and you look exactly the same."

"It's twenty-eight," I said, and I hoped I wasn't blushing. I turned to the kettle to make the tea in case I was. He was right about my hair. My mum used to do it in a centre parting and two plaits, then wind the plaits around my head and pin them. I loved it when I was a girl; it felt so clean and airy to have all my hair up away from my neck and yet it felt so secure to have it pinned there, safe and tight. It wasn't until I had left college and started working that I realised people were laughing at me: the girls in the buying office calling me Helga and the men in packing asking me what time it was, because I looked like the wife in a cuckoo clock. I kept thinking of cutting it or leaving it hanging down, but every morning I could see the kinks of the plaits, my hair telling me what it wanted to do. And even after I washed it — especially after I washed it — I couldn't resist the way the wet hair would really bite and the plaits would be so hard and tight and it would dry kind of crisp and tingly.

Coming up to my wedding day, I mentioned going to a salon for an up-do and my husband (not quite my husband then, and not my husband again now) said he forbade me to mess up my hair on the very day I should look most like the girl he loved.

"You forbid me?" I'd said, not quite sure enough to smile.

"You'll have to obey me as of next weekend," he'd answered. "Why not start now?" Then I was sure he was joking, and I laughed and did my plaits as usual on my wedding day. I tucked little white silk rosebuds in around them to have something special, but he plucked them out during the first waltz and let them drop on the floor.

"So why is it the worst night of your life?" I asked Stig, setting a mug of tea down in front of him and pushing the sugar bowl close in case he wanted any. I couldn't stop watching him. The way his hand curled around the teaspoon was the same way it curled around a pencil when he turned it upside down to rub out a mistake. The way he plucked the wet shirt away from his back was the same way he had pulled at his school shirt when it was hot at playtime and he got sweaty running round the football pitch.

"I can give you a dressing gown," I said. "I haven't got a dryer, but I can spin your things and hang them over the rail there."

He smiled and it was the same smile, stolen from the boy and used by this man, shining out from the middle of his plump face. "I'm going out again," he said, "and I don't think turning up in your nightie would be a great idea." He took a slurp of his tea. "It's the worst night of my life because I've got a stalker and I've agreed to meet her."

"Dressing gown," I said, "not nightie." And then: "A stalker?"

He put his mug down, put his head in his hands, and groaned. "A girl I was at school with. Nice enough lassie, but she's popped up again out of nowhere and kind of got her claws into me."

I hadn't felt this for years, this burning in my cheeks and the heavy feeling in my middle. Not that people didn't still tease, but these days I usually didn't care. I tried to sound light when I answered him.

"I think someone might have been playing a trick on both of us," I said. He looked up sharply. "Because . . . this girl from school. Do you mean me?"

"What?" he said. Then he laughed again. "No! You bampot. Her name's April Cowan. From *high* school, Gloria. Well, from Eden. That's why I'm here."

Eden. I had almost forgotten. The care home had been a care home for nearly twenty years and I'd been there every day for the last ten until it was like the back of my hand, like my face in the mirror. But before that, and very briefly, it was a boarding school. Eden, they called it, and they couldn't have been more wrong.

"I don't think I knew you went there," I said. In truth, when we scattered after primary I paid no attention to anyone who didn't just trot along to Castle Douglas High School like me. I knew some went to St. Joe's in Dumfries, some with enough money went up to Ayr to Wellington's, but I had forgotten — if I ever knew — where Stig had disappeared to. "Were you there when . . . what was it?"

"We both were," Stig said. "April Cowan and me."

I was trying to remember the story, but I had been twelve (and quite a dreamy twelve) and my parents hadn't wanted to tell me. I knew they didn't approve of Eden. *Hippies,* my mother had said. *Running wild.* And when it happened, whatever it was that I could only just remember, she had said, *Well, what do you expect if you let them just* — But my dad had shushed her. He was always the kind one.

"Then Moped died," said Stig, "and the school closed and I never saw her again." He was gulping his tea and his face was turning a more normal colour from the warmth and the sugar, neither the white I had seen in the headlights nor the blue-pink from the freezing rain. "Never heard from her again until a couple of months ago."

"That's right," I said. "I remember now. There was an accident. 'Mo-ped'?"

"Mitchell Best," said Stig. "He drowned."

"And this April Cowan . . . what?"

"She found me on Facebook, usual story." Walter Scott had finally got his gums around the last of his mushy dinner and he lum-

30

bered back into the kitchen. He stood in the doorway a minute, tail waving, looking at us. Maybe he was as surprised as me to have a visitor. Then he went straight to Stig, ignored his basket completely, and rested his muzzle on one of the wet trouser legs. Stig fondled his ears absently, hardly looking.

"Divorced, of course," he said. "Hitting forty, looking back and wondering where it all went wrong. Aren't we all?" I didn't say a word but he put a hand up, the one that wasn't resting on Walter's head.

"Sorry," he said. "Maybe your life's working out fine. Anyway, April and me started messaging back and forth: 'Ever see any of the crowd these days?' Chitchat, chitchat. Then it changed. I remember it really clearly. I was at work on my lunch and she sent this text. 'The worst thing, Stephen, is not knowing who knows what. Not knowing who knows.' I remember it because who sends a text that long that just says the same thing over and over again?"

"Bingo Little," I said. "Except with him it was telegrams."

"What?"

"Sorry. It's in a book."

"Still got your head stuck in a book then, eh Glo?"

"What did she mean?" I asked, ignoring him teasing me.

"Moped," said Stig. "She was talking about the night Moped died."

I said it over to myself: *The worst thing is not knowing who knows what.* Then he was talking again.

"That was when she started asking to meet. She said something like 'if I could just talk it through once and for all, face to face' and after that there was no stopping her. Where did I live, what sort of free time did I get, wife, girlfriend, how about a coffee then?" He laughed, a harsh sound that made Walter Scott jerk out of his standing-up doze and move off to his basket at last. Stig shivered as though the old dog leaning against his legs had been keeping him warm.

"Starbucks at lunchtime, Glo. Like I was some kind of Internet guy. As if for fuck's sake *she* hadn't been the one pestering *me.*"

I tried not to look startled. Everyone says that word now; I know that. Even the nurses at the home say it sometimes, though not in front of Miss Drumm, and the nice ones don't say it in front of Nicky.

"But she never showed up. I waited an hour then left. Told myself I'd delete her next one, shake her off. But it was a phone call and she caught me. Said she was sorry, said she'd chickened out. I told her she was doing my head in. That was when she started pleading. Really going for it — begging nearly. 'I just want to talk to you. I need to talk. I need to straighten things out. Whether it's you or not, Stephen. I've got to talk to someone.' "

"That doesn't sound like begging," I said. "That sounds like threats."

He frowned and for a minute he seemed to be thinking hard. Then he nodded. "But what would she be threatening me with?" he said. "Or about? Or however you — And now tonight she sent me an ultimatum." He dug in his back pocket and pulled out a phone, clicked, scrolled, and passed it over.

I'M AT THE HUTTIE. COME NOW. I'M WAITING.

"The huttie?" I said.

"At Eden," said Stig. He shivered again as a fierce squall of rain hit the window and the gale moaned in the chimney. "She'll be freezing to bloody death."

"If she's actually there."

"Yeah," said Stig. "If."

"Do you think you could find it? In the dark?"

"I could find it dead drunk and in a blindfold," he said. Strange to think that

33

Stig of the Dump drank. Stig who used to pour his school milk down his throat from a foot above his thrown-back head because he hated straws, cardboard cartons, and the taste of milk.

"If it's still there," I said.

"It will be," said Stig. "It's not really a huttie. It's this wee stone building, pretty amazing actually, like a chapel or something."

"Wait," I said. "You don't mean the crypt? Round building with railings outside?"

Stig stared at me. "How do you — A crypt? God, if we'd known that we wouldn't have —"

"I know every inch of the grounds," I told him. "I used to ramble all over the woods with Walter Scott, before he got too frail."

"I suppose you would, living here," said Stig. "How did you end up here, Glo?" He was looking around the kitchen as if noticing it for the first time, and I tried not to care about how shabby it all was: the old, green-distempered walls with the damp showing through; lino down to the backing weave; everything plugged into a six-way board at the only socket. Maybe I made the suggestion to distract him.

"I could come with you," I said. "It's better to have a witness in case she turns nasty."

He waited a long time before he answered. "Who's Walter Scott?"

I pointed at the basket. "The dog. Not the real Walter Scott, obviously. For one, I don't believe in ghosts, and for two, I prefer Stevenson."

"Who?" said Stig.

"Writers," I told him.

"You and your books, Knickerbocker Gloria," he said, standing. "Okay, you're on."

So it was my idea. It was never him who asked me. That's one thing to be clear about straight away.

THREE

We took my car because I knew the service roads through the estate and could get closer to the crypt — the *huttie,* I'd rather call it, going there in the dead of night this way — and Stig insisted on spreading a bin bag over the seat between his wet clothes and my precious upholstery. If he'd seen my car in daylight, he'd not have bothered. I told him that, but there was no arguing.

"You're doing me a massive favour, Glo," he said. "I'm not leaving you with mildew as well."

"Glad to help," I said. "I'm glad I nearly ran into you."

"Yeah, how about that?" We had bumped back along the track from my place and were out on the lane, just about where the near-running-into had happened. "You living here, right on Eden's doorstep. What are the chances?"

"Small world," I said. I didn't want to get

started on it.

"*Isolated* isn't even the word, though, Glo," said Stig, peering out past the windscreen wipers at the blackness. "Do you like it? Must do or you wouldn't have bought it, eh?"

"Well, it's handy for me," I said. "I work just up the road."

"Doing what?" he said. "Not like jobs round here are easy come by."

That was true. It was like a miracle when it happened. I went from being totally lost and alone, divorced, desperate, homeless, and broke, to having this lovely house and a good job and Nicky happy and no one watching me and judging every move I made. Miss Drumm made her offer, the job was advertised, and I never looked back.

"I'm a registrar," I said. "Up in Dalry."

"Not shifts then?"

I shook my head. "And my son lives nearby."

"Your son?" said Stig. "You've got a son?" I knew what that tone of voice was. I was used to it. Something about me made people think I wasn't a mother. But I am. I might not have a big handbag with baby wipes and fruit snacks, or wear yoga clothes and be in a book group, but Nicky was there and the skin on my tummy was still soft and crumpled fifteen years later. No one could take that away.

I swung off the road at one of the back ways into the estate. No sign, no gateposts, just a break in the bramble-laden fence. The trust kept the track narrow and uninviting to stop people getting nosy, but round the first bend it widened out again and cut through the pines growing close on either side.

"This goes to the boiler house," I told Stig, "but it passes close by the cr— the hut-tie. I mean, we'll still get soaked but less than the other way."

"And I think we'll get soaked for nothing," Stig said. "I don't think she'll be there. I think it's a game."

I was peering hard into the trees, looking for any trace of the cupola on the top of the crypt or any glint from the railings around it. Gamekeepers from the next estate sometimes drove over the top fields in spring looking for foxes, lamps on top of their Land Rovers that always made me think of lighthouses the way they swept around and then suddenly stopped, picking out the scared little fox in that harsh white light. A scrap of orange against Day-Glo green. I always turned away before I heard the crack and told myself the fox fled, hid until the

38

gamekeeper gave up and was down in the pub, cursing it. Anyway, Miss Drumm was *fully apprised of her rights* and *specifically withheld permission from any vehicle desiring to cross her land for the purposes of so-called vermin control.* She made me learn the words and promise to say them *should the occasion arise.*

"It all helps, Gloria," she told me. "Keep everyone out and no one will ever know."

"Can you shine that torch out the side window?" I asked Stig. I was pretty sure we had missed it, so I turned carefully, back and forth, back and forth, feeling the wheels slip in the mud when I went too far. Once we were on our way back again he leaned across me and clicked on the torch, but the reflection made it useless.

"You'll have to wind it down," he said. "And you'll get drenched."

"Not so bad under the trees, really." My throat was tight, filled with the smell of his body, he was that close. Stig of the Dump in primary seven had smelled of Palmolive soap and the earth that got stuck to his shoes and ground into the knees of his grey school trousers every playtime. This man smelled of aftershave and fabric softener.

"She won't be there," he said again. "This'll be just like Starbucks."

He was trying to convince himself, it sounded like, and so I faced him with the contradiction.

"If you're so sure, why did you come?"

Before he could answer, there was a sudden flash in the trees off to our left. I stopped and he played the beam around to find it again, the glittering spangled light of a leaded window.

"No sign of her car," said Stig, his voice pitched higher than usual.

"Switch off and look," I told him, thinking surely this April Cowan would keep a light on, even her phone just, and not stay in a crypt at night in a storm, waiting. But when he killed the torch and I killed the headlights, we were wrapped in instant inky blackness.

"She's not there," he said. "I told you."

"But we've come this far, so why not check?"

It was only twenty yards, but getting there was tricky. Stig leapt over the ditch, taking the torch, and then turned and shone it back to me. I picked my way down the steep side, sliding a little, then stepped over the water and clambered up again. He put his hand out and hauled me, gripping me hard just below the elbow like for an eightsome reel. Then we turned. For a wonder, there were no fallen trees in our way; most of the woods at the home were so neglected the trees leaned into each other like drunks, and everywhere you turned trunks lay across your path, roots sticking up in the air. Some of them have been there so long, they've re-rooted where they fell and become mis-shapen sideways trees, grotesque somehow but pitiful too.

All Stig and I had to deal with were the mossy lumps, knee high, that were some-times soft tussocks and sometimes had rocks under them. So although they rose up like stepping stones, we ignored them and splashed through the boggy dips in between.

"Jesus, it's freezing," he said. "No wonder April's car's nowhere to be seen. Who'd come this way?"

"The proper path's just as bad," I told him. "And longer."

We were there. A low stone wall with rail-ings above it circled the crypt and we fol-lowed it round to the gate on the far side. Stig trained the torch on the gate lock and drew in a breath. The padlock and chain were as rusted as the railings, but quite clearly in the torchlight we could see a little shiny lozenge shape — the raw place where wire cutters had snipped the chain. And recently too.

"April?" Stig shouted. "Are you in there?"

The path, no more than ten feet from the gate to the door, was paved in mossy slabs. I remembered it from summer walks here. Remembered thinking that they looked like gravestones, and Miss Drumm saying they probably were. Old ones turned face-down and put to use.

"April?" Stig shouted again and banged on the door. He handed me the torch and grabbed the tarnished doorknob. "You wait here," he said.

"I'm a witness," I told him. Then I raised my voice. "April?" I called. "My name's Gloria. I came along to keep Stig company. I hope that's okay."

Then we both listened. The rain hissed in the high branches and dripped miserably off the low branches, but otherwise there was silence.

"Might as well check," I said.

He tried the door. It opened about a foot with a grating squeal before it grounded out on the stone floor inside. Stig grabbed the handle harder and tried to lift it clear but it wouldn't budge, so he turned sideways and squeezed into the gap, breathing in and wriggling his shoulders until he was through. I followed. It was touch and go if I would fit, but the thought of how embarrassing it would be helped me ignore the pain of the door latch scraping across my front and the way the frame bruised my vertebrae as I forced myself past it.

"Oof," I couldn't help saying when I got inside.

"I told you!" said Stig, playing the torch around. It was about twelve feet across maybe, just that one window we had seen, and nowhere for someone to hide. Nothing in there at all except for a stone shelf that ran round the wall and an alcove at the far side. The place was absolutely empty, just dust and cobwebs.

"Jeez. Memories," Stig said. "We put beanbags in here, and those Indian cotton things." He moved forward. "Better than wooden benches any day, but it looks terrible now they're out too."

"Wait," I said, putting an arm out to stop him going in. "Shine the torch on the floor, see if there's footprints. *Someone* cut that wire. Someone's at least *been* here."

He trained the torchlight downwards and I saw that it was shimmering a little as if his hand was unsteady.

"Look," he said.

There *were* footprints. The dust around the edges of the room was so thick that the mortar lines between the stone flags ap-

43

peared soft, the way the garden softened under the first thin fall of snow. In the middle though, footprints criss-crossed, leading away from the door to the far side in front of the alcove. There they were muddled and scraped about, and at one spot the floor was completely clear. A square with no dust at all.

I walked over and looked down at it. Stig followed me, the torchlight sending a monstrous shadow dancing on the wall.

"Why would she clean off that one slab and leave footprints everywhere else?" he said.

"She didn't," I answered. "I think the dust slid off when the stone tilted." I crouched down, feeling along the edges.

"Tilted?" said Stig. "Like a trap door? Glo, this place is freaking me out. Let's get ou—"

I had found the spring, or the latch or whatever it was, and the clean stone slab lifted at one end. I grabbed it and pulled until the slab stood up like a gravestone. I don't know what I had been expecting: a staircase, a tunnel, treasure? Or maybe deep down inside I knew what I was about to see. And there it was.

Nicky!

"Oh Jesus fuck," said Stig behind me. A

brutal, needless pair of words, so wrong to put them together that way. But looking into the hole, I nearly echoed them.

"Is that April Cowan?" I whispered.

"Oh Jesus fucking Christ," said Stig, and I knew from the way his voice had softened and grown guttural that he was almost retching. "It's been so long. It's — But I think so."

I reached down and pulled the thick brown hair away from her face.

"Yes, yes, that's April. Jesus," he said. "Oh Christ."

She was cold, but it hadn't been long. I brushed her cheek, moving her hair, and it was still soft to the touch. Her eyes were half open and still shining. The knife was shining too. Blood had poured over the handle and coated her hands, drying in the creases of her knuckles and around her fingernails, but its stubby little blade was clean, wiped clean when she'd pulled it out of the long gaping gashes on both her arms. I remembered a nurse at the home telling me one time that someone crying out for help slashes sideways, but if they mean it they open the veins from wrist to elbow.

I heard electronic bleeps from behind me and saw a new bluish light added to the torch beam.

"What are you doing?" I shouted, standing, turning, and grabbing Stig's arm all in one movement.

"I'm calling the police," he said.

Nicky!

"No. Don't."

"Gloria, what are you talking about. We've got to."

"There's no signal," I said. "You won't get a signal until you're back on the road at Crocketford. Let's go. And use my landline."

"What are you doing?" said Stig. I had pulled my coat sleeve down and I wiped it over her hair where I had touched. Then I pushed the stone until it was closed again and wiped my fingerprints away. "Gloria? Why are you doing that?"

"Ssh," I told him. I pulled the scarf from round my neck and, walking backwards towards the door, pushing Stig along behind me, I swished it over the floor, wiping all the footprints, his, mine, and the ones we had found. Mixing them all up into a churned mess of dust. He squeezed out through the door first. I followed, took the torch, and ran it all up and down the opening looking for fibres. But my anorak was shiny and Stig was so wet that nothing would have come off him. I pulled the door closed, surprised I was strong enough to shift the swollen wood, then I polished the handle.

"What about them?" said Stig, pointing to our muddy prints on the gravestone path.

"It's going to rain all night," I told him. "Let's go."

"Back to yours and call the cops?" he said. "Only why did you wipe —"

"We need to talk," I said.

The silence lasted a long time. I thought it was because I had shocked him. But then he spoke again.

"Yes, we do," he said. "I haven't been completely straight, Gloria. There's something you should know."

FOUR

"I didn't do it."

That was the first thing he said when we were back in the car, crawling along the track to the gap in the fence. I would have driven like a bat out of hell if I could have, but my limbs had turned leaden on me, my feet sludgy on the pedals and my arms so heavy I thought they might drop from the steering wheel and just lie in my lap like sandbags.

"So if you're protecting me for some mad reason, you don't have to. I didn't do that. I could never . . ."

I believed him. I knew without a flicker of doubt, right from the off that Stig Tarrant hadn't killed April Cowan. It wasn't sentiment. It wasn't old times. It was the way he had called out her name, so hopeful, and the way he had said she wasn't there, so torn between relief and disappointment, and the way he had said those terrible words:

48

Oh Jesus fuck. He wasn't acting.

I can smell insincerity at fifty paces. I can hear the lie under the kind word every time. Lynne at work calls it a certain kind of detector, and though I don't like the sound of having one of them inside me, I suppose it's true. One of the orderlies is always saying Nicky's a lovely boy and I'm a lucky mummy or he's a lucky boy and I'm lovely mummy, and she might as well shout at the top of her lungs that she despises me and Nicky gives her the creeps. But then there's this old Irish orderly, Donna, and she says, "Ah, the poor soul, but he's still your blessing." And she means every word.

"I know you didn't," I said to Stig. "She did it herself."

"But I mean I didn't *drive* her to it," Stig said. "I don't know why she picked on me and set me up for this. I don't understand anything that's happening."

"I know."

"So why aren't we dialling 999?"

"Listen," I said, "and I'll tell you."

Back in the kitchen the Rayburn was teetering. When the wind gets up in the north it sometimes just snuffs it out, and then Rough House is a miserable place to be. I usually light a fire in the living room if it looks likely, but tonight I didn't have the energy to strike a match, never mind lay the paper and twigs and nurse it. The chimney's as bad as the stove when the wind blows.

"Tea?" I said.

"Whisky?" said Stig. I went through to the living room to get the bottle from the press. When I got back he had dragged two chairs from the table, set them close to the oven, and opened the door.

"I know it'll cool your hot water, but needs must." His teeth were chattering.

I turned and left again, went upstairs to my bedroom, got a tee-shirt and a sweat suit — a plain one in pale grey with no sparkles — thick socks and a fleece hat.

"Here," I said, when I got back to the kitchen again. "Strip off and get into these. I'm going to change too. Shout when you're ready."

I managed not to laugh at the sight of him, bundled in my clothes with the hat flaps pulled over his ears. I just sat down beside him, kicked off my slippers, and put my feet on Walter Scott's back. He thumped his tail once but didn't open his eyes.

"Think my size nines would flatten him?" said Stig, his voice sounding rough from a big swallow of whisky.

"Not Walter," I said. "Sometimes at night he burrows under me so I'm right on top of him, and he stays there till morning."

I blushed then, but who knows if it was from admitting I slept with a dog, alluding to my figure, or just the whisky.

"Okay," I said. Stig wouldn't know I was blushing. Only the lamps were on, not the big light, and the green distemper makes everyone look like a vampire. "Why I live here. It's not my house. It belongs to a friend who's not in good enough health to stay here alone anymore. So I'm long-term house-sitting."

"Glo," he said. "That's all very — We've got more impor—"

"Wait," I said. "Just listen. It's Nicky."

Nicky! I thought when I swerved to avoid Stig on the road. *I can't have a car crash because who'll be there for Nicky?*

Nicky! I thought when the knock came at the door. *I can't be attacked in my home by a crazed madman because Nicky needs me.*

And crouching in the huttie looking down at the curled shell of April Cowan's body, my only thought was *Nicky!*

"My son, Nicky, lives at the home," I said. "I go every night after work. I've never missed a day in ten years and if they were to close it off — for an investigation — and I couldn't go . . . Well, it maybe doesn't make much sense now, but that's why I wiped the prints."

"What's wrong with him?" said Stig.

"That's why I wiped the prints," I said again, ignoring the question. Nothing is wrong with Nicky. "For Nicky. Because never mind an investigation. They might have to close the home."

"They wouldn't."

"I can't chance it."

"We can't just leave her there!" said Stig. "We have to phone and tell someone. People will be worried about her. Her family."

"If they close the home . . ."

"They won't. Things happen, Gloria. Bad things happen. People die. Very unhappy people kill themselves. There's a pub in Edinburgh where a girl was murdered and it's still open. It's only a pub and that was a murder. They won't close a *care home*."

"But what if someone who works there is mixed up in it somehow? If there's a scandal and they lose their license?"

"They won't," he said again.

"How can you say that!" I said. "It happened before. It happened when the home was a school. It happened at Eden."

"Exactly," said Stig and drained his glass. "What happened tonight is nothing to do with the home. What happened here tonight started with Eden."

52

"You know that for a fact?"

He nodded.

"Okay," I said. "Phone them."

But he shook his head and laughed very softly.

"No," he said. "Now it's my turn."

Dorothy had been sitting on the floor looking up at us and now she finally made her choice. She sprang up into Stig's lap, kneaded the grey sweatpants for a moment and then curled into a ball, purring. He stroked her back in slow gentle movements. I noticed because he had patted Walter Scott before and usually someone who knows how to pat a dog is too rough with a cat, ruffling them up and confusing them. Stig smoothed Dorothy's fur from just behind her head all the way to the tip of her tail, and she uncurled and stretched along the length of his legs to let him make a proper job of it.

"What is it you need to say?" I asked. But he just kept stroking the cat, not looking at me. His head was sunk down onto his chest. The cat purring, the aftershock, the whisky. His breathing sounded halfway to snores, but then some heavy men do breathe that way.

I tried again.

"Earlier you said you knew April was talk-ing about Moped. Was that because she said more then you've told me? Because just from what you've told me, it could have been anything."

He roused himself at last. "You're sharp," he said. "You always were even though you never looked it." He was staring down into his empty glass, but he didn't reach out to the bottle for more. "I would have guessed if she'd said even less," he went on quietly. "It was my first thought when the first message came. Before I even read it. I saw April Cowan's name and thought, *Moped*! Just like that.

"One time years ago I passed another girl from Eden in the street in Glasgow. Rain Irving. I recognised her and I thought, *Moped*! And she recognised me and thought the same. Her lips moved, saying his name. I bet that sounds crazy."

"Not to me." It sounded like my life. "Except that a tragic accident years ago . . . you'd think it would have faded by now."

"It would have," Stig said. He stroked Dorothy. "It wasn't a tragic accident," he said at last, and the low light, the cat, and the whisky made the words seem gentle. I nodded when I heard them.

"Is *that* what you needed to say?"

"Not really," said Stig, "but we can start there. Have some more whisky. I feel as if once I start talking, I'll never stop."

"Okay," I said, "but —"

"She's not going anywhere," Stig said. "And they'll not get wired into the crime scene till daylight and the rain stops."

"I suppose not," I said, "but that's not what I wanted to say." I knew I was blushing this time. "Can we swap sides?" Because in primary seven, in Mrs. Hill's class, I was on the left and he was on the right, and if I was going to look beside me for Stig Tarrant it seemed that, even all these years later, I should look that way. Maybe it was the whisky, but in that moment it almost seemed like all these years I'd been looking that way, wondering where he'd got to, and now at last things felt right again. *Right!* Even after what we'd seen.

Stig moved carefully, keeping Dorothy as still as he could. She stopped purring, but she didn't jump down.

"Eden had just opened up in the September," he said, when he was settled again. "We were the first ones there."

"I remember," I said. "It was in the news. I remember my mum and dad talking about it."

"Hippies running wild, trouble waiting to happen?"

"Like *Lord of the Flies*," I said. Only this

time, when I explained it, he spoke too.

"Book," we both said, and then we both started laughing.

"It's not like I know your family that well," I went on, after a bit, "but I'm surprised you went there."

Stig laughed again. I thought about the Tarrants, what I knew of them. Five years in Saudi. That marked them out from most of the people round here, who had to psych themselves up for an hour-long drive to Carlisle. They were certainly different enough when they came back — Big Jacky, Wee Jacky, Angie, and Stig — and from the things my mum said, I took it they'd changed while they were away. *Look at her! Dressed like that to nip out to the shops.* I remember wondering why someone in nice clothes would make my mother angry. *She's freezing cold and won't admit it.* That was another one. Angie Tarrant had a sunbed and she wore bare legs and short sleeves from early spring till late autumn, again at night at Christmas, showing off her tan. All my dad said was, *Good luck to them. I hope it works out.* That was when the Tarrants bought a big chunk of land at the old station yard, talking about a leisure complex, a pool and a gym and flats for the sort of people who'd want to live in them.

"You don't know the half of it, Glo," said Stig. "I don't suppose Wee J would have been packed off to live in the woods if Eden was still going when he left primary, but BJ reckoned it would do for me."

I didn't know what to say to that. A lot of kids think they're not the favourite and hardly any kids think they are. Even *my* sister moans about my mum and dad favouring me. "The right can do no wrong," she said when she found out I was getting divorced and Mum hadn't told her. Truth was my mother didn't mention the divorce because she was ashamed, was still campaigning to stop it.

"There's never been a divorce in this family," she'd said. "Never. Your grandma gritted her teeth and stuck it out and so can you." There was no use telling her it wasn't my decision. All she said was, "Well, whatever it is he wants from you, give it to him. You made vows, Gloria, and you should keep them." She had looked me all over, as if whatever had disappointed Duggie would be there for her to see. "At least you could take more care of yourself," she said. "Tart yourself up a bit. He's a red-blooded male."

I could have pointed out to my sister that a doting mother doesn't say things like that to her favourite child, but my sister agreed with every word of it and she'd only chip in with her tuppenceworth. I'd heard it before: *Cut your hair, Gloria. Lose some weight, Gloria. Get new clothes, shoes, nails, teeth.*

"So what happened to Moped?" I asked Stig.

FIVE

"It was May Day," Stig began. "The Beltane. The girls wanted to get up at dawn."

"And wash their faces in the dew," I said. "I used to do that. My mum used to wake me."

"And it sort of snowballed into all of us sleeping out all night in a clearing in the woods."

"What clearing?" I said. "The one with the flowers and the birch trees all round?"

"Yeah, bluebells it was in May and — don't laugh — fairy rings."

"It's a fungus," I said. "Nothing to laugh at."

"Anyway, we were going to build a bonfire and make our beds out of bracken, the whole bit."

"Like the Famous Five."

"More than five, more like twelve," said Stig. He must know who the Famous Five were, but it didn't sound that way.

"That was your whole class?"

"That was the whole *school* that first year," said Stig. "That was the plan. Start with the first year then, when we went into second year, start another first year, get new staff and all that, and by the time we were in sixth year, the school would be up and running."

"You were guinea pigs."

"Miss Naismith said a school should grow *organically.* She said we were pioneers."

"Was she the head mistress?"

"She was it. The only teacher. She did English, French, and art. And all the other crap like gardening and woodwork. She was winging it for history and geography — taking us to Hadrian's Wall and calling it both — and they got some guy in from Kirkcudbright to do maths and science. But you could tell she couldn't give a stuff about them, really. The next teacher was going to do all the boring useful stuff."

"You know a lot about the plan," I said. "Was it one of these student council commune things?"

"Nah," said Stig. "Anyway, yeah, so there was me, Van the Man, Moped, Bezzo, Jo-jo, Ned, and Nod — they were the boys."

"But wasn't Bezzo . . . Hang on, Bezzo Best?" I said, sorting through the names.

The Bests had been at our primary school. Good friends with Stig. Friends of the family. "*Alan* Best?" I said. "Wasn't he Mitchell Best's brother? How could they both be in first year at the same time?"

"The school did some kind of deal," said Stig. "Cut price kind of thing. And that was nothing. There were three Irving sisters there. All different ages. Okay, one of them, Sun Irving, was special needs so it didn't really matter, but Cloud and Rain should have been in different classes."

"Cloud, Rain, and Sun?" I said. "At least they're the type for an organic school in the woods." Then hearing myself, I thought I sounded like my mother. "So that's ten."

"And the Scarlets," said Stig. "Scarlet Mc-Farlane and Scarlet McInnes. We called them Scarlet McFarlet and Skinny McInnes. God, kids are cruel."

"And April Cowan," I said. "What did you call her?"

"What did we not?" said Stig. "April Showers. And that turned into Golden Showers, but with any luck she didn't know what that meant — and I can tell that you don't either, so don't ask me. We called her Cowgirl. And Cowface sometimes. And Skinny McInnes called her a different name every month. September, October, November . . . We thought that was the funniest thing out."

"You bullied her," I said.

"Everyone ripped the piss out of everyone," said Stig. "Miss Naismith called it bonding."

"Miss Naismith sounds like an idiot," I said.

"If there was a bully," said Stig, "it was Van. Van the Man. But then, after what happened, he probably never said a cross word to anyone ever again. He still lives round here."

"After what happened," I repeated.

"Yeah." He drained his whisky glass for the second time and set it down on the edge of the Rayburn top with a clunk, as if it was a gavel and he was calling himself to order. "So we slept outside. Dead excited. And we stayed dead excited until about ten o'clock. By then we'd eaten our midnight feast hours early and we were freezing cold and getting sore from lying on bracken beds, so we thought when Miss Naismith came to check on us, like she said she was going to, we'd ask to go back inside."

"Why didn't you just go?"

"Couldn't see a thing. We hadn't taken torches, planning to look up at the stars. But it was cloudy. Pitch black once the fire burnt down. So we waited."

"Pitch black at ten o'clock in May?" I said.

"Really thick clouds," said Stig. "We waited. The girls were all huddled in together. Or at least the weathergirls and the Scarlets were. April . . . I don't know where April was exactly. I was freezing — feet numb, fingers numb, back killing me — and none of the boys would get zipped into sleeping bags together to stay warm. Nod and Ned McAllister were sort of spooned in, but the rest of us were nearly getting hypothermia."

"Nod and Ned?"

He had to think about it, finding it as hard to dredge up their real names as I would find it suddenly to call him Stephen. "Nathan and either Edwin or Edmund, I think," he said at last. "Anyway. We fell asleep in the end, at least I did, and slept until it was getting light. Must have been four-ish and the sky had cleared. It was — just for a minute — it was what we had been after when we asked to stay out, you know? I opened my eyes and the sun was shining through the trees, but white and kind of . . . milky. And there was dewdrops all over my blanket. I could see them, like every one was shining, balanced on the ends of the threads sticking up, see it clear as anything.

Dewdrops all over the pine needles too, even on the cones lying on the ground. Everything was sparkling.

"Then I moved and, just like that, the dew was soaked into the wool and I was shivering. It was . . . this sounds mad, Glo, I know it does. But it was a perfect moment. It was like pure peace. Have you ever had a moment like that?"

I couldn't answer. All I could do was stare at him.

"Well, anyway, maybe it only seems that way looking back because there hasn't been a moment of pure peace ever since. I moved, the dew soaked in, I was freezing cold and soaking wet."

"Then what? Did you go back to sleep? Or was that when you realised something was wrong?"

"Oh. No, I didn't go back to sleep. No, I never slept another wink until Van was shaking me, white as a ghost, saying Moped was missing.

"We weren't that worried at first. We thought he must have woken up and gone back to the house. We thought maybe he wasn't feeling well. We'd all been eating sausages we'd cooked in the fire, black on the outside and raw in the middle. So anyway, we packed up and headed back.

And then when we were crossing the bridge by the Tarzan swing — do you know where I mean? Where the river's cut down really deep and there's sort of cliffs on either side?"

"I think so," I said. "There's no Tarzan swing now, but a little wooden footbridge with arches at either end?"

"That's it. We put those arches up. Naismith loved a bit of woodwork."

"So that's where it was?"

"Yeah. We were crossing the footbridge and Scarlet — Skinny McInnes — started screaming and pointing and we all looked over the side and there he was. Face-down. You could hardly see his head at all with his hair so black like it was and his legs were sunk down, not floating out behind him. So it was just his anorak — he had this really minging orange anorak — and he was turning round and round and round in the current, must have been turning like that for hours."

"And his brother saw him like that?" I said. I remembered Alan Best from primary school. He was the only one in our class who got *Mad* magazine and he used to lend it out to the other boys for sweets and marbles.

"Yeah," said Stig. "He climbed over the

side onto the ledge, but Van grabbed him in time."

"Van the bully?" I said. "What's *his* real name?"

"Van's real name? Something like Douglas or Dougall," said Stig. "Anyway, we ran back to the house and after that, it was chaos. Pure hell. The girls were all hysterical. Bezzo was just sitting in the corner with his arms round his shoulders, rocking. Miss Naismith started out like a zombie and then, when she realised what deep shit she was in, she started screaming at us. And she kept trying to phone people and not getting them or not getting the numbers right, because it was like six o'clock on a Wednesday morning and where would anyone be? I don't even know who she was calling except that it wasn't the Bests, because the police did that later — when they finally got in. The gates were padlocked and they couldn't get through. In the end, one of them had to get out and jog all the way up the drive, then Miss Naismith had to calm down enough to find the keys. Anyway, it was bad.

"And the scariest thing of all was . . . We were just kids, right? But none of the adults were . . . they didn't . . . they were all so *angry.*"

"They were scared too."

He nodded. "I know that now. Naismith must have been terrified. She told so many lies trying to cover her arse. Said she *had* been out to see that we were all right, asked if we wanted to stay or come in, and that we'd elected to stay out. She said we were all covering for each other, trying to blame her. No one believed her, but she went into orbit with it anyway. Said she'd been out not just once but *twice.* The first time to ask if we were okay and the second time to persuade us all to come back because she was worried about us and couldn't sleep." He laughed and shook his head, remembering. "Twelve of us all saying the same thing and she just stuck with her story."

"It does sound traumatic," I said. "But —" I bit my lip.

"Yeah," said Stig. "I know. *But.* There's no glitches. So far the story makes sense, right?"

"Kind of. Sorry."

"So here goes. The reason I woke up, when I was covered in dew and it was like diamonds? Something woke me. I heard a car, Glo. A car door slammed and the engine started and it drove away. Roared away. There was someone there that night. Someone who didn't belong there, and they left like a bat out of hell."

I waited. I could tell there was more.

"But the others said they hadn't heard it." He was agitated all of a sudden. He lifted Dorothy under her front legs and dropped her down onto the floor. "All of them, all eleven of them, said they hadn't heard a thing, and that's just not possible. There wasn't a breath of wind, and you know what it's like up here on a quiet night. You know what a car sounds like."

I nodded. The quiet at Rough House had saved my sanity. Except it wasn't quiet at all: it was swifts and tits and wrens and sparrows and oystercatchers up from the Solway, and geese and ducks, bees and owls, a thrush some lucky summers. It was the wind streaming over the grass and making it whisper, shushing through the trees, moaning where it was caught in the dips and rises. Sometimes I thought I could hear the stars turning on in the evening and the sun sighing like an old lady when it set. Sometimes I thought I could hear the worms in the soil and the flower buds popping open. After the rain, I thought I could hear the roots of the trees pulling the water up their trunks and sending it out to the ends of their twigs. Sometimes up here I thought I could hear the slow grind of the earth turning.

"No way," I said. "A car starting at Eden would be like a bomb going off."

"Exactly," said Stig. "So when April started texting me —" He stopped.

April! We were sitting here in dry clothes in this warm kitchen, sipping whisky and she was there in that hole, cold and getting colder, her spilled blood drying.

"Go on," I said.

"So when she started texting me about needing to straighten things out. I thought, *You and me both.* I thought, *At last.*" He took a deep breath. "And then tonight she finally said it. 'I heard the car.'"

"She texted it to you?" I said. "Or voice-mail? Because one thing that occurred to me was —"

"Neither," said Stig. "And this is the thing I really need to tell you."

"A good thing or a bad thing?" I said, not even knowing what I meant, just needing to brace myself if there was going to be any more.

"I don't know," said Stig. "I'll show you what I found and you tell me."

Six

He left by the front door and it banged out of his hand like always with a bad north wind, slammed back against the porch wall and rattled. There was a deep gouge in the plaster there from all the years that door had been flung open. Over a hundred years of north winds and children in high spirits rushing in and out from the garden. Maybe even a young wife taking time to settle and flouncing off in her clogs and apron to fume out there in the open air, where the view could calm her. I liked to think that Rough House saw some life before Miss Drumm and then me.

He was more careful on the way back in, and he locked it after him.

"It's not letting up," he said, using one of his hands like a window washer to scrape the rain from his forehead. He had a woman's handbag in his other one.

"I've started coming to see my mum and

dad," he said, sitting down again with the bag in his lap. "Trying to build bridges, you know. Tea at my mum's every Monday, like a happy family. And Wee J's there with the wife and kids, so that takes some of the pressure off. What I'm saying is, usually I'd have been here — or ten miles off — when the text came to meet her at Eden."

"But?"

"But what with the weather, I'd decided to skip it. I was sitting in a sushi bar in the West End when it came. So I decided to go back to my flat, get wellies and Gore-Tex."

"What happened?" I asked, thinking about his thin dress shirt and suit trousers, his ruined leather shoes.

"I found this." He put the bag in my lap. It was one of those squashy ones with too many buckles.

"I thought at first it was Carol's — she's my ex — from how it was tucked under the hall table like someone who lived there would put it down. I nearly didn't see it except I was guddling around in the hall cupboard for wellies.

"So I shouted, 'Is anyone there?' You wouldn't believe how long it took me to open the damn thing and look through it, Glo. And I was still waiting for a slap on the back of the neck. My mum used to go ballistic if you went in her bag and even my dad, even today, if she asks for her specs or her ciggies, he'll hand the whole thing over and wait to take it back again."

"Stig," I said. For the first time it seemed as if he was just talking to fill the air. Or maybe talking so he didn't have to say what needed to be said, if he would only shut up long enough to say it.

He leaned over and opened the clasp, springing the fake buckle at the first go.

"It's April's," he said, poking at the wallet, make-up, keys, phone. "All her stuff's in here. And look." He jabbed a piece of folded paper, but he didn't pick it up or open it. I did that.

Stephen, it said on the outside. And on the inside, in a round hand, plain blue biro, it said just what he told me: *I heard the car.*

"But why would she do that?" I said. "Why would she do any of this? Even though she wanted to kill herself, why would she involve you?"

"Just trying to mess with my head?" He looked upwards and spoke loudly as if shouting to someone upstairs. "Nailed it, April."

"But why?"

He closed his eyes and stayed like that with his head back.

"Was it definitely her?" I said. Stig sat up and blinked at me. Who knows where his thoughts had taken him, but it looked like a long way back to meet mine.

"Look at the picture." He took the wallet out of my hands and slid a travel card out of its plastic folder. "It's her."

He was right. The face staring out of the card was the same one we had seen in the hole under the crypt, as round and plain as the signature under it and the writing on the folded note.

"That's not what I meant, though," I said. "Was it definitely April who was contacting you? Isn't there a chance that someone else was messing with you both?"

"I wondered that," he said. "Not at first, because she knew too much for it not to be her. But when she phoned, I couldn't get the voice to fit the picture in my head."

"What did she look like when you knew her?" I asked, still staring at the photo.

"A skinny wee girl with her hair dyed burgundy, and all that zigzag way."

"Crimped," I said.

"Yeah. Bad skin, too much make-up, like it helped."

"You liked her," I said.

"Eh?"

"That's a lot of noticing for a teenage

boy," I said.

He shrugged, half-smiling. "She was my 'girlfriend' for about ten minutes," he said. "We all paired off and reshuffled till we'd been right round. You know what we were like back then."

Only I didn't, not at all.

"So, she used to be your girlfriend," I said. "And you'd been phoning and texting recently? And you were only at your flat tonight because of the weather?" He nodded. "Any other Monday you'd have got the text at your mum's, driven to the huttie, found April, and phoned the police. Like you were going to."

"After I'd checked to see if she was really dead and probably got covered in her blood. You see?"

"I see. And if they got a warrant for your flat, they'd find her bag."

"After me telling them I hadn't actually seen her for twenty-odd years and certainly — definitely — she'd never been at my place. What's going on, Gloria?"

"I tell you one thing that's going on," I said. "You're in a world of trouble."

He looked me straight in the eye then and spoke in a steady voice. Not a single tremor despite what he was saying, which would have given me the collywobbles.

"Tell me right now if you want me to go, and I'll leave. I'll call the cops as soon as I get a signal, I'll tell them I was at the huttie on my own. I'm innocent. I've got nothing to fear."

I took a long time to decide. It was a good offer. He would drive away and keep my name out of it. Nicky and I could carry on the same as ever.

"I know you didn't kill her," I said.

His relief made him sag down in his chair. "Will you help me?" he said.

"You didn't kill her," I said again. "But you're not innocent. You stopped being innocent when you found her and didn't call it in."

"But it was you that —"

I held up my hand. "Let me think!" It didn't take long. "It needs to be anonymous," I told him. "And it's better coming from a woman. I'll call."

I knew I lived too much inside my head. How could I not? Where else was there? I was the onlooker to so many human dramas every day at work: small joys, small sorrows but big to the people they happened to. So maybe I'd got the idea that I could see things clearly. Maybe I'd got an inflated opinion of myself. There's that.

And it was a chance to *do* something. I

wasn't much for praying by then, but one I never got tired of is the one that goes: God grant me courage to change what I can, strength to bear what I can't, and wisdom to know the difference. So much of my life was *bearing*. And then tonight, all of a sudden, here was a chance to make a *change*. To take injustice and change it.

And another thing too. Usually I only get to read the stories that other people make up. I see them when they're done, for good or bad. Brilliant stories locked tight and unbreakable — *The Count of Monte Cristo, The Return of Martin Guerre* — or stupid stories full of holes that leave you let down and restless — *Cyrano de Bergerac, Persuasion,* although that wasn't her fault because she died. It had never happened to me before that I got bits of a story before it was done and had the chance to sculpt it and polish until everyone saw what I wanted them to see. Until everyone listened to me.

"You need to get your car out of sight," I said. "Probably for nothing, because the postie only comes as far as the first grid and that's not till after two in the afternoon. But if it's Parcel Express it could be any time, and sometimes they miss the box and drive right in. And I've got an Amazon order outstanding."

"Stay here?" said Stig.

"I thought you wanted me to help you."

"Yeah, like lend me some cash for a room and say you hadn't seen me if anyone asked."

"But where could you go that's better?" I said. "You're invisible. Ninety-nine percent of the country's useless for hiding now. Your phone says where you are unless you switch it off. You're in about the only place for four hundred miles where no one can track you."

"Still," said Stig. He reached into a back pocket, pulled out his phone, and killed it. I woke April Cowan's and did the same.

"Also, someone should get to the bottom of this," I said.

"What are you talking about?" said Stig. He rubbed his hands over his face. "This is real, Glo. April Cowan is lying dead in a hole. This isn't . . . you're not . . ."

"St. Mary Mead," I said. "Miss Marple. But it doesn't add up. I mean, your story about what happened that night at Eden? Already I can see loose little threads I can pick at."

"Oh?" said Stig. "Likes of what?"

"Likes of why was Vanman as white as a sheet and using words like *missing*?"

"Van *the* Man," said Stig. Then he thought about it and his eyes opened so wide his

77

glasses slipped down his nose. "You're right. It didn't seem weird, looking back, because it *was* terrible, so it was like he was right to be in a state from the off. But he shouldn't have been, should he?"

"But people are strange," I said. "That might have been something or nothing. Maybe he had a bad dream. I tell you what's *really* off. How did a car roar away in the night if the gates were locked?"

He blinked at me, stunned. "Jesus Christ," he said. "Thirty years I've been thinking about this and that never even occurred to me."

"Twenty-eight," I said. "And there aren't that many possible explanations. We just need to narrow it down."

But he wasn't listening. He was looking around the kitchen, not judging it now, just getting familiar. He laughed suddenly. "Have you ever seen that film *Misery*?"

"No," I answered, "but I've read the book. I'm a friend, Stig, not a fan."

I keep the spare bed made up more because it looks pretty with the quilt and pillow slips than in hope or fear of sudden guests. No one has stayed in this house except me since I moved in ten years ago. The nearest miss was one night when my mother and father came to see Nicky and came back here after. Dad was too shocked to drive and I got as far as boiling water for hot bottles before Mum came to her senses and realised what was happening.

"We haven't set the alarm," she'd said. "We haven't set light timers. I've left a washing out." As if Castle Douglas was some hotbed of crime. "Come on, Trevor, stir yourself. You'll be fine when you get going."

She had turned back at the front door as my dad weaved towards the car; doddered almost, suddenly an old man.

"Look what you've done to your father," she said. "How could you be so thoughtless?"

"Mum, I honestly don't know what you're talking about," I said.

"The way you puffed it all up. A new place, better care. You got our hopes up, Gloria. I'll never forgive you."

The only bright spot in the whole episode was Miss Drumm the next day. She'd been listening through the connecting door.

"So that's your mother, is it?" she'd said. "That's Nicky's grandmamma? She's one you'd leave inside the wolf."

"What are you smiling about?" said Stig. I was concentrating on filling the bottles, hadn't realised the thoughts were showing on my face.

"A happy memory," I said. "And an appropriate one too. You can't choose your family, but friends are a fine thing."

I love Rough House for saving my life, but showing Stig round, I saw it through his eyes. The only bathroom is downstairs, with just a bath, no shower and no heater either, and the rickety window lets the drafts howl through. It's a long way upstairs to the bedrooms, four of them, the two big ones facing the sunny garden and the two little ones with the arrow-slit windows facing out the back to the yard. *Facing the sunny garden in the daytime in the summer if and when the sun shines,* I thought, leading Stig into the room at the top of the stairs. On a night like this, it looked like where Jane Eyre saw the ghost. The furniture was something Miss Drumm called pickled walnut. The wallpaper was a sort of colourless pinky beige in a raised pattern that looked a bit like fungus, and the carpet and curtains were much the same. The crocheted mats, worked in white and stained with tea, and the crocheted, tea-stained handles on the brown-paper sun blinds didn't help. Cat sick, Miss Drumm called it, which made me shudder, but at least the quilt and the pillow slips were satin. I drew the line at

80

candlewick; all her candlewick covers were in the linen cupboard, dry cleaned and stored in bags sucked small with the hoover.

"I'll put towels in the bathroom for you," I said, as I slid the two hot water bottles in under the bedclothes. "And a toothbrush. And I'll set out a razor. Can you sleep in the sweat suit for now? I won't be long and no one will come to the door, I promise, but if they do, don't answer. No one's got a spare key. No one can get in."

"What?" he said. "Where are you going?"

"Phone box at Shawhead. It's tucked well away and nobody's even going to be walking a dog at this time of night when it's like this, are they?"

"You're really going to call the police?"

"I've got to. We can't leave her there on her own in the cold and dark."

"I can't ask you to do that," he said. "You don't owe me."

"Anonymously and a woman's voice," I said. "It's best that way. They'll probably want to ask me if I heard anything or saw anything, but they'll get me at work tomorrow. They won't come round here. There's no reason for them to connect me with April."

He nodded. I held out my hand.

"I'll put your car away while I'm out."

He nodded again and fished his car keys out of the sweatpants pocket. I was almost out the door when he stopped me.

"Glo?" he said. "You know earlier, when you were freaking out about them closing the home? Thinking someone who works there might be mixed up in this?" I nodded. "Why would you want them looking after your boy if you reckon that's possible? Why wouldn't you want the place closed down if there's someone there who might harm him?"

I took a long time deciding what to say, but in the end I was as straight with him as he'd been with me. "What's the worst they could do?" I asked.

"I don't want to say it."

"Say it."

"They could kill him."

"And his troubles would be over. Don't look at me like that."

"Or they could hurt him."

"No, they couldn't," I said. "Wait here." I walked along the corridor to the big bedroom at the other end and lifted Nicky's picture from my bedside table.

"Oh," said Stig, when I came back and handed it to him. "What's caused that then?"

That's a fair enough question, and so I

answered him. "Pantothenate Kinase-Associated Neurodegeneration," I said, taking the picture back and polishing the frame with my cuff. "PKAN, for short." I kissed the glass over Nicky's face "My little PKAN pie. Nothing hurts him, nothing helps him, nothing ever will. I'd best be off."

"Of course, if you're going to tell them that Stephen Tarrant drove a woman to suicide and you've got him locked in your house without his car keys, there's nothing I could do to stop you," Stig said. He was smiling at me.

"You could overpower me now before I start," I said, smiling back. "If you're going to leave one woman's body behind you, why not two?"

We considered one another for a long minute. I'm not sure who broke eye contact first. Probably me since I'm not much of a hard nut.

"Drive safely," he said.

"Sleep tight," I said back.

SEVEN

I practised what to say all the way on the back lane to the Shawhead phone box. Just as I had imagined, I didn't pass another car and I drew off the road before the start of the houses, made my way to the kiosk on foot with no torch. It was lit up, but there was no one to see me as I slipped inside and fumbled the buttons with my gloved fingers. I had never dialled 999 before and my pulse started racing as I waited for the call to go through.

"What service?" asked a bored voice.

"Police," I said, trying to make my voice sound gruff.

"Are you in a safe place, madam?" asked the exchange. Obviously I sounded like exactly what I was: a scared woman.

"Police," I said again. "There's been a death."

When I got through to them, I didn't chance the gruff voice again. I whispered.

"There's a body," I said.

Then I froze. I felt a sick swirling in my head and my vision blurred. I couldn't believe I hadn't seen it until that moment, couldn't believe I had got that close to blurting out the words that would wreck everything. I crashed the receiver down, burst out of the phone box, ran to my car, and drove away.

He didn't come to meet me at the door and I wondered if he was sleeping. It was hard to imagine that sleep would have come to him, but then shock does strange things to you. When the doctors told us about Nicky — finally told us straight, laid it all out, stopped spinning fairy tales — I slept for thirty-six hours. I've never been so ashamed of anything in my life. Just when he needed his mother most of all, when he was trying to deal with such bad news, I abandoned him and slept. I even remember what I dreamt of. A childhood summer, a room with floating white curtains and a shining wooden floor and me sitting up in bed with a nightcap on, eating soup from a cup and playing with tiny little wooden soldiers that turned into chessmen and then marbles and rolled away. I've never been in a room like that in my life. More's the pity.

I turned off the kitchen lamps, rubbed

Walter's head, and said a prayer to keep the Rayburn lit until morning, then slipped out into the hallway. That was when I heard him snoring. I put the light on and looked down at him, sitting at the bottom of the stairs with his head against the banisters, his mouth open and his hands hanging down between his knees. A scrap of paper had dropped from his grasp and lay on the floor.

I bent and lifted it, seeing that it was a clipping from a newspaper. A tiny thing; it hardly took a moment to read it.

McAllister, 1 May 1995. It said. *By his own hand, Nathan McAllister. Private funeral. No flowers.*

I hadn't had any dinner, beyond the bit of gingerbread and chocolate biscuit they'd brought me at the home with my cup of tea. They're good to me there since I'm in every day. So I was lightheaded by this time. Never mind the whisky that I'm not used to. And the newspaper clipping was one thing too much. *By his own hand.*

The words danced on the page and all I could see was April's hands, curled round the handle of the knife with the dark blood in the creases of her fingers. And then Nicky's hands, curled round the rolled flannels they give him to stop them spasming up so tight I can't wash them. I wash them every night. Well, boys his age get mucky. I wash them and rub lotion into them and once a week I trim his nails and take off his friendship bracelets, rub his wrists underneath in case they're itchy. April wore no jewelry. Her sleeves were pushed back up her arms as far as they would go and there was nothing.

"It was in the bottom of her bag," said Stig. I hadn't noticed him waking. "It's Nod, from our class. If that's real, and it looks real, he's dead."

"Since 1995."

"First of May, 1995. The tenth anniversary of the night Moped died. Gloria, what the fuck's going on?"

I took a deep breath to answer, but I had no idea what to say.

"Let me sleep on it," I went for in the end. "It might look different in the morning."

Then I went to the bathroom to undress for bed. I peed, washed my face, and undid my hair to brush it, but as the cistern finished filling and quieted, I thought I heard something. Yes! There was a car bumping along the track. I switched off the bathroom light and crept through the hall in the darkness just in time to hear two car doors.

"Glo!" Stig's voice, a fierce whisper, came

from upstairs.

"Ssh," I whispered back.

"Be careful!" He probably meant *don't open up in case it's a madman.* But I had heard the radios and I knew I had to be careful in very different way. I didn't understand. Had they traced the call? Had someone seen me?

The knock, when it came, was loud enough to set my heart hammering, but they probably meant it to wake someone sleeping upstairs. I clicked on the porch light and opened the door. Policemen don't like to look surprised, but their eyes were wide and one of them moved his feet.

"I heard you coming," I said. "Is it Nicky?"

"Mrs. Morrison?" said one of them. The rain was dripping off the peak of his hat.

"Harkness," I said. "I went back to my maiden name. Is it Nicky? Is something wrong?"

"Can we come in, Ms. Harkness?"

My mind flashed to the kitchen. The two chairs by the stove, Stig's clothes drying on the pulley, April's bag wherever he had left it.

"Of course," I said, "but please, I'm begging you, tell me what's wrong." I ushered them in and steered them to the right, along

88

the hall to the living room, cold as the grave, the fire full of ash from last weekend. They didn't sit and neither did I. We just stood there in a ring, our breath pluming.

"We've had a report of suspicious behaviour," said the one who hadn't spoken before. My stomach dropped and then bounced back up all the way to my throat.

"Have you been out tonight?" said the other.

"I went to see my son, at the home," I said. "Is it nothing to do with Nicky, then?" How could someone have seen my car? There wasn't a single house between me and the huttie the way we had gone. There hadn't been a single set of headlights either. And the road to the Shawhead phone box was deserted too. Who had seen me?

"A red Skoda," said the older of the two policemen. Stig's car, in the byre now with the door padlocked. "Did you see a vehicle answering that description?"

"I don't think so," I said. "There were cars parked at the home — the backshift staff, you know — but I don't think I saw a red Skoda. I can't be sure, I kept my head down. This weather, you know. Should I be worried?"

"The driver's not a very pleasant chap, Ms. Harkness. Given to stalking. We had a report that he was prowling these back roads tonight. Scared a young woman enough that she called us."

"When?" I said. "Now? He's out there now? Did you tell them up at the home? There's a lot of vulnerable people there. My son, Nicky, and lots of others."

"We've just come from the home," said the older cop. The young one had lost interest. He was rubbing his hands together, blowing on them, ready to be away from this cold house and this hysterical old bag who kept on about her son. I could tell what he thought from the way he had stopped looking at me.

"Probably long gone," said the other one. "The call came in at eight."

"And you waited until now?" I said, after only a second's pause. "Too bad if he *was* here. He's had three hours to chop me into pieces and drive away again."

They didn't like that, but they were too well-trained to show it much.

"He's only accused of prowling. So far."

"Well, I didn't see him or his car," I told them.

"And so we'll leave you to get on with your evening," said the copper.

The young one looked at me again now, my face shiny with cream and my feet in

90

my yeti slippers that should be white but pick up all the dust going and Walter Scott's hair too and have always got a border of grey around the bottom.

I shut the door behind them and bolted it.

"—uck's sake," I heard the younger one say as they splashed back to their car. "She's as bad as the freak show up at the loony bin."

I waited for his boss to scold him, but all I heard was a snort of laughter, so I clicked off the porch light. Let them find the rest of their way in the dark.

We waited, me in the hall and Stig up on the landing, until the sound of the car had faded into the hissing rain. Then I switched the light on and went up.

"Did you hear that?" I said.

"Every word," said Stig. He breathed in and out very fast four times and rubbed his face hard with the palms of his hands. "I didn't stalk April Cowan," he said. "That was a pack of lies. I can show you my phone and her phone and the call history. Jesus fucking Christ." He had started pacing up and down the hall, in and out of the bedroom. I'd never seen anyone pace before. "She really had it in for me."

"No sugar, Sherlock," I said.

"Jesus, Glo, if they *had* come right up here as soon as they got the call they'd have found us parked up in the lane and mucking about in the huttie." Then he fell silent, stopped pacing, and stared.

"Yes," I said. "Well spotted. April Cowan wasn't on the road at eight. She was bled out and stone cold by nine. Telling the cops you were chasing her was just about the last thing she did. She must have called them right before she —" I stopped, frowning.

"Yeah," said Stig. "We've got her phone."

But I thought of a way to explain that. "We've got *a* phone."

"But you said there was no signal."

"Maybe the huttie's a hotspot." It was all I had, but it didn't seem likely.

Stig thought it over. "Do you think they'll come back when they get radioed through about the body?"

"They won't get radioed," I said. "I didn't tell them. I hung up. Thank God, as it turned out."

"Why not?" said Stig. "Why thank God?" He was watching me very carefully.

"Because it suddenly occurred to me that if she tried to get you to the huttie and she planted her bag at your flat, what do you think she's left behind at her place? I bet if there's a suicide note, your name'll be mentioned."

His face, I was sure of it, turned pale. "But we've got to tell them, Glo. We can't just leave her there."

I shook my head. "We've got to help April, that's true. But we don't need to tell *them* anything. They are not good people."

I was rummaging in the deep bottom drawer of the dressing table in the spare room.

"What are you doing?"

I hadn't taken down the little eyes from either side of all the windows and I had kept the elastic wires coiled up in a drawer. The net curtains themselves I had dipped in Glo-white, just like my mum did, and then folded them away when they were dry.

"And how do you know they're worse people than me? Why did you cover for me when they said I stalked her?"

"I asked them five times if Nicky was all right," I said. "Five times. You heard me."

Eight

Tuesday

It was strange the next morning, waking up with the windows muffled in net, like being inside a cocoon that turned the weak wintry daylight drab and grey. I missed the sight of the hill from my bedroom when I opened my eyes and the view of the garden laid out like a tapestry as I passed the landing window. Stig opened his door when I got to the top of the stairs.

"I've been awake for hours," he said. "Nod *and* April. I can't believe it." He shivered.

"Let's get into the warm," I said, and together we hurried downstairs to the kitchen. The cats were out, must have disappeared off through the flap as soon as the rain stopped, but Walter Scott was there, standing with his nose practically against the back door, waiting. I opened the door and he plodded down the steps to the yard and squatted.

"Oh great, Walter," I said. "Lovely." When I first came he used to burst out of the back door like a whippet and race twice round before he could even stop long enough to sniff. Then he'd mark every downpipe and doorjamb all over the farmyard and bucket off across the field to do his business some- where far off down the hill. I hadn't had to put my hand in one of those bags and scrape up his mess until just earlier this year. "What if I get germs from this and give them to Nicky?" I had asked, turning the bag inside out and tying it. "Nicky can't fight infection like you and me, you know. One morning bundle of yours could carry him off. Think I'd stick around here clean- ing up after you if I didn't need to be close by?" Walter Scott had just leaned against my legs and looked up at me, sneezing and snuffling that way he does when he's trying to say I love you. "Yes, I love you too," I'd told him. "And yes, I'd stay."

"I'll get that," said Stig behind me. "Where's the bags?"

"I've been thinking, Glo," he said, when he was back inside and had scrubbed his hands and then warmed them on the Rayburn. His voice had that defeated sound again, so I cut him off.

"I've been thinking too. Tonight, after work, I'm going to go back to the huttie and check that she's got no ID on her anywhere. That'll buy time. And then tomorrow —"

"You can't be serious," he said. "You're going to go back and rummage around in her pockets." His face was so white that his stubble stood out like iron filings on his cheeks. Then he shook his head. "Gloria, you're doing it again," he said. "This isn't one of your books. This is the real world. Large as life. Plain as day."

I get sick of the way people patronise me. I don't know what it is about me, but everywhere I go people pat me on the head and chuck me under the chin. Not literally, but everyone from my mother and my sister if they're in the right mood, to Lynne at work and people in the village. They're *kind* to me, patient with me, like they've got to be kind and patient to poor Gloria. The only place it doesn't happen is the home. There I'm Nicky's mum and Miss Drumm's friend and I fit right in. Deirdre's mum and I can have a nice chat like two women at the school gate, and for once no one's pitying either of us.

Stig must have wondered why I sounded so angry when I answered him, because what he'd said was pretty mild. But it was the last move in a long game. *This isn't one of your books, Gloria. That's a lovely cardi, Gloria. How's that handsome son of yours?* I slammed the microwave door and turned to face him.

"I'm not a fool, Stig," I said. "I'm being completely realistic, and books are nothing to do with it. Tonight I check her body and tomorrow I go to her house or flat or whatever and get rid of anything there that could harm you."

"You can't," he said. "I don't know where she lives. I looked through her stuff and there's no address anywhere."

"Which is odd, right?" I said. "Where's her driving licence? Why isn't it in her purse where it should be?"

"Maybe she hasn't got one. Maybe she doesn't drive."

"But how else would she get way out here?" I said. "The buses —" The thought hit both of us at the same time, but it was Stig who spoke.

"Where's her car? I know there's no buses, practically. A taxi?"

"Pretty memorable, once someone reports her missing," I said. "I need to check her pockets and her flat."

"We don't know her address, remember?"

said Stig. "We're stuffed."

"No, we're not," I said. "Because you told me she was divorced. Married and divorced? Her address'll be in the system. On the FER. Forward Electronic Register," I added before he asked me.

"You can just look everything up from your office?"

"Everyone can," I said. "Birth, marriage, divorce, and death. The FER is public record. Only, the public have to log in and it leaves a trace. And anyone looking up April Cowan's address today would be really interesting to the cops, wouldn't they? But I can look things up and no one will ever know."

"Birth, marriage . . ." he said. It had dawned on him.

"Exactly. If Nathan McAllister really committed suicide in 1995, I'll find the record. Meanwhile," I said, popping open the microwave door, "I want you to write down everything you can remember about that night and everything before it and after it. Anything at all. Just like remembering April had crimped hair and bad acne. Anything you can get out of your brain. Write it down. Okay? Any questions?"

"Just one. Are you going near any shops today?"

"I could do," I said. "But only in the village, so don't ask me for men's things."

"Pinhead oatmeal and full-fat milk," said Stig. "And real salt instead of this crap. Why do you make quick oats in a nuker when you've got a Rayburn stove?"

I poured the porridge into two bowls and banged them down on the table beside the semi-skimmed milk and Lo-Salt.

"Sorry," he said. "Ungrateful."

"I'll be back at about ten past five," I told him, "and then out again to the home and when I'm back for keeps, we can discuss everything."

"Sorry," he said again. "Do you usually stop in here first? Because if not, then don't. You should stick to your usual routine."

"I don't want to leave you that long," I said. "I'll blame Walter. Say he needs checking in on. He nearly does anyway."

Stig stirred his spoon round staring into his bowl. "It doesn't feel real," he said. "It's like we're at one of those parties where you get a card: murderer, victim, detective."

"Detective," I said. "And listen, speaking of routines, what's going to happen when you don't show up for your work?"

"Nothing," he said. "They'll change the combination on my locker and have someone else in by next week. Won't be the first time."

I wondered then. That didn't sound like the sort of job BJ Tarrant's son would have. They were business people, the Tarrants. Bought adverts in gala programmes and donated prizes to raffles. *Flash Harry,* my mum said, *and that leg of mutton he's married to.* I thought Stig would be the boss, unsackable.

"You've not had it easy, have you?"

He said nothing, just turned away from me and went to stand at the front kitchen window now, resting his head against the net curtain, staring out. "There's plenty had it worse," he said. "But honestly, I don't think I'm up to this. April dead and trying to take me down as she goes? Why? Why did Nod kill himself? Why did she have his obituary with her? There's too much and it's too complicated." His breathing was starting to sound panicky again, like the night before when he was pacing.

I didn't tell him to slow it down, but I breathed slowly myself, hoping he would follow. Modelling. I learned it in the conflict resolution bit of my induction training. All registrars get it, I think, but you only need it in big cities where weddings can get raucous and when there's two lads wanting on the birth certificate and a girl that won't give a glance to either. That doesn't happen very much in a place like Dalry.

"What's that thing?" said Stig, still with his head against the window.

I knew what he was talking about, of course. It's hidden from the lane and the gate and the path. The only view of it is from the kitchen.

"That's the only possible problem with you lying low," I said. I joined him and looked out at it. Six feet tall, six feet round, mossy and lichened on its shady side and bleached pale grey where the sun hit it, it sat basking in the dawn, enjoying the dew rising from it for the day. "That's the Stone of Milharay. It's the reason I'm here. Well, that and Walter."

"But what is it?" said Stig.

"Come and see," I said. "What size are your feet? You can jam on my crocs and shuffle out there."

It was cold, of course, but with that fresh, keen wind that makes me think of hares streaking across the fields, so different from the bellowing storm last night. Over by the stone we could hear the wind whistling.

"It's a rocking stone," I said. "Push it. Gently!"

He set one hand against its shady side and

pressed. His eyebrows shot up. "Whoa!" he said, jumping back. "That felt really weird."

"I'm pretty sure it wouldn't pass health and safety."

"It felt like it was going to roll on top of me," he said, putting his fingertips against it again.

"It doesn't matter where you push, it always does that."

"Why would you ever push it?"

"Old wives' tales," I said. "Twelve pushes for luck."

Even more gently, he rocked it again, not even hard enough to whiten the skin around his fingernails. He was so restrained — not like my brother-in-law shoving it with the side of his arm as if he was trying to break down a door and then just laughing when it threatened to topple.

"I'd have been homeless," I'd screamed at him. "And thousands of years of history gone because you're such a He-Man."

"Who says He-Man?" Scott sneered. "You're a throwback, Gloria."

"Fishwife, more like," said my sister. "Don't screech like that. You'll upset the baby." She rubbed her stomach that way she was always doing.

"What about *my* baby?" I'd roared at her. I knew I shouldn't be raising my voice, but their visit had made me scared of what they were up to, why all of a sudden they wanted to be coming to see me. "Eh?" I demanded. "What about how upset Nicky would be if I didn't live here any more and couldn't get to see him every day?"

"Nicky," Scott had said, "would be as upset as this bloody rock." And my sister, Marilyn, actually smirked. She had the decency to turn away, but she was smiling. So I never met my niece, or the nephew that followed, and Nicky hadn't seen his auntie and uncle since he was six.

"Hardly any of them still move," I told Stig. "They get choked up with leaf litter or tufts of grass or people try to clear them and go too far and they roll off. Miss Drumm's been looking after this one since she was twelve and her dad trained her. Then when she got too frail, she trained me."

"And how exactly could this thing scupper me hiding?"

"Because the only time in ten years anyone has ever turned up here unannounced is once when some archeology or history buffs — not sure who they were — came to ask about a stone. But you can't see it over the wall and they came to the back door, so I said I didn't know what they were talking about."

I hadn't told Miss Drumm in case she burst a blood vessel. The Stone of Milharay wasn't on Wikipedia and it wasn't on Historic Scotland and that was purely because — as she explained to me, gripping my arm hard with her callused old hand until her yellow nails nearly dug into my flesh — that was purely because the estate had been in her family for four hundred years and even though they lost more and more of it until she, the last of the Drumms, was forced to live in a shepherd's hovel, the fact that Rough House and its grounds had never passed through the office of an estate agent kept the secret safe.

"Why does she care so much?" said Stig, when I'd explained to him.

"Well, standing stones and circles and menhirs, you know," I said. I didn't want to tell him, because Miss Drumm is my friend and there's no way to say it without making her sound like a lunatic.

"I really don't, Glo."

"Druids, Wiccans, Pagans, all that lot. A standing stone — I'm quoting Miss Drumm now — 'is like catnip, and a rocking stone that still rocks would be like catnip rolled in cocaine.' The place would be overrun with them, she reckons."

"And she likes her peace and quiet, eh?" said Stig.

"That's it," I lied. And changed the subject. "So I'm here guarding the stone and feeding Walter Scott. Miss Drumm would shut the place up if it weren't for Walter, but as long as he's here, I'm here, and as long as someone's here they can . . . guard the stone." *Rock* the stone, I had almost said, but I stopped myself before he got the chance to laugh at me. "And because I don't pay any rent I can afford to keep Nicky in the home, which I couldn't otherwise, because being a registrar doesn't pull in much of a wage really. But as long as Miss Drumm lasts long enough, everything will be okay. So I spend just about as much time making sure they take good care of her as I do making sure they take good care of Nicky, and that does her no harm either."

"Lasts long enough for what?" said Stig. I tried to answer him. I opened my mouth and closed it enough times to feel like a fish, and God knows what I looked like, but I've never said the worst even to myself and certainly not out loud. I wouldn't know where to begin.

"Poor wee guy," said Stig, showing that I didn't need to.

"And speaking of my job, I need to go and do it," I said. I only cried a little bit while the bath taps were going and, anyway, even if you're doing a wedding, I always think people will just assume that a registrar with red eyes has just recorded a death.

NINE

" 'Nothing in the world is single,' " I said at the end of the ceremony. " 'All things by a law divine, in another's being mingle — Why not I with thine?' " There wasn't a dry eye in the house.

It would get me struck off if the Humanist Society could hear me. I could just imagine Bryan — the sergeant-at-arms, Miss Drumm called him; actually the HS regional coordinator — choking on the word when he tried to accuse me: *A law divine, Gloria? Divine? If they wanted divinity they'd cough up for a church.*

"That was absolutely lovely," said one of the mothers. She was neck to knee in lavender chiffon, like a mother should be, a fascinator like a giant insect landed on her head. "Are you coming to the reception?"

"Oh, how kind you are!" I said. "If only I could. But I've got to get back to the office and enter all this to make it legal." I patted the folder where the signed register extract was waiting. That usually did the trick. The thought of the registrar kicking up her heels at the party and the precious documents getting shoved under a banquet table and lost was enough to stop nearly everyone.

"Well, then for God's sake, come to the reception," sneered the other mother. She was wearing a herringbone suit that had seen better days. Even I was more dressed up, and I try not to be. Neat and smart but no competition. Lynne at work had been kind anyway.

"Gorgeous!" she'd said when she saw me. But no one who dressed like Lynne could think someone who dressed like me was gorgeous. "One of these days, Gloria, there's going to be a jilting at the altar and a groom's going to whisk you away."

"Not today," I told her. "It's two grooms."

Lynne narrowed her eyes. "Bloody gay weddings." But she didn't mean it unkindly. "I've only just learned the forms for civil partnerships and here we go again. Moderate pace of change, my arse. They never think about the paperwork, do they?"

I ignored the scruffy mother and turned to the giant fascinator one.

"How lucky Carl is to be joining *your* family," I said, squeezing her hand. Some of

Miss Drumm was starting to rub off on me. I would never have been so rude before I started spending so much time with her. But I put it out of my mind. It wasn't as though the torn-faced mother was going to complain about a sour note spoiling her son's wedding when she didn't want her son married anyway. And besides, I had to make the most of the time I was alone in the office this afternoon. Lynne only worked mornings.

Nathan McAllister. Born 17-3-1972. No occupation. Single. Aged 23. Found dead 8.16am 1-5-1995. Stirling University Sports Centre car park. Usual residence: Flat 4, 38 Horne Terrace, Edinburgh. Cause of Death: (amended) (i) suicide by carb.mon.tox. Certifying physician pppf [signed]. Registered by: Edmund McAllister (brother) Central Reg. Ed. 10-5-1995.

I read it over and over again, then clicked back to the index screen, feeling my eyes start to swim with tears. Twenty-three years old and he'd fed a pipe from his exhaust into his car and sat there in a car park until he poisoned himself. No time of death, just when he was found. And a doctor appointed by the procurator fiscal. His brother registering his death for him. I could imagine the parents, sitting in a silent room with drawn curtains, unable to move, unable to speak. The words danced in front of my eyes, doubling and dazzling.

Then I blinked, leaned forward, and looked again. The words weren't doubling at all. I was reading the next entry down.

Edmund McAllister. Born 17-3-1972.

Ned and Nod, Stig had called them, and they were both dead. They were twins, otherwise they wouldn't never have been beside each other in the record — plenty of McAllisters in Scotland, after all. They were twins and they had died within a year of each other. I clicked through and kept reading.

Found dead 7.15pm, 8-11-1995. Hermitage, Dunkeld.
Cause of Death: (amended) (i) suicide by drowning.
Certifying physician, pppf [signed] Registered by:
Phillip McAllister (father) Central Reg. Ed. 20-11-1995.

The Hermitage at Dunkeld. I knew the place. It was a beautiful spot — a high waterfall with a little stone folly. If someone wanted to blend the Eden crypt and the place where Moped Best fell into the river, then the Hermitage at Dunkeld was about as good as it could get. And this time his poor father had to go and register the death himself. Presumably because there was no one else to do it for them. I thought about my colleagues up there in the central office in Edinburgh, in that gloomy looming building, and hoped that Mr. McAllister had got someone kind, someone still able to share a little in the pain, even if they saw it every day.

I printed the two entries then wiped the history and switched the computer off. Sat there looking at the wall of fame, all the babies and couples in their wedding clothes. We never got funeral photographs, not of the flowers or the coffin or even the mourners. And I always wondered if it was worth trying to start the tradition. You heard it over and over again at the funeral teas afterwards: how the family only ever saw each other at funerals these days, how the last time they'd seen the departed was at so-and-so's funeral. *Well, stand up and smile and take some pictures,* I always wanted to say. *Chances are there's someone here today you'll never see again in this life.*

But what, I asked myself as I sat there staring, was bothering me? Some thought had flitted over my brain and now it was gone somewhere I couldn't follow.

I tried all the memory tricks I knew as I waited for the clock to tick round to five, then I washed out the coffeemaker, set it up for the next day, put the printouts in a plastic sleeve, and went home, like I always do. If anyone was watching from one of the cottages on the long main street all they'd see was that woman who lives up the hill going home like clockwork, or maybe fat Gloria setting off for another thrilling night at someone's bedside, or that nice registrar who was so kind when Auntie Joyce died; that's her off home.

I didn't usually wonder what anyone thought of me or even whether they did, but tonight I felt like an ant crawling across a sheet of white paper under a microscope, with the printouts in my bag and the unfamiliar groceries in a basket over my arm.

"Been watching Jamie Oliver?" Mr. Slocombe in the shop had asked at lunchtime. "He's the women's Nigella, isn't he?"

"Been on the Internet, Mr. Slocombe," I said, hoping I wasn't changing colour. "It's all about sugar now. Fat and salt are fine."

Only now I was worried that he would ask

himself *where* I had been on the Internet, because the WiFi at Rough House would make you weep. And I didn't want him to think I had been abusing the machine in the office. Especially because today, for the first time, I had. I mean, there was nothing illegal about me looking up entries, or even printing them, but I had stolen two sheets of paper and a plastic sleeve. There was no denying that.

At first I thought he'd gone. Rough House was as still and serene as ever. The house cats and byre cats were sitting on the wall by the gate, the two camps keeping their distance. Walter Scott was nowhere to be seen. The nets blinding the windows didn't move and no shadow passed behind them. When I opened the back door, though, everything was different, the kitchen fragrant and steaming, but empty.

"Stig?" I called out.

I heard the bathroom door unlocking and he appeared, still in the sweat suit but with Miss Drumm's old crossover pinny on top. Walter was with him.

"Had to be sure it was you," he said, his voice sounding tremulous.

"What's that smell?" I asked him.

"Meatballs Arrabiata. Or as close as I

113

could get with what I could find. Your cupboards are pathetic." He saw my look. "I had to do *something* cooped up all day. You didn't give me your password and there's no telly."

"There's a radio," I said, nodding at it up on the high mantelpiece above the Rayburn. "Was there anything on the news?"

He shook his head. "An accident on the A75 and a break-in at the furniture showroom in Annan. Ask me anything. I've heard it seven times. I could go on *Mastermind* and my specialist subject would be Southwest Scotland on the eighth of October, two thou—"

"Ssh," I said. His voice was shaking, as though he was cycling over cobbles, and his eyes were getting shiny too. "Let's just talk about something else for a couple of minutes. Try to slow down your breathing and you'll feel more calm."

"Oh, yeah great," he said. "Fucking yoga. That'll solve everything."

"What's this?" I said, lifting the edge of a tea cloth covering something on the warming rack. He batted my hand away.

"Rosemary flatbread," he said. "That wouldn't be you subtly trying to distract me, would it?" But at last he did take a big breath in and let it out again. "Pretty good herb garden you've got out there, but you'll need to wrap the bay before the frost comes."

"You're a cook," I said. "And a gardener."

"Not a gardener," he told me. "But yeah, I'm a chef. Why did you have a two-pound bag of bread flour and no yeast?"

"I bought it by accident," I said. "A chef?"

I remembered cooking classes in primary seven. We studied a country, learned the dances, made the national costume out of crepe paper and then, for a finale, went over to the new bit of the school and cooked a traditional meal. Moussaka, burritos, chow mein. I remember Stig and Bezzo mixing up flour paste and bits of carrot and corn to make a puddle of sick and freak out the teacher, then thinking of Bezzo reminded me of Moped and the double entry under *McAllister,* and I had to sit down quickly in one of the kitchen chairs.

Stig didn't notice. Looking down into his pot, he just kept talking.

"Wee J did business studies and hospitality so he could be the manager, and I got a chef's apprenticeship so I could stay in the kitchen. My mum trained to run the spa and my dad was going to stand behind the bar and tell jokes. A perfect little empire with BJ at the top, like the fucking Godfather." He lifted a spoonful of sauce out of the pan and, holding his other hand underneath it so it didn't drip on the dog, he turned to let me taste it.

"You swear quite a lot," I said.

"All chefs swear a lot," said Stig. "If you had a telly like normal people, you'd know that."

"I'd rather have a cheese toastie and no effing," I said.

"What's wrong?" he asked, looking properly at me for the first time.

"Are you sure you'll be okay if I tell you?" I said.

"I promise," he said. "I'm sorry. Being cooped up is —"

But still I chickened out of telling him at first. "I got April's address." He raised his eyebrows. "And I looked up Nathan's record." I took the plastic sleeve out of my bag and handed it to him.

"Fucking hell," he said, reading the two printouts. "That's three, Glo. Ned, Nod, and April."

"Four counting Mitchell."

"It can't be coincidence," he said. "But what's the connection?" He stared at the paper, as if he could work out the answer from those few brief notes. On the Rayburn, the pot was bubbling harder, sending out

116

splats of sauce that sizzled on the hotplate.

"I don't know," I said. "I don't understand. I suppose it's possible that the trauma about Moped affected Nathan so badly he killed himself, and that that might do his twin brother's head in. And then April saw the death notice and that finished her off." I was babbling, but I couldn't stop myself.

"I could have stopped this," said Stig. "If I'd listened to her. Insisted on seeing her. God, if I'd even got to the huttie a bit quicker. I don't suppose you looked up any of the others?"

I flushed. "I don't know their real names. Or couldn't remember them, anyway."

"Alan Best?" said Stig, and I flushed deeper. I could feel the angry blotches creeping over my chest and was glad that I still had my coat on.

"I wasn't thinking straight," I said. "Look, I really need to go and see Nicky, but while I'm out you write down all their names. Full names if you can."

"I've already done it," said Stig. "I've written everything I can remember, like you said."

"I'll go over it when I get back. Over dinner."

"Can't you take it with you?" he said.

"Read it while you're there?"

"Read it to *Nicky*?"

"No! Sorry! Sorry."

I was too angry to speak. I just stood up and walked out. I'd stay longer than usual, I thought, getting in and slamming the car door, and if his Meatballs à la Profanity were dried up when I got back, then tough cheese.

Ten

The McAllister brothers, April Cowan, and poor Moped faded a little as I rolled up to the home to see Nicky. It was always my favourite bit of any day, rolling up to the home to see Nicky. Even Miss Drumm was like family now after ten years.

It used to be that I'd stop in on her every few days, let her know how Walter Scott was getting on, reassure her about the stone, share news of the brambles in the hedgerows and how the potatoes were doing. I sometimes wondered if she knew that I had never made a pot of bramble jelly in my life and wouldn't know potato blight if I caught it, but I thought maybe she liked the pretence, found it harmless, since she'd never see the garden again or find out that the vegetable patch was overrun with those sunflowers and the great-great-grandchildren of her last lettuces.

Besides, since they were in adjoining

rooms, I could hardly visit Nicky and ignore her. It was good of her to have him, really; he still cried out back then, and it wasn't a noise you'd choose to hear if you didn't have to. It wasn't all that different, when I came to think of it, from the noise Walter Scott made when I tried to get him to leave her behind, the few times he visited. Miss Drumm turned her head away, her mouth trembling, and Walter dug his toenails into the polished floor of the hall and sat down hard. If the doors on that side of the corridor were open and the morning sun was shining, you could still see the scratches on the parquet where I'd dragged him.

But Walter hadn't been here for nine years now and Nicky had stopped making any sounds at all about six years back, so now the arrangement worked perfectly for everyone. Miss Drumm listened in on the nurses to check they weren't teasing him, and he was the only resident who didn't mind a connecting door with "that chopsy old B" as Mr. Ainsworth called her.

"Do you know, Gloria," he'd said, "she had the cheek to tell me well-done steak was wasted beef and I might as well have a slice of luncheon meat and leave the fillets for more discerning palates."

"Why did you tell her?" I asked him.

"She's blind. You could have said it was ooz-ing with blood and she'd not have known any better."

"She could tell from the sound of me cut-ting it," Mr. Ainsworth said. "She's got ears like a bat."

But it was her bat ears that I valued most, her chopsy ways too, and even her hector-ing. I couldn't think of anyone better to be looking out for Nicky all day.

Little Deirdre was sitting on her stool just inside the front door as ever. She was only in her fifties, but her hair was like thistle-down, her cheeks as withered as week-old balloons.

"Hello there," I said.

Deirdre beamed at me. Her teeth were gruesome; she'd neither brush them herself nor let anyone else brush them for her, and a rinse with strawberry mouthwash twice a day over the years had fallen far short. When the pain got bad, they sedated her to get her in the car and then knocked her out completely at the dentist. It wouldn't be long before the next visit was due.

I usually paid no attention to the house as I made my way to Nicky and Miss Drumm, but tonight I found myself wondering about all it had seen in its years. About when the Drumm family used to hold balls and shooting parties in the winter, about the soldiers from both wars who recuperated here, the years it stood empty, ringing with silence and filling with cobwebs, then those children at Eden and the morning that Miss Whatshername was screeching and the kids were terrified and the police were at the gate trying to get in. And a boy in a bright orange anorak was facedown in the river, turning with the current, all his secrets locked inside him forever.

"You're late," said Miss Drumm. She put out a hand and slapped the outsize button of her clock. *Five-fifty-three,* said the robot voice.

"Are you bursting with news for me?" I managed to get my tone very breezy, but even just asking had made my pulse beat faster. Could I fake surprise if it had broken?

"News?" said Miss Drumm. "In this place? Chance'd be a fine thing. Then I could give up on those soap operas that are rotting my brain like ergots."

"So no gossip then?" I asked.

She moved her thumb over the nodule on her chair arm that controls the direction until she had swung round to face me. "What is it?" she said.

The light shining in from the bright corridor bounced off the lenses of her spectacles and hid her eyes. If I hadn't known she was blind, I'd have sworn she could see right through me.

"What?" I said. "Nothing. What do you mean?"

"Is Walter all right? Have you had the vet out? Has some nosey parker come sniffing?"

"Walter's fine. No one's been anywhere."

"Are you rocking the stone?" she said.

"Of course," I said. "I did a wedding today. Two lovely boys who've been together for seven years. And old Mr. Thorne died. His children are coming to register it tomorrow."

"Oh?" said Miss Drumm. She couldn't care less about weddings, but a death in the village was always something.

"Yes, he went to a nightclub in Glasgow and snapped a vertebra break dancing."

"Typical," said Miss Drumm, grinning to show me she appreciated the joke. "I remember Sandy Thorne when he was a paperboy for Slocombe's back when it was Ainslie and Sons. He used to bring our *Times* on his bicycle and leave it in a tin box stuck to the gate. I had a bit of a soft spot for him when he was fifteen and I was seven, and I used to swing on that gate for hours waiting to catch a glimpse."

"I think that's the box that's on the gate

at the Rough House road-end now," I said. "For the postie."

"Don't interrupt," said Miss Drumm. "And one day I turned up a bit late to find Sandy trying like billy-oh to stuff the *Times* into the slot. But it wouldn't go. I had the key for the box, being a child of the family, and I opened it up.

"Well, lo and behold, inside there was a robin's nest with two blue eggs and the fiercest little robin ready to defend them with her life."

"How marvellous!"

"Marvellous indeed. Sandy Thorne took both eggs and pelted them at the trunk of a rowan tree, then he swiped the nest out of the way, put the newspaper inside, and slammed the door shut."

"No!"

"I never spoke to him again. I can still hear that little robin crying if I listen."

I should be used to her by now; Miss Drumm delights in the sort of mawkish stories even Thomas Hardy would edit out with a blue pencil in the second draft. Normally I can roll my eyes and ignore them, but the horrors of the day had built up inside me until I was fit to burst, and for some reason the two blue eggs and the grieving robin mingled in my imagination with Mrs. McAllister and the two dead boys, and suddenly tears were very close. I had never cried in front of Miss Drumm, who was savage about what she called *blubbing.*

"Gloria," she said, "I'm going to ask you again. What is wrong, my dear?" *My dear!* "Has there been bad news about young Nicky? None of these nurses ever tells me anything."

"No," I said again.

"So why are you troubled? You *have* been rocking the stone, haven't you?" This was what I hadn't wanted to tell Stig. Miss Drumm and her stone. "Twelve times, mark you!" she said. "If you miscount and do thirteen, carry on till twenty-four, I mean it. Don't you scoff at me, young woman! Don't think I don't know just because I can't see you."

"Every day. Twelve times."

"Hmm," said Miss Drumm. "And yet you seem to be exhibiting just the same malaise as engulfed our old shepherd's wife when she stopped. They tested her for everything under the sun and none of the doctors could tell what ailed her. Then when she was too ill to carry out her duties anymore, and her husband took over, she rallied. She'd been to see that dreadful Billy Graham fellow in Glasgow, you see, and got the idea that rocking the stone was godless."

"It's good to hear a story with a happy ending," I said, ignoring the sideswipe at Billy Graham, who'd brought me great comfort when I read his sermons.

"Happy ending, my eye," said Miss Drumm. "Once she was better the stone was neglected again, and she died a year later with a growth the size of a medicine ball in her belly."

"For crying out loud."

"And even the hallowed place couldn't save her," Miss Drumm said.

"Lourdes, you mean?"

"Popish claptrap."

"Walsingham?"

"Next door to the same thing."

"Mecca?" This was just devilment but I couldn't resist it and, recognising that, she smiled at me. "Well, what then?" I said.

Miss Drumm sucked her teeth for a minute. She had good strong yellow teeth, not many at the back these days (although more than Walter), and she sucked them with relish whenever she was thinking hard. "I've never told you about the hallowed place," she said at last. "And I make no apology for that. You didn't need to know."

I had the oddest feeling I knew what she

was going to say.

"But you must have seen it," Miss Drumm went on. "The little place in the woods half a mile from the footbridge at William's Leap?" She paused, but I knew if I tried to speak my voice would betray me. She really *was* talking about the huttie. "My uncle William leapt across the gap on my father's mare taking a shortcut on the Boxing Day chase in 1920 and ribbed Fa about it until the day he died. Fa didn't dare to try and couldn't bear it that his brother had bested him. So he built a bridge — against my mother's express wishes and his own better judgement. He built a wooden footbridge."

I had calmed my breaths enough to talk again. "So the hallowed place is the crypt?"

"Never!" said Miss Drumm. "Monstrous! The Drumms wouldn't dream of such a thing. Every Drumm there ever was is decently buried in the good earth at the parish church at Corsock, where I shall be before too long, I hope. Crypt! What nonsense."

"Sorry!" I said. But still I was sure. And bewildered. In ten years she hadn't so much as mentioned it until today, when April's body lay under its floor.

"What do you mean, 'hallowed place'?" I asked, trying to sound as interested as I guessed I should, but no more.

"Gloria," said Miss Drumm. "You are un-nerving me."

"Is it a chapel?" I asked, guessing that would be as bad as a crypt in her eyes and, if I annoyed her, she might stop scrutinising me. But Miss Drumm, for the first time since I'd met her, looked — there was only one word for it — *shifty.*

"Consecrated," she muttered at last through gritted teeth.

"And what is it you've never told me about it?"

"You've tired me out with your nonsense," she said. "Get on through and see that boy of yours. Let me rest." Then she set her jaw as though she would never open it again, slightly off-centre but tightly shut.

Nicky's room must have been the old serving pantry, adjacent to the breakfast room, back when the care home was a fam-ily house. It was smaller than the others, so between that and the connecting door, I got it for a good price. Or rather the money I gave the home bought more one-to-one care than I could have afforded if I'd insisted on a bigger bedroom. He didn't need the space. His narrow bed with the oxygen on one side and the fluids on the other left enough room for a chest of drawers where his pyjamas were kept folded. An armchair for me and a lamp to read by and there was no need for more. It was quiet, warm, tidy, and softly lit — my favourite place in the world.

"Hallo, my darling boy," I said, bending over to kiss him. "Hallo, my little Harlem Globetrotter. That's some excellent dribbling you're doing today." I picked the top pad from the pile of soft gauze we keep by his bed and wiped his chin. They used to use kitchen roll and once I was shocked to come in and see a toilet roll there. Then I was given these pads at the dentist one time after I'd had a tooth out, and they were so soft and so snowy white that I went back in and asked the receptionist for the company name and then told the home to buy them for Nicky.

"I've had quite a time since I left last night," I said, settling down. "I don't want to burden you with any of it, but believe me — it's like a day at the beach coming here."

"I'm not listening," shouted Miss Drumm through the open door. "Say what you like and don't mind me."

"I spoke to an old friend," I said to Nicky, ignoring her. "Someone I haven't seen since I was younger than you. People don't change though, do you know that? You haven't changed since the first minute I set my eyes on you, not in any way that matters. And neither has my friend."

"I have," Miss Drumm shouted. "I used to have feet. And eyes that worked."

"I thought you were tired out!" I shouted back and went to close the door, picking up the book on the way back again.

"Now then," I said. " 'The Moon'. Except there isn't one tonight. 'The Moon has a face like the clock in the hall . . .' "

The poem was so familiar after all these years, that I could let my mind drift, read it without thinking. What I should have foreseen, though, was that my mind would drift to that other night when children hoped for a moon as they lay in a clearing.

" 'And flowers and children close their eyes till up in the morning the sun shall arise.' " Stig and the dew and his moment of perfect peace. I remembered his voice saying *I was wet through and never slept another wink until Van was shaking me.*

"That's not right, Nicky, is it?" I said. "If you're awake you don't get shaken. Why did he say that?"

I turned the page.

" 'The Swing,' " I read and felt a jolt inside me. A Tarzan swing used to hang over the river near the bridge. Stig had said *the footbridge by the swing.* And the huttie was the hallowed place half a mile away. And Dunkeld, where Ned McAllister had gone to die, had a huttie of its own, by a waterfall. Something about all of that bothered me.

I kissed Nicky again after I had finished reading, stroked his face, remembered his smile. Once, a year or two ago, I tried to move his face into a smile shape, pushing the sides of his mouth with my hands, but it was so horrible that I frightened myself, and that shocked me. And I went home and cried, hugging Walter Scott and bellowing into his solid side.

"Night-night, darling," I said. "You've helped Mummy a lot tonight. Magic kisses. One on each eye to send you to sleep, one in each hand for you to keep." Then I turned away.

Miss Drumm had wheeled herself over and pulled the door open. She was just sitting there.

"Helped you with what?" she said.

ELEVEN

"Have you been absolutely straight with me?" I asked as soon as I was in the kitchen door, unwinding my scarf and kicking off my boots. The table was set with a cloth and a jug of water instead of just a filled tumbler.

"What?" Stig turned round and stared at me. His glasses hid his eyes, the light bouncing off the lenses just like Miss Drumm's. But she could see better, despite her blindness. "What do you mean?" he asked me.

"For starters, you said last night that you didn't sleep again after you moved and the dew soaked in, but then you said the next thing you knew was that Vanman was shaking you."

"Van the Man," said Stig. "After Van Morrison, not after white-van man."

"Van *Morrison*?" I repeated.

"He's a singer," said Stig. "Come on,

Gloria. I know you go more for books than records, but you must have heard of Van Morrison."

"But why was he shaking you if you weren't asleep?" I asked, trying to wrench my mind back to where it should be instead of jumping to crazy conclusions.

"Because he didn't know I was awake, I suppose," said Stig.

I felt all my held breath leave me in a rush. Of course, there was an explanation for everything. And I couldn't actually remember which one of the Eden kids was *something like Douglas or Dougall,* if he'd ever said. They were common enough names, like Morrison. There was an explanation for everything.

"Okay, next question," I said. "This occurred to me tonight reading to Nicky. Why the huttie?" This time Stig didn't try to fend of the question. He nodded slowly with his lips pushed out as if he was thinking. "You were camping in the clearing with the fairy rings that night. Moped died at the bridge. And yet April texted you to meet her at the huttie. Why?"

"To stay out of the rain?" said Stig.

I shook my head. "I don't think so. And it's bothering me." Miss Drumm was bothering me too. If she wanted to tell me about the hallowed place, and it was half a mile from the bridge, why did she mention the bridge at all? "Listen," I said. "Poor Edmund chose the Hermitage at Dunkeld to commit suicide, didn't he? And if you were going to describe the Hermitage you'd say . . ."

"A wee building and a waterfall," said Stig.

"Why didn't he choose somewhere with a bridge and a swing?"

"His brother chose a car park."

"Yes, but . . ." I was thinking so hard than when Stig smacked his hands together he startled me.

"You're right," he said. "Oh my God, Gloria, you're right! Nod killed himself in a car park because all he wanted was to die. But Ned wanted to say something. He wanted to leave a sign. But it's the wrong sign. It's not a bridge."

"But April knew what that sign meant," I said. "And that's why she told you to meet her at the huttie."

We stared at one another for a long time after that, both of us trying to work it out. Then Stig glanced at the stove and stood up, unhooking the oven gloves. "Did anyone up at the home say anything about the police?" I shook my head. "So they haven't found her. Are you still up for . . . what you said?"

"After dinner, yes, I'll go."

Which was delicious, of course.

"This is actually worth a bit of bad language," I said mopping up the last of the sauce with some of the rosemary bread.

"Wait till you taste my chocolate cheesecake," said Stig. "I'll get to say cu—" He bit the word off and winked at me.

He cleared the plates, wrapped all the leftovers in foil, and put the kettle on. Then he handed over the A4 pad I had given him that morning and started running hot water for the dishes.

"I could get used to this," I said.

"As long as you don't mind the shopping," said Stig. "I've done a list."

But I was looking at his other list.

Moped Best—Mitchell	*D*	
Ned McAllister—Edmund	*D*	
Nod McAllister—Nathan	*D*	
April Cowan	*D*	
Van the Man Morrison—Douglas?	*Then: CD*	*Now: same*
Jo-Jo Jameson—John? Jonathan?	*Then: Moniaive*	*Now: ???*
Bezzo Best—Alan	*Then: CD*	*Now: ???*
Scarlet McFarlane	*Then: London*	*Now: ???*
Scarlet McInnes	*Then: Glasgow*	*Now: ???*
Cloud Irving	*Then: Borgue*	*Now: ???*
Rain Irving	*ditto*	*ditto*
Sun Irving	*ditto*	*ditto*
Stig Tarrant—Stephen	*Then: CD*	*Now: Gloria's house*

I stared at it for a long time, that one name looking bigger and blacker than all the others. My heart was hammering. Did this bombshell change everything? How far back did it stretch and how deeply into my life had it got its tentacles?

"Well?" said Stig, tipping out the dishwater and wringing the cloth so hard I could hear it squeaking.

"I can check these names against the computer the day after tomorrow when we're open again," I said, amazed at how steady my voice sounded compared with how warbly it felt inside me. "And then I'll just have a general look online. How many Rains, Suns, and Clouds can there be?"

"You're still on the first sheet?" he said, giving me a puzzled look. I could tell from the way the pad of paper was ruffled into little seersucker shapes, the way it gets when someone leans hard with a biro, that he had filled a good many pages.

"What about Miss Naismith?" I said. "She should have an entry. What was her first name? And there must have been someone else. Secretary, janitor? Someone."

"No idea what Naismith's first name was," said Stig. "And no, no one else. It was sort of on a shoestring. A cleaner used to come, but nobody else lived there."

"How late did the cleaner work? Did she have a key to the gate?"

"Couldn't say," said Stig. His voice was low and gruff. Was I getting near something he didn't want to tell me? *Were* there things he didn't want to tell me? I looked at the list again. There must be.

I told him I would take the notes to bed with me later, after I'd been to the huttie again. Told him that was where I did important reading because that was where I concentrated best. He believed me.

"Takes all kinds, Glo," he said. "If I tried to read in bed I'd be asleep in seconds.

Maybe not tonight, mind you."

"Try it," I said. "I've got most things. Except Westerns."

"The last book I read was at school," he told me.

"Nick Hornby," I said, calling over my shoulder as I walked along to the living room to the big bookcase. *"High Fidelity."*

"I've seen it."

"About a Boy then."

"That was a girl's film. Carol tried to make me, but I got out of it."

"It was a boy's film, actually," I said. "And it's a boy's book too." I came back to the kitchen and put it in his hands. "Don't turn the pages back. Use a bookmark. And I'll go to the chemist tomorrow and get you some sleeping tablets. I'll be back as soon as I can."

This was either the bravest thing I had ever done or the worst idea of my life, and I would never have dared to go through with it if it had been a night like the one before, black as pitch and freezing cold with lashing rain. But tonight was dry with a thin fresh wind and a good bit of light from a three-quarter moon.

Anyway, I had to. When I stopped Stig from phoning 999 it was like jumping off a cliff. A split-second decision and no way back. Now, if the police broke into April's flat and found a note casting suspicion on Stig, and then they found he'd disappeared, they'd be looking for him so hard it would be like a manhunt. I pictured them in Rough House opening doors and swiping at curtains with their truncheons. And even though I knew that was nonsense, once the idea had grabbed me, it wouldn't let go. There would be traces of him everywhere. If they asked the residents, Miss Drumm would say I was on edge. If they looked in my byre, they'd find his car. If they checked to see if I was connected to Eden . . .

I shook the thought away and tried instead to concentrate on April.

Finally she would be taken care of, taken somewhere safe, given somewhere proper to lie down instead of staying curled in that hole. Her poor arms would be bathed, her eyes closed, and she'd be at peace. And as long as she lived alone, the other half of the plan would work too. Stig said she was divorced, so chances were she did.

Stig had said a lot of things. The names on his list danced in front of my eyes again, and once again I forced the thoughts away.

Did I have the courage to look at her, touch her, check her pockets?

I pulled off the lane in the same spot as

the night before, stepped out of the car, and played the torch around. Our footprints were gone in all the rain, as I'd said they would be, and there was no sign of any new disturbance. I slipped through the gate again and up the path to the door.

I wasn't as strong as Stig, and I had to haul on it and shove it hard with my shoulder to budge it. Already I was sniffing, couldn't help it, even as I tried to tell myself that it was almost cold enough for frost out here and she'd been there only a day. There would be no smell yet. There *was* no smell except earth and leaf mould, that mushroomy pungent smell of Milharay in a wet winter. Once the door was open, the dust and damp of a cold, closed building was mixed in there too but there was nothing stronger, and that made it easier for me to squeeze through the gap and into the deeper darkness, where the torch made shadows leap and shudder all around. It took every scrap of my nerve to steady the beam and train it on the far side of the floor where the tilting slab lay.

We hadn't made as good a job as I'd thought of wiping away the evidence of our visit; the edges of the slab were smudged and there was a smear on the floor in front of it too.

A smear of what? I wondered, crouching down and peering at it in the torch light. It could have been coffee or ketchup just from the look, but there was no question here, in this place. The only puzzle was how.

I'm not a fanciful woman. I couldn't afford to be, living all alone in that isolated house, with the stone outside and Miss Drumm's stories ringing in my ears. I'd read Wilkie Collins, Edgar Allen Poe, and Thomas Harris and go to bed quite happily in the dark to dream of old friends and exams, just like everyone. But at that moment, crouching there, all I could think was that those smudges were April's fingerprints from where she'd grabbed the slab and pushed it open. And that smear was a trail of her blood from when she'd hauled herself out or perhaps from where she had slithered back in again.

"Nicky, Nicky, Nicky, Nicky," I said to myself as I set the torch down and took a firm grip. When the slab shifted, I grabbed it and set it upon its edge. Then I held my breath, took the torch, and shone it down into the hole.

She was gone. Nothing left of her except a small rusty stain.

I took the moment needed to kick the slab back down again, but I didn't bother with

141

the door. I just squeezed through and left it open. The raw edge of the cut chain would attract attention soon enough anyway, I told myself. But really, I just wanted out of there. As far away as I could get, as soon as I could get there.

TWELVE

"That was quick," said Stig.

I shrugged out of my coat, letting it fall onto the floor behind me, and then dropped into a chair. "She's not there."

"Who's not where?" said Stig. Then he put both hands up to the back of his head as if to stop it hurting.

"Maybe the police —" he began.

But I shook my head. "No chance. There was no tape, no signs up, nothing to show there's been a stretcher or medics. It looked exactly the same, except she was gone."

"Why would someone move her? And keep it quiet?"

I had a head start on him from the drive back, and I was almost calm as I laid it out to him. "I can only think of one reason someone would move a body," I said. "And it explains why we couldn't find the car she came in too. And why you're involved."

Stig opened his mouth to speak, but after

a frozen silent moment he slumped back. "Yeah," he said. "There's no such thing as being framed for a suicide, is there? Someone —"

"Say it."

"Someone murdered her."

"At least now you don't need to go to her flat," Stig said, and his words shoved the new truth into my head

"Oh yes, I do," I said. "And tonight too."

"At this time? Why?"

"He moved her because it didn't work. You didn't call it in, and then even trying to get the cops prowling around here looking for you didn't get her discovered. So he's moved her somewhere she'll be found. And where do you think would that be?"

Her address was on King Street, right in the centre of Glasgow, in the Merchant City, which was good. There'd be lots of bustle even on a Tuesday night, but it was two hours hard driving to get there. An hour on the empty twisting roads out of Galloway up as far as Ayr, threading along the valleys beside the rivers that had made them, over stone bridges meant for carts, through pine woods planted for profit not beauty, and growing so close on either side of the road that they blotted out every gleam of moonlight and sucked at the headlamp light too, swallowing it, leaving me blind at every corner, so that I pushed the car into blackness praying — *Nicky!* — not to meet someone pushing through the blackness the other way.

And the second hour was down out of the hills, onto the plain, into the traffic like a fish joining its shoal, swept up in the surge. Trying at first to ignore the other cars as they wove in and out around me, then speeding up, keeping pace, hanging onto the taillights ahead, not a fish anymore; more like one of those bulls in the stampede that doesn't even need to touch its hooves to the dusty ground, letting the herd carry me.

Then after the suburbs and city lights, eventually, at getting on for ten o'clock, I turned onto King Street and noticed nothing wrong, not at first anyway. I was crawling along, peering at the shop fronts and the fanlights above the tenement doors, searching for numbers and not looking beyond the lights of the car in front of me until the flashes of red and blue were sweeping across my face, bathing everything warm and then cold. Then finally I flicked a glance along the street and braked hard. The car behind me hit its horn, but what was in front of me was worse than an angry driver. Six police, in their bright bulky jackets, turned and stared to see who was tooting.

Carefully, I pulled into a parking space outside a little corner shop, lit up and welcoming, still with its trays of fruit outside on the astroturfed tables. The shopkeeper was in the doorway, holding up his phone to the cops, filming them. I looked at the number in peeling gold on the window above him and counted forward to where the police were clustered around, their cars double-parked, a van with its doors open and the gleam of metal machines inside, bathed red then blue then red again.

The knock on the window was soft, but it still shot me hard against my seat belt.

"Whoa, whoa!" I saw the shopkeeper mouth it even before I rolled the window down. "Sorry, sorry," he was still saying, once I could hear him. "Are you okay?"

I stared at him, then back at the colours, the red and blue lights, the yellow jackets, and the fierce white of the high-sided van.

"I'm having a better night than some people," I managed to say. "I'm just trying to work out whether to carry on or go round another way."

"The road's open," he said, nodding.

It was down to one lane, though, between

the double-parked cars and the open white van. Drivers were taking turns, slow and steady under the gaze of all those police. And they *were* gazing too. Cop habit, I suppose, unbreakable. Every car that drove by got a flick of a glance at the licence plate and another flick at the driver.

"Pretty disrespectful, though," I said. "That's a mortuary van, isn't it?"

He stopped smiling then. Must have thought I was calling him a gawper.

"I think I'll go round," I said, rolling up the window, hoping he wouldn't remember me because I'd insulted him, wouldn't mention me when the door-to-door started.

Just then, something caught his attention and he hurried away. They were bringing the stretcher out. A green cloth mummy strapped to a board, the wheels dropping down when they got to level ground and then folding up again as they shoved April Cowan into the back of the van and slammed the door.

I drove in a trance with the herd, in a deeper trance down through the dark folded hills, and pulled in at home after midnight, cold, crabbed into the shape of seat and steering wheel, my head as numb as my toes.

Walter was awake. I could hear him shuffling around on the other side of the door waiting for me to open it. Stig was still up too. I let myself in and saw the back of his head in the light of one lamp, his chair still drawn up close to the open stove.

"We were right," I said quietly.

"I know," said Stig without turning. "It was on the news. They know she didn't die where they found her. They're looking for me."

I stood there, one hand on the kitchen door handle, letting all the heat out into the scullery. My excuse, if he'd confronted me, would have been that Walter was out in the yard. The truth, if I'd asked myself, was that a bit of me didn't want to put my keys down and step away from the door.

Stig of the Dump! I had thought when I saw him at my door. I knew what kind of sandwiches he liked best and what kind he'd rather go hungry than eat. I knew he couldn't spell *except* and *exact* and couldn't draw horses, and I knew he loved his little brother and his brother loved him back.

But whoever killed April Cowan had been to school too, gobbling Marmite and spitting out egg, talking about brothers and sisters, and asking the little girl at the next desk to do the hooves and hocks for payment in bubblegum.

148

"What did the news say?" I asked the back of his head.

"Named her, said she was dead under suspicious circumstances; named me, warned people not to approach."

"She was in the flat. I saw the police and the mortuary van, saw them taking her away."

"Did they see you?" said Stig.

I thought of them turning to look when the horn behind me blared, thought of the shopkeeper filming with his phone, and still told him no.

"Where are my car keys, Glo?" he said, still without turning. His voice was dull and empty. "This has gone far enough. I'll keep your name out of it somehow."

"Where are the cats?" I said as Walter lumbered back in again. I couldn't think of anything else to say.

"Here," said Stig, and I stepped closer to look. Both house cats, Dorothy and William, were crammed onto his lap and he had his hands laced together, making a sling out of his arms, to keep them from falling. They were deeply asleep, heads lolling.

"How long have you been sitting there?"

"Since I switched off the eleven o'clock news. My shoulders are killing me."

I lifted one cat and then the other, dropping them down into the other chair.

"Mitchell Best, Nathan and Edmund McAllister, and April Cowan are in the clear," I said. "And you are too."

I thought he would look up at me, but he bowed his head even lower.

"That still leaves eight," I went on. "Do you really think if you turn yourself in, the Castle Douglas cops are going to track down eight more people before they start the paperwork?"

Stig laughed. "I'm fu— I'm stuffed," he said.

"No," I answered, thinking if I was going to do this, I'd better toughen up quick. "You were right the first time. Okay. I'll start in the morning. I'll start with Duggie Morrison because he's easy to find, but I'll track them all down and I'll . . ."

"Unfuck me?"

I actually laughed. He was ruder than anyone I'd ever liked before, but I laughed because it was funny.

THIRTEEN

Wednesday

Duggie Morrison was more than easy to find. He was hard to avoid. Morrison's Carpets and Flooring, Morrison's for Beds, and Morrison's Kitchen and Bathroom spread out along the top end of Castle Douglas High Street as they had for sixty years, ever since Duggie's grandfather and great-uncle came back from the Ideal Home exhibition with pounding hangovers and a vision of the future. In other towns, less staid and settled, Morrison's would have been long gone, but in Castle Douglas with its butcher's shops and greengrocers, its bakers and cobblers and gentlemen's outfitters, IKEA was defied and the townspeople, along with the farmers from all around, got their laminate and granite islands from the same dependable family business where their fathers had bought their wine racks and black ash, and their grandfathers had bought their breakfast bars and knotty pine.

That's why the likes of the Tarrants can't waltz in and take over, my mother had said, when the station-yard development plan had fallen through. *Castle Douglas has its own way of doing things.*

I parked outside the carpet shop and tried to prepare myself. I couldn't help my pulse starting to race, and I knew my cheeks were starting to colour too. I'd never stopped hoping that every time could be *the* time. It could easily be today.

But it wasn't Duggie behind the reception desk in his shirtsleeves and tie for once, with one phone to his ear and another in his hand rubbing its surface with his thumb, like a child with a blankie. It was a woman. She was somewhere in her forties, with sleek tawny hair and a suit of caramel-coloured moleskin. Her fingernails were bubblegum pink with rims so white they were almost blue, and when she stood up and walked around the desk to greet me I could see that her toenails were done the same way and she wore a gold ring on her middle toe. Smiling, she tugged the jacket straight before she stretched out a hand to shake mine. The jacket was too short for her figure, cutting her off just above the swell of her bottom so that her thighs looked like hams. And the caramel-coloured trousers were too short too, half-mast above her chocolate brown mules, shortening her legs and turning her dumpy.

She had probably paid a fortune for the outfit and it did nothing for her. I — clever with my needle — once I found a pattern that suited me, made it up in every colour in my palate, perfect fit, perfect length, like the button-through dress I had on under my Mackintosh today. *You look like you're in costume,* Lynne at work had said once, and I thought I knew what she meant: that it was unusual to see someone in clothes specially tailored for their shape. One other time a girl on a bus had called me a Texas polygamist, which had puzzled me until I Googled it at work and saw them, with their beautiful hair and their handmade dresses. Only those frocks were hanging off their shoulders like sacks and mine fit me like gloves. Like *my* gloves, which I also make to fit.

"Can I help you?" said the moleskin-suit woman.

"Is Duggie in?" I said.

Her smile didn't falter, but something behind her eyes clicked from warm to cold and her voice was different when she spoke again. "Who should I say is asking?"

"Gloria," I told her. "His wife. His son's mother."

I could tell two things from the flash in her eyes: she was more than just an employee, and she hadn't heard a peep about Nicky and me. She gave me an incredulous look up and down and then disappeared into the back office.

Duggie appeared like a jack-in-the-box ten seconds later. He always dealt with me quicker in person than on the phone.

"*Ex*-wife, Gloria," he said. It was true and he was right to point it out, but I could never bring myself to say it. We got married in a church, in the sight of God, and those papers he sent me to sign didn't have any power to change that.

"Nicky's fine," I told him, "in case you were wondering." Then I bit my lip. I don't know why, but dealing with Duggie always turns me into a nag.

"Nicky's your son?" said the woman. She was leaning in the office doorway, exploring the side of her mouth with her tongue.

"Nicky's our son," I confirmed. "I've got a picture of him if you'd —"

"Zöe, why don't you take a quick coffee break?" Duggie said. He put his hand out and actually touched my arm to stop me rummaging in my bag for my purse and flipping it open to the picture of Nicky. "It looks as if I've got a bit of family business to take care of."

"I'll bring you back a latte," she said. She hooked a bag — a soft one with lots of buckles just like April's — off the back of the reception desk chair and stalked out. She looked less polished in the cold daylight as she got to the front of the shop and plate-glass windows. Her make-up was thick and her hair coarsened with dye. I've got the skin you get from never smoking or tanning and the hair you get from not washing it every day and never blow-drying it at all. Not that it was a competition, but if it was, I was winning.

"What do you want, Gloria?" said Duggie once she was gone.

"Have you heard the news?" I said. He cocked his head. "A death in Glasgow."

"And?" he said.

"There was a prowler up in the grounds of the house," I said. "Did you hear about it? He didn't go inside — he was stalking this woman and she took the back roads to shake him off and he got lost or something. But now a woman's dead and I think it's the same one."

"And this matters to me why?" said Duggie. He had taken out his phone and was caressing it with his thumb. I bit my lip again. *Everyone does that now,* I reminded myself. *He's not any ruder than anyone else.*

"Your son lives close by," I said. "Ask me why I think it's the same woman."

"Go on then," said Duggie. "Amaze me."

"Her name was April Cowan. She went to Eden."

He didn't look up, but he hesitated in his scrolling. "I'm still not with you," he said. He put his pursed fingers against the screen and opened them, enlarging something, then he gave a huff of laughter.

"Why did you never tell me you went there?"

"It didn't come up," said Duggie.

"How?" I said. After twenty years, this man still mystified me. "When I found the perfect place for our son to live and you railed at me and forbade it and told me you would never set foot in the place to visit him, how could it not 'come up' that you'd been at school there?"

"Great summary, Gloria," said Duggie. "That pretty much covers it."

"Stop looking at that ridiculous device and talk to me with some respect," I said, grabbing at his wrist. He held the phone up out of my reach. "Treat me with some civility, for heaven's sake," I said. "You're forty, not fourteen." He had done it to me again — turned me into a harpy.

"You're the one snatching at my stuff like we're in the playground," he said, and I knew from his voice that I had needled him. We were always like this: a disaster. We'd been a train wreck from the time of Nicky's diagnosis, since I — as my mother put it — *turned away from my husband and let the inevitable happen.* Only it hadn't felt like that to me.

"I'm sorry," I said.

"It was nothing to do with Eden that made me against the idea," said Duggie, putting his phone away. "For one thing, it was expensive."

"He's your son!" I wailed.

"As long as he's warm and dry and got a drip and a catheter, he might as well as be in a kennel," said Duggie. He had said things just as ugly before, but it never stopped hurting. I could feel the tears bulging up and trembling on my lashes. "And there'd have been even more expense if the place folded again and we have to shift him."

"But ten years later it's going strong."

"As it turns out," said Duggie. "But who was to know that? That stupid school the Tarrants tried to start was over before it began."

"Exactly!" I said, blinking my tears away. "The school did come up. It should have come — What?" I had only just got what he said. "The Tarrants that had the station-yard thing? They *owned* Eden?"

"It's your pal Helen Keller that owns the site," said Duggie. "But they owned the business, yes."

"Miss Drumm isn't deaf," I said. "Duggie, why do you say such things?"

The door opened and Zöe, balancing two coffees in a cardboard tray, walked back in. "Bad moment?" she said.

"*What* was it you wanted, Gloria?" Duggie said, taking one of the cups out of the tray and giving Zöe that smile of his. I remembered that smile.

"You were at Eden," I said to Duggie. "You were there when that boy died."

"What's this?" said Zöe. She was hovering at his elbow.

"Was April Cowan close to him?" I said. "Was she his girlfriend? Do you think it's connected?"

"Gloria, love, what are you on about?" said Duggie. "An accident decades ago and another one yesterday? Why would it be connected?" He turned to Zöe and rolled his eyes, but she just frowned at him and then held out her coffee cup to me.

"Here," she said. "You need this more than I do." I was so surprised, I took it. "What's happened, Dougall?"

"Nothing," Duggie said.

"It's connected because she was down here before she died," I said. "Two of them were." I was looking at Duggie but then switched my gaze to Zöe, taking a sip from the cup. "Thank you. That's really kind of you. Did *you* hear the news this morning?"

"I had it on," she said, screwing her face up as if trying to remember.

"April Cowan was at Eden and the guy that was following her down here on the back roads was Stephen Tarrant. They were there together when that kid Moped died."

Duggie laughed. *"Moped!"* he said. "God, I'd forgotten we called him that. Moped — haven't heard that for years." He turned to Zöe again to share the joke, but she was looking at him with a kind of look that I recognised, only from the inside. I knew the feeling that made that look. But she wasn't me. I always started in on him; she just shook her head and then looked away and took a step towards me.

"It must be worrying for you," she said. "Is that right? You live up there where that Tarrant guy's been hanging around?"

"I — Thank you," I said. "I'm just — So I

thought I should tell Duggie to keep his eyes peeled."

"You think I'm next, eh?" said Duggie. "Wishful thinking, Gloria." He was joking.

"In case he's still around and you see him," I said. "The police would want to know."

"You set the cops onto me?" said Duggie, joking again. His jokes started out making me laugh, but over the years they began to exhaust me. I didn't notice whether Zöe smiled at this one.

"No, of course not," I said, in that way of mine that made Duggie think I had no sense of humour. "But if they come round."

"Why would they come round?"

I hadn't even realised I was dropping a bomb until the silence that followed it.

"To see where you were on Monday night and then again on Tuesday," I said. "Since you knew both of them."

"He was with me on Tuesday," said Zöe. "What's Monday?"

I couldn't answer, couldn't tell anymore what I would know from the cops at the door and the radio news and what I only knew because I had seen it or Stig had told me. The sooner I shut up and got away, the better. I held the cup out to Zöe.

"Thanks," I said again. "You can have the

rest. I haven't got cold sores or anything." Duggie snorted, but Zöe smiled as if I'd said something really funny.

"Let's share it," she said. "I'll get my mug and nick some and then you take that away with you." She disappeared through the back again to the little kitchen.

"Thanks a fucking bunch, Gloria," whispered Duggie, looking over his shoulder to make sure she was gone. "Cheers for showing me up in front of her."

"I have no idea what you're talking about," I said, which was true.

"You're losing it, love," he said "You're seriously losing your marbles with this latest crap."

"Duggie, I'm not being funny, I don't know what you mean."

"Barging in here, banging on about shit from years ago. Yes, I was at Eden. Yes, Mope died. Yes, Golden Boy Tarrant was nowhere to be seen and no one ever asked why. If he's finally gone too far and he gets done for it — great. But it was a long time ago and it's nothing to do with me or you, so leave it, okay?"

"Nice mug," I said to Zöe, who'd just pushed the door open again.

"Spode," she said. Duggie was standing as rigid as a totem pole, glaring at me, but Zöe came up beside him and put an arm round his waist and leaned her head against his shoulder.

"I'm divorced myself," she said to me. "You wouldn't believe the way me and my ex talk to each other sometimes. Even after ten years." She turned and smiled up at Duggie. "Don't look so worried, you numpty. I've heard worse. I've *said* worse. And not when there's dead bodies and prowlers involved either."

He didn't snarl at *her* for showing him up. He just shook her off without a word and threw himself down into his desk chair as I turned to go.

I watched them through the window while I was putting my seat belt on and fitting the coffee cup into the holder under the dashboard. I don't usually get takeaway coffee and I didn't think I'd ever had a cup in there before today.

Duggie was still at the desk and she was sitting on it, like a secretary from a *New Yorker* cartoon. One of his hands rested on the desktop, gently holding the curve of her round, trousered bottom. He was laughing.

He had probably had girlfriends before, I told myself. It didn't mean anything. In fact, he might be playing it up just to make me jealous. I wished I could have told him that

I had an old boyfriend staying for a few days and return the favour. *Golden Boy Tarrant,* he had said, which sounded jealous already. Then suddenly, the rest of his words struck me. *Nowhere to be seen and no one ever asked why.*

Finally I knew what had really been troubling me about the bridge and swing and the huttie and the clearing — what I had so nearly grasped last night. I had a firm hold of it now.

FOURTEEN

Incarceration was starting to show on him. His scalp, which had been so gleaming, was dull now, even flaky in places, and the corners of his mouth looked dry and sore too. His eyes were hollow above and puffy below, his glasses magnifying both.

"You don't look well," I said. He was kneeling in the living room laying a fire, with Walter Scott lying on his feet and both cats watching him, one on each arm of the couch.

"Glad you're back," he said. "Can you get some coal? I'll carry it from the back door."

"Stig, you can go outside," I said. "Honestly, no one ever comes and you can hear them from the top grid anyway."

"No one except those cops," he said.

"And it's logs anyway," I told him. "In the wee shed by the bottom door. Through the scullery, through the old farm office, and out the far end."

He blanched, gazing at me. "There's a third door?" he said. "Is it locked?"

"Maybe you'd feel less tense if you weren't keeping so many things quiet," I said to him. I picked up Dorothy and tried to use her as a muff, hoping she'd stay draped over my hands as long as we were in here — there is nowhere like Rough House for cold — but she wriggled, all four legs splayed and all claws out, then she jumped down, going to sit near Walter and giving me an imperious look.

"What things?" said Stig.

"I'll go first," I said. "No, don't turn away; look at me. I want to see your face when you hear this. Duggie Morrison is Nicky's dad."

For a minute it looked as though he couldn't understand me, as though he couldn't parse the words to make the meaning. And then his eyes opened so wide that his glasses slipped down his nose.

"Van the Man was your husband?" he said. He sat right back, trapping Walter's paw under his leg. Walter struggled free. *"You* were married to *Van?"*

"What's giving you all the trouble?" I said. "That he snagged me or that he let me go?"

Stig hung his head then and tried not to laugh. "Sorry, Glo," he said, rubbing his face. "No offence, but . . . Van was always a bit of a . . . flash git. And you're . . . with the books and —"

"So you being here is quite a coincidence," I said, ignoring him.

"Hand to God, Gloria, I hadn't even thought about you for thirty years when I saw you driving the other car. If you'd changed your hair like everyone else, I'd have kept driving."

"Twenty-eight years," I said. "And none taken." He started to bluster, but I shushed him. "It's okay. I know how uncool I am. I know what an odd couple we made, Duggie and me."

"Don't say that!" said Stig. "Don't put yourself down."

"Is that what you heard me doing?" I said, and he blushed again.

"What went wrong?" said Stig. "Was it . . . you know?"

"No!" I said. "Was it Nicky? No, of course not. I mean, a new baby's a strain on any relationship. But no."

The truth was I found it hard to remember the end of my marriage. I was clear about the beginning. Duggie swept me off my feet. He brought flowers and little stuffed animals with satin hearts and messages written on them. *Be mine* and *Sweetie-pie* and once a white kitten with blue glass eyes and a pink velvet tongue that said *Your Purr-fect.*

My purr-fect what? I had asked him, but he didn't understand.

He had come for Sunday lunch with my mum and dad. My mum flirted with him and my dad simply stared as if he didn't believe it. That hurt me more than anything in our five years of marriage: the thought that my own father didn't get what a tall, good-looking, successful, confident man like Duggie Morrison saw in me. That hurt more than I could say.

When he proposed, when we were planning the wedding, decorating that first flat above the kitchen and bathroom bit of Morrison's, I was happier than I had ever expected to be. I gave up my job, like some fool from the fifties, concentrated on the house and the wedding plans. I thought I'd get work in one of the shops after the honeymoon, join the family business, learn all Mrs. Morrison's family recipes and have her and the old man and the rest of the clan round for supper at our new place, show them how well I'd look after their boy.

But the job never happened, the Morrisons never visited the flat once, and cooking turned out to be a lot harder than it looked. *Now you're wishing you'd done something sensible at college, aren't you?* my mother had sneered one day towards the end. *Romance literature!* I didn't even try to explain that Romantic Literature was nothing to do with love and marriage and happy endings. I just looked for a job where they wouldn't mind what degree I had, and then for a job where they wouldn't mind that I had a degree. Assistant registrar at Dumfries came up, I applied, they accepted, and I fell into my round hole. The third one. The first one was being Nicky's mum, and the second one was Rough House. In the end, I think I barely noticed Duggie leaving me. My mother probably had a point there.

"And speaking of lies, Stig," I said, "one last chance for you to come clean and then I'm going to have to ask you."

"I haven't lied," he said.

"And I quote," I said to him, " 'Golden Boy Tarrant was nowhere to be seen and no one ever asked why.' That's word for word what Duggie just said to me about the night Moped died." Stig had turned to carry on with the fire, and I stared hard at the back of his head. "I wondered what was troubling me about your story. It's this: you went to sleep in a grassy clearing surrounded by birches and you woke up in the pine trees with dew on the cones and needles."

He said nothing and after a minute of watching the way his scalp moved above his ears as he worked his jaw, I turned on my heel and went through to the warm kitchen.

He followed, but reluctantly. Walter came along the passageway in front of him, that's how slowly he was moving.

"Wee J's the golden boy," he said, once he was inside the kitchen. He came over to the Rayburn and put his hands down on the closed lid to warm them. Cold as he was, I could still smell a faint sweat on him and I could see the line around his sweatshirt collar where it had soaked in.

"What?"

"For the record."

"Where were you, Stig?"

He groaned and put his head in his hands. I could see sweat stains under his arms.

"You need a bath," I said. "And different clothes. And you need to go outside and get some fresh air. You look terrible. But first you need to tell me the truth about what happened that night at Eden."

"Eumovate," said Stig. "My eczema's going to be a riot unless I get some soon."

"Tell me."

"It's nothing," he said. "It's really nothing. It's just embarrassing."

I took the pad of paper full of his notes,

pulled off the written on sheets and slowly ripped them into pieces, staring hard at him.

"No!" he said. "Don't. Most of that was absolutely true."

"I've copied the biographical details into a notebook of my own," I told him. "Now you speak and I'll write down the new version."

"Like I said," he began, "it's embarrassing. We'd been cooking these sausages on the campfire and pretty much as soon as we settled down to sleep for the night my guts started acting up, so I went to the bog."

"Back at the school?"

"We didn't use the bogs in the school," he said. "Well, we did — or the girls did — for peeing in. The boys peed on the compost. Miss Naismith rigged up — what were they called? — big woven fence things."

"Willow screens?"

"Could be. She was nuts about all that stuff. Green materials and reclaimed materials, years before anyone else gave a stuff about it. The wood to mend the footbridge was so full of nails it took twice as long to get them out as the whole rest of the job put together."

"Tell me!"

"Anyway, when it wasn't a pee we went outside to these dry toilets, not as disgusting as they sound. There was a bucket of sawdust and a wee shovel and you" — he mimed sprinkling as if he was feeding a goldfish. "The girls hated them, even Cloud, Sun, and Rain, and it was their dad who'd come down to build them and show us how they worked. But twelve-year-old boys? Well, you know."

I thought of Nicky when he was ten, his eyes huge and scared when the spasms started, his arms waving wildly, and how I cried when I had to hold out a rod for him to grip instead of his mummy's hand. But the rictus was so severe by then that if he took hold and froze, I was stuck, knuckles grinding, trying to weep quietly. And then there was that one time he'd really got me in a hold and the ends of my fingers were turning purple and Rod, one of the nurses, found us and took hold of Nicky above the elbow and whacked his hand so hard against the bed frame that he let go. The sound of his cry will never leave my ears as long as I live.

"I know, darling, I know, I'm sorry. Oh you wee sweetheart," Rod had said, cradling Nicky and shushing him, but then over the top of his head, he said to me very calmly, "You caused that, Gloria. You have got to start offering the grip until we get the relaxants recalculated for him."

That was why I couldn't stand to use a robot-voice in the car. The first time I heard it, I felt bile rise in my throat. *Recalculating!* said that disembodied stranger and I was back in all those case meetings, all those times they had tried to persuade me to go for it. *Full sedation, Gloria.* Even kindly Donna was against me towards the end.

"You poor dear soul, with the heart of a mother," she'd said. "I know how precious these times are when it's balanced and he's given back to you. But he's a growing boy and the seizures are getting worse, and that's two different factors pulling two different ways. How long did it take us to get a balance last time, Gloria my love, and how long before we were recalculating again?"

"I'm not ready to lose him," I'd said. "I was reading to him this afternoon and he was laughing."

"Right," said Mr. Wishart, the consultant. "Recalculating for Nicholas Morrison. But this might be the last time, so you must prepare yourself. Nicky's distress weighs more with me than yours."

"So you went to the toilet," I said to Stig.

"Big time," he said. "I was in there for hours. Thought I was going to die. I mean I'd had Delhi belly before — from buying juice off a pomegranate stand at the road-

172

side in Saudi — and there was a pretty wild night after some steak tartare in Brussels about five years ago, but that night in the woods is the only time I've really believed I was dying. I just sat there, bare-arsed, crying for my mammy until I fell asleep."

"And woke up covered in dewdrops," I said.

"Like I said. Then I had to deal with what had happened." I cocked my head at him. "God Gloria! Do I have to spell it out? Dry lavvies are meant for healthy hippies that live on lentils and kale, not for wee boys who eat cheap sausages half-raw. It was more than a bucket of sawdust could cope with."

"Sorry."

"I cleaned myself up and went back to where the rest of them were camping and lay down and tried not to go to sleep, in case I got caught short again. But I must have zoned out because I never noticed Van until he shook me."

"So it doesn't actually make any difference where you were?"

"It could have. If Miss Naismith had really come out to check on us, she'd have known that one of us was missing."

"And she didn't know?"

"The kids blew it. When there was all the

argy bargy the next morning, Van shouted at her something like: 'Oh yeah? Well, if you were there taking care of us so perfectly, how comes Stig spent the night sitting on the kludge with his arse in tatters?' "

"What happened to her?" I said. "After Eden." Stig shrugged. "You didn't overhear anything from your mum or dad while they were shutting down the school?"

He went very still. Only his chest moved. The grey plain of sweatshirt that was stretched over his front rose and fell gently for several minutes, then rose hugely as he took a deep breath to start talking again. "Yeah, that was stupid of me to keep that quiet," he said. "It's not as if you couldn't have found out if you asked someone."

"Why did you?"

"I dunno. I didn't get it, I suppose. I never understood what that was about, starting a school. It wasn't a business thing, like the station-yard development or the hotel. It never really made any sense. And then Moped dying at my dad's school made it seem like I was responsible."

"That makes no sense whatsoever," I said. "You were twelve."

"But, it was like I should have — I don't know — taken the lead or stopped it or remembered a bloody torch. Or at least made sure the sausages were cooked so I was there when Moped left."

"Is that when you vowed to become a chef?" I said.

Stig turned to face me, and I was sure I saw tears in his eyes. "Go on and laugh," he said. His voice was rough and angry, but I could hear the break in it too.

"I'm sorry," I told him. "I didn't mean to touch a nerve."

"Hit the nail on the head, more like. The next morning we were all just milling about in the hall in the big house. You know where I mean? In that bit under the gallery that's like a room?"

I did. It was one of my favourite places in the house, because it was the only place they still lit a fire. The health and safety regulations were tight and getting tighter all the time, and Mr. Lawson, one of the long-term residents, had terrible bronchitis as well as his Alzheimer's so it wouldn't have been fair to have wood smoke in the lounge or dining room. But since there was a front door and a back door out of there and it was open to the top landing, sometimes in the winter Mrs. McTurk, the housekeeping manager, would light a fire. And if it was Christmastime with a tree at the bend in the stairs, you could almost imagine what

Milharay House was like in its pomp, full of servants and guests and music.

Even Miss Drumm would get misty-eyed then, smelling the spruce resin and wood smoke. Then she'd sniff harder and turn her blank, accusing eyes on the nearest nurse.

"Cherry!" she'd said. "Cherry wood. Did you buy that in or has another venerable old tree been left to die of neglect in the orchard? My great-grandmother planted those trees and generations of Drumms were taught their table manners with stones from those fruit."

"The orchard is fine, Miss Drumm," said Donna. She winked at me, which I always wish people wouldn't do. "The birds get as many as anyone these days, for there's few wants to be climbing ladders for fruit now we've got Tesco."

Miss Drumm sighed and slumped down in her wheelchair. "Lot of ninnies," she said. "If the Germans decided to make it a hat trick, we'd be done for."

"Miss Drumm, what has your cherry orchard got to do with a World War?" I asked. "With either of them!"

She sat up again. "Half of Corsock never tasted a bit of fresh fruit from '39 to '45 unless it came from our walled garden," she said stoutly. "Cherries, pears, plums, apples. Peaches from the glasshouse. And we made War Jam. I don't mean Victory Jam, Gloria. I mean *War* Jam. Left all the stones in, didn't use any sugar, and sent it to Hitler." She had tired herself out by this time and shook her head, laughing at herself. "I don't suppose the cook actually sent it to Hitler, but it was the best use of diseased fruit I can think of — letting two little girls believe they were going to choke the man who was shooting at their daddy."

Stig was staring at me.

"Have you ever been tested for narcolepsy, Glo?" he said. "Because you don't half drift off a lot."

"I wasn't asleep," I said. But his words had stung me. Too many people had said similar things. *Earth to Gloria! Anybody home?* And my mother chipping in with *Maybe you need some iron pills, Gloria. Or a plate of liver.*

"I do . . . zone out," I said to Stig. "I think it comes from spending so much time with Nicky. You know? I don't really want to dwell on what's actually happening so I just" — I twirled my hands in the air, higher and higher — "go somewhere nicer."

"So you usually spend more time with

Nicky? You're shortchanging him because of me?"

I knew that my face was blank and my eyes wide. I pride myself on honesty, but he had caught me out in a bare-faced lie.

"Glo?" he said. "I didn't mean to upset you."

"It used to be true," I said. "I used to spend hours there every day. After tea till bedtime every work day and all day every day that I was free. I'd take sandwiches and just . . . But lately . . . So I suppose it wasn't fair of me to use him as an excuse. The truth is I spend too much time on my own." I plumped down into one of the chairs. They were still drawn up beside the Rayburn, and Stig had added a little side table between them.

"You're awful hard on yourself," he said, joining me.

"What were you saying? Something about the morning after Moped died?"

"We were milling about," he began again. "Frozen and damp. Hungry. And then my mum and dad turned up and Angie had brought Rise & Shine. Remember that stuff? Powdered orange juice? And Pop-Tarts. Twelve frightened kids looking for comfort and my mother brings foil packets. That's her all over. I left with Nod and Ned because my parents wanted me out of the way while they dealt with the shitstorm, I suppose, and we stopped off at Littlewoods in Dumfries for their Five-Star breakfast — eggs, sausage, bacon, beans, hash browns, fried bread, mushrooms, grilled toms, and tea with three sugars. I decided to be a chef that day."

"That wasn't the Five-Star," I said. "That was the Big-8."

"Get out of town!" he said. "Another fan of the Littlewoods breakfast buffet?" Stig shouted with laughter. The happiest noise he had made in the two days he had been there.

It was a shame to take it away again.

"I can't believe you ate more sausages after the night on the toilet," I said. And it really did give me a twinge to see his face fall and his eyes grow dull again.

"Twelve-year-old boys, Glo," he said. And then my face must have fallen too.

FIFTEEN

My work computer was singing to me from across the valley. In it I would find the addresses of any of the Eden kids who'd married, had children, or (God forbid) died in Scotland. There would be far too many John Jamesons and even more Alan Bests, but the Scarlets — McFarlane and McInnes — with a rough year of birth too? That was a possibility. And those Irving girls — Cloud, Rain, and Sunshine — *must* be waiting in there to be found. Unless they had changed their names when they reached eighteen, like Zowie Bowie, poor lamb.

I remembered Duggie and me poring over the baby books when Nicky was born. I liked Robert and Thomas; Duggie liked Gareth and Ben.

"Oh not Ben," I had said. "Every Tom, Dick, and Harry's called Ben." He hadn't laughed. He didn't even realise I was joking. But *Nicholas Morrison* rolled off the tongue and we agreed.

"Nicholas Morrison breaking away for Scotland!" Duggie shouted, in his commentator's voice, holding the swaddled baby like a rugby ball, ducking and feinting along the length of the living room as if the furniture was defenders. I tried not to wince, just bit my lip down on all my cries ("Be careful!"), laughed, and clapped at Funny Daddy having a joke with his boy. But my heart didn't slow down until Nicky had decided he didn't like being a rugby ball, started crying, and was handed back to me.

But I couldn't go into work and fire up the computer on a day when our little office was closed. There was probably a way for someone at Central to tell that the machine had been on and besides the electronic record there was the whole of Main Street, Dalry, behind their curtains, watching. So, frustrating as it might be, I would have to wait until tomorrow. Do it the old-fashioned way today.

Alan Best came from Castle Douglas, and his parents probably still lived there. They were the generation to keep their landline and never take their names out of the book.

"But give me something to do before you go," Stig said. "How can you live with that

Internet connection? It's like the fifteenth century."

"Have a bath," I told him. "And try *About a Boy.*" How could anyone be bored in this house of books? "I'm going to bring some clothes back with me, so you could put those in the wash if you like."

"Bring some food," said Stig. "Get me something fiddly to cook. I'll make you a raised game pie if you've got time for a stop at the butchers."

"I don't."

"Eggs, butter, flour, and sugar then and I'll get baking," he said. "Icing sugar too. Have you got a piping bag?"

"Last thing you need if you're taking no exercise," I said. It was just a throwaway line, but I saw him suck his stomach in and could have kicked myself.

"Gloria," he said, "you read. Some people walk their dogs or grow leeks the size of telegraph poles. I cook. Please, bring me something to bloody cook!"

So I promised. And on the way to town again I made a mental list: chocolate, lemon, coconut, vanilla. Because if he really was going to bake, he might as well bake my favourite things. Then I put it out of my head, refused to think of him stuck there going crazy, with his scalp flaking, and thought instead about the four of them. Mitchell Best. Edmund and Nathan McAllister. April Cowan.

Because April's body had been moved, the police were suspicious. But if April's death was murder, where did that leave the other three? An accident, two suicides, and a murder made no sense at all.

Three suicides? But what would make a twelve-year-old boy take his own life? And anyway, three suicides and then a murder didn't make much more sense, really.

If *April* had been deliberately killed . . . I stopped, began to bring myself back to plain old reality. Not that Fiscals don't make mistakes, or pathologists, or even police, but not three times. No way.

Castle Douglas isn't a big town, and I found Alan Best's family home without any trouble. It was small, ex-council, mid-terrace and scruffy with it. They hadn't changed the windows when they bought it and now that the council houses all around had had theirs updated, not to mention that the other bought ones had hardwood and conservatories, the Bests' place looked like the only wilted flower in a bunch.

The woman who answered the door was in better shape than the house, but just barely. She looked seventy, with faded fair hair, cut short and let dry without styling, and she wore a crew-necked jersey with ribbed cuffs in that flat blue shade that only flatters if you're peaches and cream. She hadn't chosen it to flatter. If I'd had to guess, I'd say she chose it to punish herself. The ribbing clutched at the wrinkles on her neck and the cuffs clutched at the wrinkles on her wrists. Below it she wore a pair of brown nylon trousers bagged at the knees and down at the hem on one leg. The sort of trousers you'd have to go looking for these days, when it's harder to dress badly than it is to go to Primark and dress like everyone.

"Mrs. Best?" I said. To my surprise, she gave me a faint smile.

"And who are you from?" she said. For a minute it puzzled me, but before I could let the chance be lost by starting to explain, a light came on. It's not the first time it's happened. Something about me, either my face or my hair or my clothes, makes people hold out their hand for a pamphlet, or tell me they're Catholics and slam the door.

"The Church of God," I said, thinking it was bland enough to be likely. "How are you today?"

"I'm . . ."

"You're troubled in your spirits," I said. It

184

was something Donna at the home had said to me in the early days when I was still expecting Duggie to come round and I hadn't accepted the road that Nicky was on.

"I am," said Mrs. Best. "I am that."

"Can I offer you comfort?" I asked her. "I'm just as happy listening as I am talking, if that would help you."

"I don't suppose you're a mother," she said.

I beamed at her. "I certainly am," I told her. "Mother to this little chap." And I got my wallet out and showed her Nicky's picture.

She gave a very soft cry, more of wonder than pity, and stepped back from the door.

"Come in," she said. "And let me put the kettle on. Tell me — What will I call you?"

"Nicola," I said.

"Tell me, Nicola, how do you keep your faith after a thing like that has happened to you?"

Thankfully, she went to the kitchen then and left me behind her. A thing like that! If she had said *after a thing like that has happened to him,* she might have meant the PKAN happening to Nicky. But the only thing that had happened to me was my son. By the time she came back through, I had composed myself and was smiling again.

"Are you warm enough?" she asked.

It was a cheerless little room, no fireplace, which always makes a living room feel like the relatives' lounge in a hospital to me, chairs and coffee tables and those curtains that reach halfway down the wall under the window and just hang there. This place even had the bland factory pictures of a relatives' waiting room too.

"I'm fine," I said. "Have you had a test of your own faith, Mrs. Best?"

"I've no faith to be tested," she said. "But you do?"

"I do," I told her, still smiling. "He's not in any pain, you know. And he is loved. His father and I love him more than we could love any other son or daughter God had sent us."

"He's your only one?"

"He is. It's genetic, what happened to —" I broke off. If I said *Nicky* I'd look like an egomaniac. "Stephen." It was the first name that came to my mind. "My husband and I together made him what he is. So yes, he's an only one."

"There's testing," said Mrs. Best. "But I suppose if you're . . . you wouldn't . . ."

I had said it once to Duggie, when he was sitting numb with the shock, nursing a vodka so big I'd thought it was lemonade, sitting hunched on the footstool bit of his leather lounger, just staring. "There's testing," I'd said. "I'm not saying I'm not glad to have Nicky, but it's different going ahead with another one now that we know. But we can have tests. We wouldn't have to carry on."

He had shuddered. I'll never forget it. He had actually shuddered. Then he'd taken a slug of the vodka and focussed his bleary eyes on me. "Glad to have Nicky," he repeated, in a flat voice.

"Of course," I'd answered. "He's our son."

"The Church of God teaches that life is sacred," I said now to Mrs. Best. "All lives. Your life. You are as precious to God as his own son."

The kettle through in the kitchen clicked off.

"He's got a bloody funny way of showing it," said Mrs. Best, ignoring the click. "I had two boys." She nodded towards the mantelpiece where there was a school portrait of both of them. Alan Best, just as I remembered him, in a lurid shirt like they used to wear on school picture day, his hair slicked down at the front but still wild over his ears from running around the playground with Stig and the others. In front of him, as if his big brother was protecting him, there was Mitchell. The same fair fluffy hair as his brother and mum, a shirt just as snazzy in a different shade of pink, and a missing front tooth not taking an ounce of brilliance out of his smile.

"Beautiful boys," I said.

"That was about three years before Mitch died," she said. I wanted to stop this charade. Wanted to come clean to her, talk honestly. Never mind God and faith and the perfect love of my perfect husband that had only been strengthened by what was sent to us. I wanted to talk to her for real, mother to mother. Then I thought of April Cowan's mother and Mrs. McAllister, who'd lost both her sons in a year.

"Was Mitch your husband?" I asked, and I managed to look properly shocked when she put me straight. "Twelve years old," I echoed. "I am so very sorry."

"How could I worship the god that did that to me?"

"No one could fault you for doubting," I said, hating myself for the sound of it. "His brother must have been deeply hurt too. You can tell from this picture how close they were."

Mrs. Best just nodded, with her eyes filling and said nothing.

"He must be a comfort to you," I said.

Her head had sunk onto her chest, but it snapped back up again now. "Get out," she said.

"I'm sorry," I stammered. "I didn't mean to be unthinking."

"Just get out. You know nothing and you understand even less." She stood up and stalked to the front door, wrenching it open and waiting until I scuttled past her. I half-expected her to take a swipe at me. On the doorstep, I stood, heart walloping, mind racing, and I could hear the first wretched sobs being torn out of her behind the door.

I took a quick look to either side. The house to the left was neat, smart, and empty. The one to the right had Little Tykes bikes on the path and an elderly car with its hatchback open on the driveway.

I hopped over the wire fence and rang the bell.

"Just a minute!" a voice called, and I heard an enormous bunch of keys being applied to the lock before the door swung open to show a young woman — somewhere in her twenties — in the dark blue trousers and tunic of a dental nurse or a physio. She had a toddler on her hip and a phone in her hand.

"What?" she said. "Who —" Then she

looked over my shoulder at the car. "Oh God almighty, I thought I was doing well remembering to unload the shopping. Thanks for letting me know." She walked past me to the car, talking into the phone. "I've left my boot hinging open again, Mel! Some wifie's come and told me. I know! I *know*!"

"Actually," I said, "that's not —"

"What?" she said again. "Mel, I'll get back to you." She hung up and waited, still smiling.

"I um — I'm from the Church of God," I said, and the smile was gone like fan snapped shut at a ball.

"Not. Interested."

"Fine, fine, but I was just talking to your neighbour and I've upset her. I wonder if you would stop in later and see if she's okay."

"Aren't you god squad lot meant to help people?" she said. Then she shifted the toddler to her other side and looked more closely at me. "Wait a minute. I *know* you."

"She was talking about her sons," I said. "And she's in great distress."

"*She's* in great distress?" said the girl. Her tone had got so rough that the baby was starting to look troubled, gazing up at her mother with solemn eyes.

"I know one of them died," I said.

"And the other one should of. Only death's too good for him. Here, he's not back, is he? Because if he is and my Scott catches so much as a glimpse of him, there'll be hell."

"He's not back," I said.

"Is he with you lot?" she asked me, taking a step forward. "You're all about forgiveness, aren't you?"

"We are," I said. "But I have no idea where he is. Do you?"

"I haven't heard a thing about him since he went to Barrwherry," said the girl. "Years ago. Must be ten years. And I'm happy for it to stay that way." She had gentled a little. "Look, I'm sorry for Jill Best. But you've got to ask yourself, I mean, she brought them up, didn't she?"

"Maybe you could look in later," I said again, "and make my apologies. Here." I scrabbled in my purse and pulled out a ten-pound note. "If you're back in town you could maybe get some flowers or chocolates for her. You don't need to say they're from me."

Now she was almost smiling gain.

"You lot are usually taking money in, not giving it out," she said and gave me another hard look. "I *do* know you, don't I? You

191

used to live in CD. Years ago. But your hair's the same. I didn't know you were one of them."

"A god-botherer?" I said. "You don't seem surprised."

I don't even think the smirk she gave me was meant to be unkind. I wasn't suppose to get the joke; I never am. People like me are supposed to be as blind to the looks as Miss Drumm and as deaf to the whispers as poor old Mrs. Healey, who's as deaf as a doorknob.

"What's that, love?" the nurses say, when Mrs. Healy's bellowing at them, straining her voice from the effort of shouting so loud. They cup their ears and beckon. "Didn't quite catch that. Speak up, will you?" Eventually she gets it and stops, with her gnarled old hand in front of her trembling mouth.

"Was I shouting?" she asks, still quite loud.

"Never you mind," says the nurse. "Saves me a fortune in cotton buds, Mrs. H. Never need to get my ears syringed as long as you're with us, love. Might well have cleared my sinuses too."

"Even your god wouldn't bother with Alan Best," the woman said as she was closing the door.

SIXTEEN

Barrwherry, I thought, driving away from Mrs. Best's little house again. It's past Newton Stewart on the bad Girvan road, the only road that ever made Nicky carsick, after he was a baby when the movement of the car lulled him like a rocking cradle and before car journeys, all journeys, were over for good. Now his bed is his little boat, like Stevenson says. His vessel fast. And he'd be waiting there for me in the evening, no matter if I was a little late or a little early. So there was no reason not to follow the trail where it took me.

Only, the Gatehouse to Girvan road goes right past the entrance to Kennan Lodge, the Tarrants' country house hotel, and without seeming to decide or even consider it, I found myself turning in past the smart green-and-gold sign.

The drive was smooth and level, no ridges or standing water, and the rhododendrons on either side were trim and glossy, not like the half-dead straggle on the drive to the care home. At the sweep, the gravel was even raked into a shell pattern like a Japanese garden, and there were stone tubs of ivy, black pansies, and cyclamen on either side of the door. It reeked of money, and the Range Rovers and BMWs parked along the far edge against the balustrade smelled the same way.

I pulled my little Corsa up at the edge of the row and smiled at it sitting there. I didn't care about flash cars. I'd nurse this one all the way to the scrap heap. It had a sunshade with a teddy bear's face on it velcroed to the back passenger-side window and a light spot on the seat cover where the mark left from that trip to Girvan hadn't quite washed away.

Inside the vestibule, there was the regulation blue-and-white china umbrella holder, mahogany hallstand with antlers to hang the hats on, and a narrow table with leaflets advertising Girlie Spa Getaways, Weddings and Events, a Dickensian Christmas Fayre, Traditional New Year Cèilidh, and Boys' Breaks (golf, shooting, fishing). Every way food, drink, and a bed for the night could be slapped together into packages and sold, the Tarrants had thought of it and made a leaflet.

And right enough, when I got into the hallway, there were four women — two pairs of mother and daughter it looked like — sitting dressed in robes with turbans on their heads and towelling slippers on their feet, eating salad out of boxes with black plastic forks. They pretended not to see me, as if the weirdness of a packed lunch in a hotel lobby with your clothes off could be avoided that way. They'd forked over cash and they weren't going to feel foolish about it. Not out loud, not to each other, not before the end of the day.

I rang the bell at reception and couldn't help my eyes growing wide when I saw who came to greet me. If I hadn't known Stig of the Dump was in my house right now, I'd have said I was looking at him, framed in the doorway from the back office. He was taller than he'd been in primary seven, and he had that stubble that's harder to get than a clean shave. His hair was full and glossy, flopping over one eye and twinkling short at the sides, and his blue eyes shone out of a face just as tanned as when he'd got back from Saudi, on top of a body just as wiry and lean as the one that pelted round the playground every day, dribbling the football past Alan Best and the rest of them.

"Wee J?" I said.

His face broke into a grin that made him seem more familiar than ever. "You've got me," he said, searching my face and shaking his head. "I'm sorry."

"I don't think we've ever met," I said, "but you look so much like your brother. He's a friend of mine."

In one snap he seemed to take in the four women in their bathrobes, kill his smile, resurrect it, and shoot out a hand to grab my arm.

"Do you know where he is?" he asked in an urgent whisper. He looked down, saw his hand holding me, and let go, stretching out his fingers like a starfish. "God, I'm sorry," he said. "I'm just — you've heard what's happened, right?"

"I heard on the news about the woman in Glasgow," I said. "It doesn't seem possible. I just came to offer my — But condolences are like he's — I just, I'm not some kind of ghoul come to stare."

"Of course not," said Wee J. "*Do* you know where he is?"

"I haven't seen him for years," I said.

"Yeah, I believe that," said Wee J, "or I wouldn't remind you of him. Steve's not had an easy time."

The first thing I noticed was the perfume. Wee J was looking intently into my eyes and I was lost in his and the memories of Stig they had stirred up in me, so Angie Tarrant was right there before either of us knew it. There was a sudden blast of scent in the air, then her two arms wound round Wee J's neck and her face appeared hooked over his shoulder.

"Not in the front shop, Weej," she said. She flashed her eyes at me. "Come on through, sweetheart, and let's hear what you've got to say."

One of her arms, exercised ropey and tanned as dark as the wood that panelled the hall, uncoiled from around her son and reached out to me. She had those pink and white nails too and pale flesh in hoops around her finger bases where she must wear rings when she wasn't working, rings that would match the thin bangles of gold and diamonds she wore even when she was. The short sleeve of her white tunic rode up above her knotted little biceps as she reached further and further, far enough to touch me, and I saw that the tan went round her arm as dark underneath as on top. She must roast herself like a kebab to get as even as that. And it wasn't from a bottle, I could tell. It was ground as deep into her skin as the riot of smells from her massage oils was ground into her palms — citrus, geranium, lavender, and lily, all fighting each other. The spot on my sleeve where she touched me would still smell of her by the evening. Stig would say "Christ," and step back from greeting me, and Walter Scott would snuff at it and give me a look of puzzlement.

Behind reception was a small private office with two desks, and sitting at one of them was the wreckage of BJ Tarrant. If Wee J was Stig in the past, then here was Stig in the future — some unhappy future where nothing worked out for him, his body even softer and much larger, his face pouchy under the eyes and jawline. Big Jacky still had a full head of jet-black hair and his purple shirt had four buttons open at the neck, showing a turquoise and silver pendant on a leather thong nestling in his chest hair these days, in place of the heavy gold chain he had worn when I was a child. He had even more rings too. The signet and the sovereign, just the same, but also a claddagh and more of the turquoise and silver, cheap-looking against his tobacco-stained fingers. He had been the only dad who smoked cigars when it wasn't Christmas.

Angie Tarrant took her place at the other desk without so much as a glance at him.

Wee J rolled a chair over for me, smiled, and hitched himself onto the edge of a shelf running round the walls. All three of them looked at me expectantly. *What was I doing here?* I asked myself. *Why had I come?*

"Friend of Stevie," Angie Tarrant said. "She knows something."

BJ grunted but didn't speak.

"I don't know any more than I heard on the news," I said.

"Do you know where he is?" said BJ, just as his son had.

"I haven't seen him for years," I repeated. "It looks bad if he's gone missing."

"He's done a runner," Angie said. "Chased her all over the country and no one's seen him since the night she died. 'Looks bad' isn't the half of it."

"But you can't suspect your own son, surely?" I said. Neither of the men would meet my eye.

"Of course not," BJ said. "But we're worried about him."

"Doesn't matter what I suspect," said Angie, not quite interrupting him but absolutely ignoring him and answering me as though he hadn't spoken. "We're in the hotel business here. Customers have to feel safe enough to lie down and sleep, safe to eat the food we've prepared. We've just

199

spent a bomb advertising Seasonal Gift Packages. Who's going to buy a gift token to a weekend at the Slasher Arms?"

"Mum," said Wee J.

"And you can bet your life the *Galloway Snooze*'ll have plenty to say," she went on. "They'll be raking up all the shit in the world to see if it sticks."

"Crying out loud, Mum."

"Here!" said Angie, suddenly. "You're not from there, are you? You are! You're a muckraker from that tenth-rate wee pile of chip wrappings, aren't you?"

"Mum, for God's sake!"

"I'm a friend," I said. "An old friend. And a worried mum. My son lives in the care home at Milharay, you see, and I was thinking as long as the cops keep trying to find Sti— Stephen, they're not looking for whoever it was who killed April Cowan for real. I was thinking maybe when they saw his car that night, maybe it was nothing to do with April driving around down here, maybe he was just on his way to see you. And if you told the cops that, they would forget about him and start looking for the real villain."

"What?" said Wee J. "Hang on."

Angie Tarrant was frowning hard. The two black darts she had made of her brows with dye and plucking were pulled together, and a third line just as thick and black had formed between them on her skin.

"Why are you worried about your son?" she said. "April Cowan died in her flat in Glasgow. So what if she drove by Milharay?"

Too late I saw the trap I had walked myself into. Milharay only mattered because of what Stig and I had seen hidden under the huttie floor, and the police had only said a red Skoda. I shouldn't be worried at all. I shouldn't be here.

"Eden," I blurted. "I'm worried because that's the only connection, isn't it? Between April and Stig. They know each other from Eden."

"Don't talk to me about that place," said Angie. "If I never hear that word again it'll be too soon."

"Ange," BJ chipped in, sounding weary.

She turned on him. "Shut it," she said. "Sit there like a lump and leave everything up to me if you like, but don't start moaning about it too."

"It must have been a terrible time," I said. Even I knew how false the sympathy sounded in the middle of whatever was going on in that little room.

Angie Tarrant laughed, just a chuff of breath, and not so much as the hint of a smile. "And every day since," she said. Her voice was bitter. "For better or worse. Or in my case, for worse and worse and just when you think it couldn't get any worse, a bit worse."

Wee J was squirming with embarrassment, but his father looked beyond being bothered by anything his wife said. He was looking at me, studying me really. "A friend of Stig's," he said. "An old friend?"

Angie Tarrant stood up, slow and measured, as if a string on the top of her head had been pulled, lifting her. "Oh my God," she said. "*Now* I get it! Which one are you?"

"Which one what?" I said. "Mrs. Tarrant, I'm just worried about my son and —"

"What's your son's name?" said Angie. "A Milharay resident? Aye, right! Which one of them are you? Walking in here —"

"You've got to be kidding," I said. "I'm not telling you my son's name when you're acting so — What's wrong with you?" She took a step towards me and I bolted. I didn't mean to do it, but somehow I managed to send the wheeled chair spinning as I took off and it tripped her, slowing her down and letting me get clear — that and the fact that her husband reached out and laid a firm grip on her arm. Wee J was running too, but he didn't follow me to the front door; he took off the other way.

The women in bathrobes stopped forking up their salads as I shot past them. Then I was back at my car, inside, engine on, ignoring the seat belt bleeps, ignoring the spray of gravel hitting the Range Rover next to me and the skid that ruined the shell pattern under my wheels.

I was halfway down the drive when Wee J stepped out in front of the car holding his arms out wide to the sides, staring me down, daring me. I slammed my brakes on and stopped, slewing to the left. He came around to the driver's side and mimed at me to roll down the window. I cracked it. That would have to do.

"You're not any of them, are you?" he said. "A Scarlet or a weather girl. You're Knickerbocker Gloria."

I nodded. "How —" I began, but he shushed me.

"Is he okay?" he asked, and the look in those blue eyes was like nothing I'd ever seen.

"He's at —"

"Don't tell me," said Wee J. "Just tell me he's okay."

"He's fine," I said. "He's safe."

"Don't come back here," Wee J said. "And be careful, won't you?"

I closed the window and drove away, watching him in my mirror.

"Thank you," he mouthed, then he turned and disappeared again between the rhododendrons along the side of the drive.

"How did he know who I am?" I asked Nicky's picture. It smiled back at me. "What's going on?" Nicky just kept on smiling.

SEVENTEEN

The Barrwherry trip was misery from the start — maybe from the minute Mrs. Best opened that door in her ugly blue jersey and looked at me out of those tired eyes — so perhaps I shouldn't have been surprised at how it ended. For sure, by the time I had cleared Gatehouse and was heading up the side of the bay and into the hills, I could feel a weight of dread pressing down on me and, whether I looked back to the memory of Angie Tarrant rising from her chair with her eyes flashing and her voice cold, or forward to the prospect of Stig at the end of another long day full of nothing but fear, there was nowhere to put my mind that didn't press the weight down harder and fill the shadows with things I couldn't see.

The trees were almost leafless but the road, a green tunnel in summer, was no lighter for it, since it cut through deep valleys where the sun was gone by lunchtime.

And the cold, away from the sea, was seeping and sly, three parts damp with no crispness to it at all.

Barrwherry is one of those long, snaking villages, just a single street that starts spread out — farms and holdings and bungalows — then grows closer and more huddled until, at the centre, the cottages join together in a terrace for a while. Then the terrace breaks, the cottages start to thin, and eventually the village stutters out into more miles of emptiness before the next one. I've never liked them. They're like clots, like blockages. And there can't be anything pleasant about logging lorries thundering by your front windows. In the bigger towns at least there are bumps and cameras to hold the traffic to thirty, but not in places like this.

I drove to the end, turned in a field gate and came back again. There were no side streets, just that double row of windows, each house joined to its neighbours on either side, laid bare to its neighbours across the way. Everyone's business would be everyone else's; surely an incomer couldn't hide here.

The old butchers and bakers and candlestick makers had all been turned into houses, some of them still showing pale rectangles in the stonework above the front doors where signs had been unscrewed and taken down, but a newsagents cum grocer was still trading, its lighted window like a single candle in an empty church. I hadn't noticed how dark it had got until I saw that yellow square glowing in the unbroken grey of road and stone and slate and sky. I pulled in right outside and sat watching, through the decals, in between the posters and small ads, waiting for the customers to leave. It was afterschool time and children were spending their pocket money, but finally, the last of them cleared out and I made my move, hurrying into the warmth and greeting the smile from the woman behind the counter with one of my own. This woman would know. She'd sort newspapers for everyone in the place — *The Times* to *The Sport.* She'd know who came for rolls on a Sunday, who bought vodka when the shop was empty but walked out when there was a queue. She'd know which kids bought more hairspray than they needed for their hair and which housewives bought tubs of ice-cream and pound bars of chocolate on a school day. She'd know about Alka-Seltzer and condoms and who had cancelled their subscriptions when the work dried up at the quarry. If Alan Best lived here, she'd know him.

"I like your hair," she said, when I pushed my hood back. "That must keep your head nice and cosy."

"It's awful out there, isn't it?" I answered. "Miserable."

"Just passing through?" the woman said. "I can make you a coffee but it's only instant. Fine with milk and sugar, but Starbucks isn't trembling."

"Actually, I'm looking for someone. He moved here — Oh, must be nearly ten years ago now. Well, more than five." She was looking at me as expectant as a collie watching the whistle between the shepherd's teeth. She wouldn't only oblige with information, this one, she'd pride herself on it. "His name was Alan Best."

She raised her chin very slowly and further than seemed reasonable or even possible, then she looked at me down the length of her nose, talking through her teeth, barely moving her lips. "Friend of yours, is he?"

It was warm in the little shop, but her voice sent shivers down me worse than the damp cold outside.

"Absolutely not," I said. "I'm trying to locate him in connection with something, but no he is not."

"In connection with something new?" she said.

"Something very old," I told her. "Nearly thirty years old."

"Makes no difference," she said. "I'm sorry for your troubles."

I nodded and gave her a tight little smile, just the sort of smile a woman with troubles would give. Suddenly I was sure I knew where she was leading me, this friendly woman whose voice had turned to ice; where she thought I had come from.

"He *was* here," she said. "Came years back — maybe ten — with his so-called girlfriend. She was a funny one. Care worker, if you ask me, but she didn't do much of a job of caring. Her conscience got to her and she told the mums of toddlers. He didn't last long here after that."

"He was . . . on the register?" I said.

She nodded. "Nice polite way to put it. Yeah, he got caught in Castle Douglas, moving in on a single mum, grooming her kid. They found the stuff on his computer when he put it in to get fixed. So they shipped him out here, Social Services did, as if our kids didn't matter. He lasted a year, but we got him out."

My stomach had clenched, but my mind was tumbling over itself. How young could it start? Did Alan Best drive his brother to suicide that night? And Nathan McAllister too? Did Edmund die of guilt because he knew and didn't protect Nod? Where did April fit in?

"I don't suppose you know where he went?" I said.

"Maybole," said the woman. "Just up the road. Another flat, all furnished no doubt. Another fresh start. But we found him and told them, and then he was off again."

"Where to this time?" I said, sure that she knew.

"Dalmellington." Another grey Ayrshire town with more houses than tenants who wanted to live in them. I could believe that Alan Best, men like him, would be put there.

"Is he *still* in Dalmellington?" I asked the woman. I knew my voice was thick with nausea, but she didn't mind. If anything, she looked pleased with me.

"He's not," she said. "But I hope wherever he is, he's suffering."

I nodded and turned away. I couldn't believe that Alan Best, the Alan Best from primary school, Stig's friend, was —

Stig's friend! My stomach suddenly seemed to unhook inside me and turn right over, long and slow like an eel in a river. Stig was in my house. Stig who'd had a hard life, according to his brother; Stig who was single; Stig who wasn't part of the family business anymore, who was lost without the Internet. He was in my house with pictures of Nicky when he was a baby. Pictures and films and footprints of my little boy.

"Get away from that!"

He was hunched over the laptop again, as ever, his shoulders rounded and his tummy pouched out in front of him almost touching the keyboard. He started and pushed his chair back. Walter Scott had been sitting on his feet and he yelped as his roost was pulled out from under him.

"Glo?" said Stig. "What's wrong?"

"Alan Best," I said. "Your friend, Alan Best, is a paeodophile."

Stig's face drained of colour, leaving a waxy sheen over it. "Bezzo," he said. "*Bezzo?* He can't be. He fancied the teacher and she was ancient."

"It's not a joke, Stephen," I said. "I'm not as big a fool as you think. If you've been looking at pictures on my computer, if you've been looking at videos of Nicky —"

Stig's face was bluish white now. "Me?" he said. "*Me?* And kids? Where did that come from?"

I stood staring at him, breathing in and

out like a bull, trying to get on top of the sickness rising in me. Then the whole day just piled onto my head and smothered me. I sank down, put my arms around my shoulders and tried to hug myself — like I hadn't learned that *that* doesn't work — and the sobs that had been building inside me since I left Mrs. Best on her doorstep finally burst out.

"I don't know," I said. "I don't know anything. I thought I'd found a good place for Nicky and I thought I had happy memories of childhood and you, and now there's April in the huttie that's never going away and Alan Best and what he did and everyone's face when they talk about him, and his mother in that empty wee house with both her sons gone, and your mum threatening me and your dad just slumped there, and Duggie moving on and I'm so tired and you're so scared. It feels like something's going to snap and Miss Drumm's not herself and if she dies before Nicky, if she dies before Nicky, if she dies before Nicky, and what kind of mum am I to even think it?"

Halfway through all of that he was there, kneeling on the floor in front of me, with his arms round my middle, and I finished up screaming the end of it into his neck. He

212

said nothing, just rocked me. Over his shoulder I could see Walter Scott, lying listless in his basket with his muzzle over the side and his eyes half shut.

In the only future I could bear to think of, Nicky was released from all his suffering — that was how I put it to myself — and then Miss Drumm got her rest, and then Walter finally went last of all. But I knew from looking at him that it wasn't going to work out that way. Walter was going to break Miss Drumm's heart and then she was going to leave me high and dry, and Nicky would have to move to a hospital and wait there for the end. Unless I went crawling back to Duggie for money or went crawling back to my mum for a roof over my head while I kept paying for the home.

"Glo, I'm going to have to move," said Stig. "My knees are killing me."

I laughed and couldn't believe it. Two minutes before, I had thought I'd never laugh again.

"Okay," he said, getting to his feet and rubbing his legs through his sweat suit bottoms. "First things first. If Alan Best was caught messing with children — when was this supposed to be?"

"It started ten years ago at least," I said. "Did April have kids? Did she take a carv-

213

ing knife to her veins because she didn't protect them?"

"That wasn't a carving knife," said Stig. "You saw it, Glo. It was an oyster shucker, like a chef would use." My head jerked up. "Yeah," he said. "Nice touch. But listen."

I rootled in my sleeve for a hankie and blew my nose. It sounded so disgusting that I expected Stig's lip to curl, but he just raised his eyebrows.

"Impressive," he said. "Now, listen to me. If Alan Best had hurt children, he wouldn't be sent to Barrwherry. He'd be sent to Barlinnie. He'd be inside. I don't know who you've been listening to, but whatever they've told you is gossip, not news."

I opened my mouth to argue with him then closed it again. He was right. Between the miserable woman in the empty house, the neighbour vicious with anger at his name, and then that long dreary road to that long dreary town, I had been ready to believe any horrors at all by the time I got there. And so the poison of that shop assistant had found a home in me.

"But if it's not true then he's been hounded —"

"It's *not* true," said Stig. "Believe me, I would know. I shared every magazine Bezzo Best ever laid his hands on from before

Eden to the end of high school, and it wasn't little girls he went for. Or little boys either."

"Before Eden?" I said "From Mrs. Hill's class? You were twelve!"

"Yeah? And?"

"So . . . what was it? That he went for."

"Big and Busty," said Stig. *"Juggs.* There was this one mag called *Mambo Mamas* and —"

"You were twelve!" I said again. "You sat next to me and drew a love heart on my pencil case."

"That wasn't a love heart," said Stig. "That was Mambo Mama's mammoth arse, seen from over her shoulder."

This time I laughed until I wept, rocking back and forward again. At some point in the middle of it, Stig came and sat on the arm of my chair, putting a hand on my back and rubbing me like a mum burping a baby.

"I did draw a love heart on your pencil case," he said, when the tears had subsided again. "And you just said you had happy memories of childhood and me. Maybe we should stop pretending we were just two random kids the teacher made sit together."

"We were."

"To start with," said Stig. "But when my mum and dad were talking about Eden, I asked them if there would be scholarships. They laughed their teeth out. *Scholarships!* Where had I even heard that word?"

"From my school stories."

"Exactly. You and your books."

"And one of these scholarships was going to be for me?"

"That was the plan," said Stig. "Thank God there weren't any, eh?"

"Except if a butterfly flaps its wings," I said. Stig shook his head, not understanding me. "If I had been at Eden, it would have been different. Moped wouldn't have died, because all the things that happened to bring him to that moment would have been changed."

"What are you talking about?"

"Maybe I'd have caught a cold and given it to him and he wouldn't have slept out. But I wasn't there to catch one. Or maybe I'd have had a torch and woken up when he started moving. Or anything. There's a thousand ways for things to go, and almost all of them are fine."

"It's a Wonderful Life," said Stig, and I smiled with relief that he understood me. I couldn't have faced explaining it the only way I knew how. Cells and genes and alleles, recessive and dominant, like shuffling a pack of cards.

"Exactly," I said.

"A wonderful life, except everyone's either dead or we haven't checked yet," he said. "Apart from Duggie and me."

"I'll check the rest in the morning," I told him. "The Scarlets and the weather girls. That's what Wee J called them."

"Yeah, about that," Stig said. "You said my mum threatened you? Why'd you go to Fawlty Towers, Glo?"

"I don't know," I said. He waited for me to go on. "I suppose I thought they must have some answers."

"Who did you ask — Mum or Dad?"

"They were all there," I said. "But your mum was the one doing most of the talking. Stig . . . your dad." He looked up at me. "What happened?"

He shook his head slowly a couple of times before he answered. "What do you mean?" he said. "He got older, like all of us. His health isn't great, but he's fine."

This was so far from being true that I didn't know where to begin, but then I thought of Nicky and how I would feel if someone asked me *What happened?* in that heartless way and how I would do anything rather than answer.

"I never really got the chance to ask your mum anything much," I said. "She was pretty upset. Well, angry. I'm sorry, Stig, but she doesn't seem completely convinced that you're innocent."

Stig gave that bark of laughter again; I was getting to know it now, getting to recognise the pain of it so well that it hardly sounded like laughter at all. "I'll bet she's not," he said. "And yeah, she's angry. See, the thing is, my mum didn't have much to do with Eden. It was always Dad's thing."

I could certainly believe it wasn't Angie Tarrant's thing. A spa and a gym and hen weekends were much more her line. But the BJ Tarrant of my childhood was Angie all over again except for being a man.

"Wee J guessed who I was," I said to Stig. "He's worried about you. He told me to tell you to stay out of sight and be careful. Does he know what's going on?"

"No, but he trusts me," said Stig. He leaned back against the Rayburn rail and smiled, staring into the distance. "He was a nice wee boy and he's a good bloke now," he said. "It's not his fault." He paused and I was going to ask, but then he started speaking again. "When we came back from Saudi there was a lot of family visits and that, and one of my uncles brought a girl-friend to meet us. And there we were, sitting in the house having a beer, coke for the kids, and she asked why I wasn't called Jacky after my dad. Why it was the *second* son who was Wee J."

"Was Stephen your granddad's name or something?"

"No, it wasn't that," said Stig. "My mum explained it to the girlfriend that day. I'll never forget it. She stubbed out her fag in this big glass ashtray and said, 'We didn't think he was going to make it — a lot of complications at the birth — so we didn't want to waste the name in case it ended up on a headstone.' "

I could feel my face falling. "With you just sitting there? Did she know you could hear?"

"Oh yeah," Stig said. "It wasn't like some big secret she'd finally decided to tell. It was more like it had never come up before and then it did, so she answered the question. Like if *I'd* asked one day, she would have told me, just the same."

"That's horrendous," I said.

"Well, it is and it isn't. It made sense of things. Why Weej got taken on holiday with them to Turkey and I went to stay with my granny. She said it was too much to handle two kids at once."

"But that's ridiculous," I said. "It would have been much more fun for you and Wee

J to be together, so you could play. Whether it was Turkey or your granny's makes no odds."

"Yeah," he said. "And then birthday parties too. He had a party in the middle of July and I didn't in the middle of December. She said it was because it was easy to have the kids out in the garden and mine was too near Christmas."

"What did your dad say?"

"He told her to knock it off and stop being such a cow. When we were wee and then in Saudi. After Eden, he never said boo. But Wee J was never spoiled by it. He shared his birthday cake, made me blow out the candles with him and everything. And he even sent me a postcard from Turkey. Just scribbles and my dad wrote the address."

"But I don't understand," I said. "How can your mum *be* like that?"

"I suppose," said Stig, "she didn't want to get attached. In case I died. And then it was too late. Or maybe she felt guilty and took it out on me. Dunno."

I couldn't speak. I shouldn't have judged Angie. I knew from Duggie's grief that it was normal to feel that way. Nicky made him angry because he was guilty because he was ashamed. He even accused me to trying to make him look worse by — I'll never forget the word he used — *overacting*. I was puzzled. Overacting how? I wanted to know.

"Putting it on and going too far. *My son this* and *my son that*. Like this, bringing him to the Gala Day and introducing him."

"Why would I not introduce him?" I said. "I'm proud of him. You should be proud of him. He's our son."

And then Duggie had said, "Come off it, Gloria. Nobody's bringing the cakes that didn't rise and the jam that didn't set to the Gala Day and saying they're proud." And Nicky was right there when he said it, just like Stig and Angie.

"Who's mummy's little pot of runny jelly?" I'd said, wheeling him over the bumpy grass of the temporary car park to take him home. "You're mummy's little flat sponge, aren't you?"

"You know who you remind me of?" I said to Stig. "Harry Potter. It always bothered me that a boy who was kept in a cupboard and given clothes hangers and tissues for his birthday ended up so well adjusted. He should have been setting light to cars and drinking in the swing park."

"A whole cupboard?" said Stig. "All to himself? Luxury."

"I'm going to see Nicky now," I said. "I'll be back by nine o'clock. What will you do?"

"More dead-slow-and-stop Internet."

"But nothing . . . ?" I flicked a glance at the computer.

"Don't worry," said Stig. "I'm not in the mood anyway."

"Just tell me," I said. "This teacher that Bezzo used to have a crush on. It wasn't Mrs. Hill, was it?"

"God's sake, Gloria, that's sick!" said Stig. "No, of course not. It was Miss Naismith at Eden. Tie-dyed t-shirts, hairy legs and all. I knew he fancied her because he never stopped giving her a hard time."

"Poor thing. All on her own there with you lot."

"Yeah, we were wee shites. One time she locked herself out on the roof because we wouldn't stop tormenting her."

"Some people are just not cut out to be teachers," I said.

Eighteen

But still, when I looked up at the chimneys — dark against the moonlit sky — as I was getting out of the car ten minutes later, I felt sad to think of it: a teacher, overwhelmed by naughty children, sitting crying on a roof. And not just her; how many times in the life of the house must it have harboured people quietly weeping, quietly falling apart while they tried to hold it together. And, as I was just about to find out, it was happening again.

"Gloria?" said Miss Drumm at the sound of my footsteps. "At last. I need to talk to you."

I sat down at her bedside. That was the first worry. She usually insisted on what she called *the niceties*. Dinner at a table with an ironed linen napkin and sitting in her chair until a decent bedtime. But tonight she was in a flannel nightgown and bed jacket with her hair pinned back off her face, gleaming from the cold cream she'd been rubbing into her skin every night for sixty-five years until her pores were monstrous pits, black around her nose and in the crease of her chin, while her wrinkles only looked deeper for the shine on their slopes.

"The hallowed place," she said. "Is everything as it should be?"

I felt my insides drop and then bounce back to settle higher than they should be. What should I tell her? The chain on the padlock was cut through and the door wasn't closed or locked, but she couldn't know that or I'd have heard about it too.

"I can't think why not," I said.

"And the stone?"

"As ever," I said, although I felt a twinge of guilt saying it because the truth was I hadn't rocked the stone today, and yesterday I had only rocked it once, showing Stig. "I meant to ask you about the hallowed place, actually," I said, hoping to distract her. I would rock the stone when I got home.

"Oh?" said Miss Drumm. She sat up, searching my face with her blind eyes.

"It's just what you said about it not being a crypt or a chapel but being consecrated. I realised I didn't know what else it could be."

"Memorial," said Miss Drumm, gruffly.

"It's an odd one," I said.

"Granted. It was an odd circumstance that led to it being built." She tugged at the pillow behind her until it was bunched enough to support her neck and then she let her head drop back. "It's a memorial and a sanctuary both, I suppose you would say. A haven."

I wondered if she knew it was full of beanbags and teenagers once.

"A haven from what?" I asked her.

"I'm not in the mood to be scoffed at," Miss Drumm said.

"I promise."

Miss Drumm gave a faint smile, satisfied. "I've been feeling most uneasy," she said. "*Most* uneasy. And I haven't felt that way for decades. The last time, I was hale and hearty enough to do something about it, but those days are over and so I'm relying on you."

"But what does the stone have to do with the temple?" I asked her. "You said yourself it was about half a mile away."

"It's exactly half a mile away," said Miss Drumm, "as the crow flies. It's half a mile from the stone to the hallowed place — it's not a temple, my girl; we're not swamis — and it's another half mile from the hallowed place to the house. A mile in all between the stone and the house and the only way to go is by the bridge. So it seemed a good idea to build a little sanctuary."

I turned all of this over carefully, not wanting to scoff or be accused of scoffing. But after almost a minute's quiet thought, I could make no sense if it.

"I'm not with you, Miss Drumm."

"Promise me you'll be a good sensible girl. Walter Scott would be lost if you took a fit of hysterics and ran away."

"I promise," I said again.

She munched her teeth together for a while but took it up again eventually. "It isn't always safe to run through the forest at night, you know. Nor to cross a bridge to get home."

"I agree about the forest at night," I said carefully, more lost than ever. "Although I've always thought the Milharay woods were friendly."

"Of course they're friendly woods! As safe as Oxford Street on a Saturday afternoon." She reached out, feeling for my hand. When I put it under hers, she patted it. "As long as you're rocking the stone."

"Miss Drumm," I said, "the stone isn't in the woods. The stone's in the garden. It's —"

"I might be old, girl," Miss Drumm said,

back to her peppery self after the compliment and the hand-patting, "but I am not senile. I told you not to scoff at me. If you won't listen, I'll need to find someone who will."

"I'm listening," I said. "I apologise. I'm listening, really."

"Well now," she began. "The Stone of Milharay. Everything I've ever told you about it is true. But it's not the whole truth. The whole truth, Gloria, is that the Stone of Milharay has something inside it. Someone, I should say."

I said nothing. I only stared at her shining face. Was she really telling me that the stone that sat outside my kitchen window and that I laid my hands on every day, except when I forgot like this morning, was some kind of sarcophagus? How could that be?

"Who?" I asked gently.

"Remember your promise."

"I remember. Who is it?"

"The devil," said Miss Drumm. My mouth dropped open. "You'll catch flies," she snapped. "I heard your breathing change." I shut my mouth and swallowed hard. "That's better. Manners are so unpolished these days. When I was a girl, no young lady would sit gaping with her mouth open. Mind you, it made life terribly difficult for anyone who suffered from adenoids and it did mean that, when one had a cold, one was banished from society. But I daresay that was healthier than the way everyone just slugs down Day Nurse and goes about their business spreading germs."

"Miss Drumm," I said. "The devil?"

"He's been in there near enough full time for more than three hundred years, since my ancestor Margery Drumm tricked him into it in the 1680s. Of course, Rough House wasn't built until 1820 and even this place wasn't around. The old house was a terribly draughty place with seven storeys and no bathrooms."

"Three hundred years?" I said, nudging her back to the point.

"More or less constantly. And I know you've been doing a splendid job for the last ten. And yet still I've got the oddest feeling that something is wrong." She broke off and lifted her head. "I'm baring my soul here, girl," she said fiercely, then dropped back again.

"And the last time something went wrong, I was responsible. I went away from home and didn't make provisions. Didn't want to tell anyone, you see. I vowed then I would never let it happen again and I shan't. So you make sure and rock that stone. Every day. Morning and night. And if you wake up in the small hours to spend a penny, go out and rock it again."

"What exactly does rocking the stone do, Miss Drumm?" I said. "I always thought it was just for luck."

"You could call it luck," Miss Drumm said, "inasmuch as it's most unlucky for someone if you don't. Rocking the stone keeps him addled, you see. It's when it sits steady that he gathers himself and grows strong."

I am, as she had said, as sensible sort, living all on my own in that big old house miles from anyone and never thinking twice about it. And I meant what I said about the woods too, how peaceful and cradled I'd always felt under the trees in the soft dark when I took Walter Scott out in the old days. But sitting there at her bedside in the low light shining in her bedroom door — a blind woman never bothers with lamps in the evening — I felt the flesh on my neck creep and tingle as a shudder rose through me and then felt my scalp shrink as it fell away again. It was terrifying listening to her sounding so old and confused instead of bright and funny. I was scared of losing her and scared too of the day I would be like her and no one would come to visit me, to listen without scoffing.

"There," she murmured. "I've said my piece. Now go and see that boy of yours. I'm tired, Gloria. I'm getting more than a day's worth of tired at the end of every day now. I'm getting once and for all tired, I fear."

"Don't," I said softly. "You've probably got a little cold or maybe you need an iron pill. But don't talk about once and for all."

She shook her head twice, and on the second shake she kept it turned away from me. And so I did a thing I never do. I stood, bent over her, and kissed her cheek.

"You are my good friend," I said. "I can't do without you." But she was already sleeping.

When I turned, I saw Donna standing in the doorway, watching us. I raised my eyebrows in question, and she gave me a sad smile and shook her head in answer.

"That you off?" she whispered.

"No, I'm running late tonight. I haven't been in to Nicky," I said.

"Ah, and he's lovely for you," Donna said. "We have him in the taupe and mauve stripes from Next, and he's a picture."

I grinned at her and dug in my bag for my phone. "I better make sure and get a snap of him."

"You do that," Donna said. "I'll be there in a minute with a cup of tea."

He really did look handsome in the pyjamas, grown-up and rakish, like the lead in a Noël Coward play.

"Hello my little West End sensation," I said to him. I took a gauze square and wiped his mouth, then carefully applied some of the salve where the feeding tube dries his lip. Sometimes in winter it gets bad enough to crack, what with the dry air from the central heating as well, and the sight of that red line and the swelling on either side of it makes me hurt in my stomach. Of course he can't feel it — he can't feel anything — but it looks as if, were he to waken suddenly and smile, it would be sore.

"Now then," I said, lifting the book and opening it at the marker. The next poem was "Time to Rise." It was short but it struck me as cruel, a little bird hopping around a windowsill chirping at a child in bed: "Ain't you 'shamed, you sleepy-head?" so I had started skipping it as we went along. "The Marching Song" too and the one called "At the Seaside." But most of the poems are about bed and dreams and life outside the sick-room window. Or they're thoughts that you could have from anywhere, like "The Moon" or the one I would read tonight.

" 'Looking-glass River,' " I said, and started in. I'd always enjoyed it before; it's got an interesting rhythm, and you have to pay attention to get the sound right. Tonight though, by the time I was halfway through it I had forgot about the rhythm completely and was speaking the words in a kind of trance.

" 'We can see our coloured faces, floating on the shaken pool,' " I said and I thought of Moped Best, the little boy in the snazzy shirt in his school picture, leaning over the footbridge and gazing down. I thought of Miss Drumm saying calmly, *it's not always a good idea to cross a bridge to get home.* " 'See the rings pursue each other; all below grows black as night,' " I read. " 'Just as if Mother had blown out the light.' " I glanced up at Nicky's face, checking to see that I wasn't frightening him. He was as serene as ever. " 'Patience, children, just a minute' " — it was the last stanza — " 'see the spreading circles die. The stream and all in it will clear by-and-by.' " Then I shrieked as Donna out a hand on my shoulder.

"Mercy!" she said, stepping back. "I didn't mean to startle you. I only just came to say it'll be a while because Iveta's emptied the

232

kettle to clean it. This hard water! And I've put a pot on the stove instead."

"Actually, Donna," I said, "never mind the tea. I'm going to have to dash off."

"Ah well," said Donna. "I've said it for years now, Gloria, as you know."

I bent over Nicky, kissed his eyes and his hands as usual. She *had* been saying it for years — telling me I should be out at evening classes or line-dancing, could just as easy pop in and see Nicky in the morning for five minutes.

"How has Miss Drumm been these last few days?" I asked, hoping to sound casual.

"She's fading," Donna said.

"And getting wandered with it," I said, keeping my voice low. The connecting door was shut, but it was better to err on the side of caution.

"I wouldn't say that. She's old and her body's betraying her, but her mind is sharp as a tack," Donna said. "Always was and I think it always will be."

NINETEEN

For the first time ever in all the years, I was glad to be out of there. I felt as if I had escaped something unclean. The woods — those friendly woods — were crowding round in on either side of the car, and the long track to the house with its cattle grids was just a stretched-out nothingness between me and anyone who would hear me and come to help me if I screamed. If Stig hadn't been waiting for me, I might have driven all the way to Dumfries to a budget hotel and stopped at Tesco for a toothbrush on the way. Stig and Walter Scott anyway.

And besides, I told myself as I stopped on the track and opened the garden gate, I promised Miss Drumm I would rock the stone.

I knew the way to it no matter how dark the night, and so there was no fumbling. Ten steps over the pebbles, up the six stone stairs, five steps over the grass where the daffodils grew in the spring. I lifted my hands as I reached it and felt the rough surface under my palms as I had every day for ten years, until these last two. *One, two, three.* I paused and did something I had never done before. I put my head against the stone between my stretched hands and listened. *Four, five, six.* I could hear the scrape of the base in its cup. *Seven, eight, nine.* But the sound was dull and dead. There was no hollow in there. This was solid rock. *Ten, eleven, twelve.*

I hesitated. Miss Drumm had always been so insistent. Twelve pushes. If I miscounted and made it thirteen, I was to keep going until twenty-four. Still I paused with my hands on the rock, chilled now against its coldness. What if I pushed one more time?

Then I gasped as the outside light clicked on.

"Gloria, you nearly gave me heart failure," said Stig. "I heard the car, but you never came round to the yard. Then I heard the front gate. I've been shitting myself in there."

"I just remembered I'd forgotten to rock the stone this morning."

"I've been rocking it all day," said Stig. "I need any luck that's going. Twelve shoves a pop, right?"

"Right," I said, making my way back to the gate to get my car and carry on round. When he had put the light on and startled me and I had flinched, had I flinched hard enough to move the stone, making it thirteen?

"You're early," Stig said when I was in the kitchen. "I've got choux buns in the oven, but they're not ready to come out yet and they'll have to cool a bit before I glaze them. But I'm glad you're back because I've got something to show — Are you okay?"

I shook my head. "I was reading this poem to Nicky and it all got too real. Maybe because I saw Moped's photo this morning at his mum's, but all of a sudden it's not just a puzzle. It's a kid younger than Nicky and he died. Two brothers died, Stig. And April. It just suddenly seemed like there was something badly wrong with this place."

"What the hell kind of poems do you read him?"

"Robert Louis Stevenson," I said. "*A Child's Garden of Verses*. It's about a wee boy ill in his bed and the dreams he has. Adventures and make-believe and all that. Because Stevenson wasn't well a lot of his childhood, you know."

"I've never heard of him," said Stig. "Robert Stevenson?"

"Robert Louis Stevenson," I said, trying not to look too astonished. "Of course you've heard of him. Jekyll and Hyde? *Treasure Island?*"

"You're kidding," said Stig. "The same guy wrote horror films and Disney films?" He winked at me. "*I'm* kidding."

"How can you be so cheerful?" I said.

"Cos I'm cooking again," he said. "Either that or past caring. And Walter Scott helps a lot." All the talk of Stevenson had confused me, and I blinked at him. "The dog," he told me.

"Right," I said. "Of course. Listen, Stig, about the dog. Before Walter Scott, Miss Drumm had James Hogg, and before James Hogg she had Robert Burns."

"Heard of him!" said Stig. "Totally heard of Robert Burns."

"And she used to walk them all over the woods, all the time. She lived here at Rough House when you were at Eden."

"Her!" said Stig. "We called her Dog-breath Dora. She was always shouting at us and shaking her stick and — sorry, animal lovers, but — that dog was a bastard."

"Robert Burns," I said. "Twenty-eight years ago, it must have been Burns. Even Miss Drumm admits he was . . . lively."

"So that's your friend," said Stig. "Jesus,

how old is she?"

"She's eighty. She was only fifty-two when you were at Eden. Twelve years older than we are now."

"Jeez," said Stig. He sucked his stomach in and pulled at his face that way he had. "I suppose I'd look like some mad old codger to twelve-year-old kids already, mind you."

I smiled at him. "I need you to cast your mind back," I said. "To that night in the woods. I don't suppose there's any way for you to remember, but you never know. Was Miss Drumm around? That night? The days leading up to it?"

"I don't need to rack my brain for that," said Stig. "I can tell you right now she was away. Scarlet McFarlet was terrified of that damn dog, and the only reason she agreed to sleep out was that Dora had gone to see relatives and she'd taken the mutt with her."

I went over to the kitchen window and poked a gap in the curtains. I couldn't see the stone, but I knew it was there. So she had been away, neglecting her duties, when Moped died. It was crazy, but then, everything was beginning to feel crazy to me.

"Stig," I said, turning round, "next time you're on the Internet, can you look up folklore about bridges for me?"

"Bridges?" he said. "Like Devil's

238

Bridges?"

I felt my eyes widen. "Why would you say that?"

He shrugged. "That's the only folklore about bridges I know. Will do. I've finished what I've been looking for anyway." I waited, but he just chewed his lip.

"It's bad news, isn't it?" I said.

He nodded. "You don't need to look up Bezzo at work." He went over to the laptop where he had set it up at one end of the kitchen table, a notepad and collection of pens beside it. Between that and the two armchairs, the side table, and a footstool he'd brought from his bedroom and squeezed in between Walter's basket and the chairs, Stig was making a little nest for himself in my kitchen. I wasn't annoyed; it looked more purposeful and lived-in with his clutter. When it was just me, sometimes I felt as if the house was no more than a shelter for sleep. As if there was no sign that I actually lived my life there. I ate from the freezer and threw the packets away in the wheelie bin, and I read one book at a time and kept the others in order on the shelves. Stig, in my kitchen, had dirtied every pan, washed most, dried some, left some steeping, some draining. He'd made notes and spread them around. His glasses were hooked over the edge of the fruit bowl in the middle of the table. A fruit bowl filled with fruit he'd got me to buy, that he'd polished and arranged. He'd even been out and picked bunches of herbs and strung them up from the hot pipe running along under the high mantelpiece, and he'd put a little tin pail lined with newspaper on the bunker near the sink.

"What's that for?" I asked him.

"Scraps for the compost heap."

"I haven't got a compost heap," I said. "If Walter or the birds won't eat it, I just chuck it."

"I've started you one," he said. "If you stick at it, you'll have a mulch for those gooseberry bushes come next year. Anyway, look at this." He beckoned me over. "It's taken me forever to get three pages loaded at once, by the way."

I sat down in the chair he had set up in front of the screen. It wasn't one of the kitchen chairs; it was a dining chair with a padded seat that usually stood on the top landing, but it was just the right height and comfortable enough for long stints at the keyboard.

On the monitor was an article from the online *Guardian*. VIGILANTISM CLAIMS ANOTHER VICTIM. The group was called

Letz Go and they had hounded a man out of supervised care in the community somewhere in Hertfordshire, sent him underground again, except that a man answering his description had been picked up from the changing rooms at a —

I stopped reading.

"Just look at the end," said Stig. "At the bullet points."

- Jack Sower of Lancaster: died in custody after his community placement broke down following the activities of a chapter of Letz Go.

- Peter Masterton of Greenwich, considered highly dangerous: dropped out of sight of authorities after a campaign of harassment targeting him and his family by an unnamed local parent organisation.

- Allan Best of Galloway: found hanged in St. Quivox Parish Church graveyard after sustained harassment by unnamed groups. Mr. Best was never convicted of any crime.

"Where's St. Quivox?" I said, once I had read it over several times.

"Ayrshire," said Stig. "Can't be too far from where he was staying. But I think I know why he chose there." He leaned over me to use the mouse and restored another page. On it was a photograph, unmistakably taken in a Scottish churchyard. Everything about the cold light, the tussocky grass, and the leafless sycamores said so. In the middle of the photograph was a headstone, ancient and weathered, the names and epitaphs worn away, but the carving still distinct. Trees, gnarled and heavy with fruit, climbed up either side of the stone framing two naked figures, hand-in-hand, who stood on something that looked like a crude gondola but might have been a serpent.

"Eden," said Stig. "I looked up *The Ayrshire Post* and found the report."

He clicked again, but I didn't have the heart to read any more. I pushed my chair away and let him in close to the screen.

"Body found in St. Quivox churchyard," he said. "Blah blah blah — suicide, no one sought in connection — blah blah. Overdose of drug from opiate family and hanged by means of a rope attached to the well-known Adam and Eve gravestone."

"What?" I said rejoining him. "Go back to the picture." I leaned over his shoulder, peering at the screen. "That headstone's only five feet tall at the most," I said. "If he hanged himself from that, it must have been by sitting down and letting his neck take the weight."

"Well, with the overdose too," said Stig. "But yeah, you'd have to be determined, wouldn't you?"

"Moped, Ned, Nod, Alan, April," I said, half to myself.

"I looked for the rest," said Stig, "but I couldn't find them. Over to you and your work computer."

I nodded. "I've even thought of something to say if I find people and phone them. I can tell them about April, let them know about a funeral."

"Who will you say you are?"

"I'll think of something," I said. "A friend. Therapist. Could even wheel out the Church of God again if I have to. If I find them. If they're somewhere I can get to."

"If they're still alive," said Stig. "That's the big *if*, really."

TWENTY

Thursday

I didn't remember what I was dreaming but I woke with a strong sensation of having seen something, like a face in a crowd or a name I recognised in a long page of writing. I lay for a while, cuddled into my soft bed, hoping that if I drifted it would come back to me. Dorothy and William were pinning the covers down around me, one curled behind my knees and one stretched along the front of my thighs. *The stone,* I thought to myself. *The bridge, the huttie, the clearing, the stream. Edmund and Nathan, Mitchell and Alan, April and Duggie and Stig.* What was I missing?

After a few minutes, I wriggled out from between the cats and stepped over to the window. Dorothy stood, squeezed herself up into an arc, then stretched herself out and settled down beside William, greeting her brother with an ear lick before closing her eyes again. I nudged the curtain open. Stig was out there already, watched by both the byre cats, Bill and Weed, hunched side by side on the top step waiting for him to finish and feed them. They had waited many times for me to do the same. They and Ben, the other male, before the night when the fox got him.

I had trembled at the thought of telling Miss Drumm, but she took it calmly. *Mousers, Gloria,* she'd said. *Nothing more. I wouldn't see harm done to them, but they're not of my heart. Not like Dorothy, William, and Walter.* I nodded my relief and tried not think about how callous she sounded. Miss Drumm could hear a thought even if she couldn't see the expression that went with it. Perhaps it was easier for me because none of the animals was of my heart when I got there and I had to work at all of them just the same. Or perhaps Bill, Ben, and Weed were just more to my liking; they asked for little — a bowl of biscuits, a paraffin stove in the shed on the coldest nights — and they repaid those little favours. They would sit, as they were now, watching me hang out washing or weed the herb bed, scurrying away and resettling if I moved too close. But then, every so often, when the sun was warm and I was still for long enough, one then two then all three would steal close to me, close enough for me to hear their rusty purring.

I'm only sorry that if one had to go it wasn't Weed, Miss Drumm had said. *Stupid name. They were christened before they came to Rough House, of course.* Or they would have been . . . I thought but couldn't come up with two brothers and a sister from literature. Unless it was Charlotte, Emily, and Bramwell with no Anne.

There went that elusive thought again, just out of reach, as I watched Stig and the cats. Bill and Ben, the Flower Pot Men. I turned and looked at the two curled up as tight as snail shells on the bed. William and Dorothy Wordsworth. Miss Drumm had her own talent for stupid names, if anyone was asking me. Moped and Bezzo Best. Ned and Nod McAllister. April Cowan and —

Nicky! I flinched and turned as a shower of gravel hit the windowpane. Stig was standing at the top of the steps, the cats gone, waving up at me.

"Come down," he shouted. "I've got something to tell you."

I shrugged myself into my dressing gown, belted it shut, shoved my feet into my warm slippers, and went downstairs.

"Eggs *en cocotte,*" said Stig, when I got to

246

the kitchen. "Ready in five. That's proper French tarragon you've got out there, you know. None of your Russian muck." He put a mug of coffee at the seat nearest the stove, took a slurp of his own, and jiggled the laptop screen back to life.

"You must admit it's better than that sewage you were drinking," he said. "Even if I did have to bash the beans with a rolling pin. How can you not have a coffee bean grinder? Or a mortar and pestle?"

"If coffee at home tastes like Starbucks," I said, "what do you do for a treat?" I ignored his look. "What did you want to tell me?"

"Devil's Bridges," said Stig. "They're all over the shop. Scotland, Wales — France is lowping with them — and the story's the same every time. It freaked me out a bit when I was reading about it last night because it all sounded so familiar and I couldn't think why. But listen."

I sipped the coffee and waited, letting my hand fall down by the side of my chair to rest on Walter Scott's head.

"There's always an uncrossable river," he began. "So up pops the devil and offers to build a bridge. The only catch is that he gets the first soul to cross it once it's finished, right? So he builds it and then either no one ever crosses it and he just sits there forever waiting and it's an uncrossable bridge over an uncrossable river. Or some sneaky villager chucks a bit of bread over and a stray dog races after it, so the devil gets a dog soul. Sometimes a rat, sometimes a pig. Or — and here's the one that's interesting — he builds the bridge but before anyone crosses it, he's — hang on." He scrolled down the screen and read from it. " 'Imprisoned by a spell so that the villagers can use the bridge without danger to their souls.' "

"Okay," I said, carefully. "When did you say for those eggs?"

"Shit," said Stig, leaping to his feet and dumping the laptop down on the seat behind him. He grabbed the oven mitts and opened the Rayburn door. "Caught them," he said. "Birl round, Glo." He had set the table with napkins and matching china and a few of the last asters in an egg-cup, and now he put down a plate of toast triangles and the little dishes of egg. "Leave it minute if you don't want to burn your tongue."

Walter, now that the opening and closing of the oven door was over, went to his basket and lay down.

"He's not used to so much action at the stove," I said. "But this looks lovely."

"Perfect," said Stig, sitting and shaking

his egg dish. "I've never worked with a single oven oil-cooker before, but once you get used to it, it's fine. Right, so I looked up spells to imprison the devil."

"What?" I said. "Where?"

"On the Internet," said Stig. "You don't even have to look hard. You need a load of people and some words and somewhere to put him — like a stone cross, or a cairn, or a standing stone or 'an ancient and sacred marker of that ilk.' And that's when I remembered. The Irving girls were all about Pagan crap, and I'm sure one of them knew about your stone, Glo. They were even talking about it that night. Telling each other ghost stories. They had started before I took off to the bog. I remember it now. Rain Irving was talking about what she called the hollow place! And I think she meant your stone out there. I think the devil's in it."

I concentrated on my breathing. My throat had closed and I knew I couldn't speak, but if I could just keep breathing I would be okay. Then Stig gave a snort that almost choked him.

"Christ sake," he said. "I don't mean I *believe* it! Jesus, Gloria. I'm saying it gives us a reason Moped took off. If the rest of them were telling horror stories and Mope was scared, then maybe that's why he hightailed it out of there. And if Nod was the one doing the worst of the scaring, maybe he felt guilty about it and that's why he killed himself. And Ned followed him because he couldn't forgive himself for not stopping Nod from doing it."

"And Alan Best?"

"Same as Nod. Couldn't forgive himself for the night Moped died."

"But what about all the gossip about Bezzo and his girlfriend's child?" I said. "Where does that fit in? You're so determined that it's not true — and that means someone started a rumour. A real live someone, not a ghost. And what about April?"

"Same thing," said Stig. "Couldn't forgive herself. Who knows what they all did that night? I wasn't there."

I shook my head. "This is delicious, by the way," I said, even though I couldn't imagine how I would be feeling by mid-morning, starting the day with eggs and cream and herbs. And I was sure there was a bit of garlic in there too.

"You think I should stick to cooking and leave the thinking to you?"

"I wouldn't go that far," I said, wiping round the little dish with a corner of toast. "But you're not quite there. For one thing,

Rain Irving wasn't saying 'hollow place.' It's 'hallowed place.' That's what Miss Drumm calls the huttie."

"And what does that mean?" said Stig. "Haunted?"

"Hallowed?" I said. "It means *hallowed.* Holy, basically. Like, *hallowed be his name.*"

"I'm not much for all that," said Stig. "Okay, though. The devil's in the huttie, not the stone."

I tried not to think about what Miss Drumm had said the night before. It didn't matter for what we were interested in.

"But what do you think of the theory?" he said. "Moped ran away from their scary stories, and they were ashamed and guilty."

"There's more going on here than a wave of guilt that won't stop. Someone hounded Alan Best. And someone's out to get you for sure. And someone moved April's body. Doesn't it make more sense to think the same thing happened to everyone? That Ned and Nod were hounded too? This isn't dominoes falling over, Stig. Someone's pushing them."

He had stopped chewing with a mouthful of food still there in his cheek. It bulged his face out and made his voice sound thick when he spoke to me.

"Who?" he said. "Mrs. Best? Mr. Best?

Who else would still be angry enough about an accident years ago? But they wouldn't *hound* their other son. That's the word right enough, Glo. Bezzo was innocent of any crime but hounded anyway."

"I don't think anyone would still be angry enough all these years later if it was an accident," I said. "But someone is. Ergo . . ." I waited, but Stig only shook his head. "Ergo it wasn't an accident. Someone's behind what's happening now and someone was behind what happened then. All the way back to Moped."

Stig was staring at me. He swallowed his mouthful of toast as though it was a ball of barbed wire and looked as if it might come right back up again. "The car," he said.

I nodded. "The car."

"You're saying someone who came to Eden in the car *killed* Mope?"

I nodded again. Stig looked down at his plate and then dropped his napkin over it, hiding the food as if it sickened him.

"But how would . . . anyone . . . get him away from the clearing so they could hurt him?"

"Maybe they just got lucky. They watched and waited, and if it hadn't been Moped it might have been someone else."

"It might have been me."

252

"Or no one. If the sausages had been cooked and none of the kids told ghost stories, you would all have been together all night." Stig's face clouded and he looked away. "But if that's what happened, then whoever's punishing the rest of the kids must know which ones were responsible for frightening Moped away into the woods on his own."

"I suppose," said Stig. "But the ones who've died aren't the ones I'd have thought. I mean, it was the Irving girls who knew the folklore, and Jo-jo Jameson and Moped himself were the biggest wind-up merchants. But if you asked me who'd be most likely to keep on and on until it was beyond a joke and Moped ran off? I know which name I'd tell you."

Duggie is not perfect. He left us, couldn't cope. But I knew he was a good man deep down. He always had lots of friends, was always standing someone a drink or lending someone a van.

I tried to think it through rationally while I drove to work, forgetting that I knew him, that for a while I thought I'd be spending the rest of my life with him.

On the one hand, I could absolutely imagine that Duggie would joke around in a dark wood and not stop even when it had gone too far. He always did play tricks like that. He'd pretend to have lost the car keys when I had an appointment I was nervous about — when we booked our wedding, or had a scan at the antenatal clinic, that sort of thing. And there *was* the fact that he didn't mention Eden to me and didn't want Nicky living there. That was secretive in a way that was hard to account for.

But the persecution of Alan Best went on for years. Could Duggie keep it up that long? Of course, he had mounted quite a campaign with me.

Our courtship took place on Thursday nights, Friday nights, and every other Saturday. Once I asked him if he was busy on Tuesday, and he grimaced at me as if it hurt him to say so, but Tuesday night was quiz night at the club. "I like quizzes," I had said, and he had gone so quiet for so long that I had never mentioned it again. Mondays he had a few quiet pints, Tuesdays the quiz, Wednesday in the football season was the midweek fixture and out of the season he got together with the same crowd to look back at where it went wrong and look forward to the next one, Thursday night was mine, Friday night we went out with another couple, Billy and Jade, and the three of them drank too much and giggled a lot and I drove them home, then dancing on a Saturday. Sunday he spent with his family. It occurred to me that I might be invited there too, but I said nothing; I just spent it with mine.

"If I didn't think you were too sensible to make up stories about a local lad, I'd hardly believe you had a boyfriend," my mum would say.

"He's stringing you along, Gloria," said my sister, "using you."

"What for? What do you mean?" I asked her.

She said nothing until my mum went to take the pudding plates through and put the kettle on, then she curled her lip and said, "You tell me what you're doing for him to keep him. He's a good-looking guy, so it must be worth his while to hang on to you."

I had tears in my eyes when my mum re-appeared.

"What's wrong with you now, Gloria?" she'd said.

"She's upset because her boyfriend's so off-hand," said Marilyn. "I would be too."

I couldn't help myself: "At least I've got one," I shot back. And then they both turned on me.

So I always wondered, after the night

when Duggie suddenly parked at Auchen-reoch Loch on the way home from seeing *Titanic* and it turned out that he wasn't planning to seduce me as I'd been expecting — actually, as I'd been beginning to think was never going to happen.

"Gloria," he'd said, "you don't need to answer right away, but I want you to marry me." He was so low-key, so un-nervous, that at first I thought I had misheard him. *I don't want you to answer right way but I want you to . . . hear me.* That was what I thought he said and so I waited, obedient as ever, for what he had to say. After a long silence, he turned to me, and the look on his face was one of complete astonishment.

"Did you hear me?" he asked.

"No," I said.

"Are you winding me up?"

"No. But why are you getting upset? You told me I didn't have to answer right away."

He started the car and jerked back out of the parking space hard enough to make the wheels screech. On the ten-minute journey home I had time to think it over, and when we parked again I plucked up my courage.

"Did you propose?" I asked him. He nodded, still looking at me with that same bewilderment. "I couldn't believe my ears." He started to smile. "I convinced myself it wasn't true."

The half-smile spread and before long he was laughing, one arm round my shoulders, shaking me and roaring with laughter. "God, you had me going there for a minute, Gloria," he said. "Come on then. Will we go in and tell your folks?"

I gave him an impish smile, my first one ever, not having the face or figure to be impish usually. "I haven't answered you yet," I said.

He clicked the side of his mouth and pointed his finger at me. "No way. You don't get me twice in one night. I'm not that gullible."

So, strictly speaking, I never said yes.

That night for the first time he came into the house with me. My mum had her dressing gown on and my sister had done a face pack earlier and was still wearing the towelling band round her hair and no cover-up on her spots. I wasn't to know that, though; it wasn't fair of them to blame me.

"I've got something to ask you, Mr. Harkness," Duggie had said to my dad. "No prizes for guessing what." He was standing in the middle of the living room floor, bouncing a bit on the balls of his feet, jingling his change, miming his golf swing. He was nervous, probably.

"Go on then," said my dad. "Ask me."

"Trevor!" my mum yelped. But my dad was looking at Duggie with an unreadable expression.

Duggie took his hands out of his pockets and cleared his throat. "I'd like to ask for your daughter's hand in marriage," he said.

"I'm not surprised," said my dad. "She's a wonderful girl."

But just like me, he didn't actually say yes either. My mum leapt up and kissed Duggie. My sister gave me the world's coldest hug, and my dad went to get a bottle of wine out of the fridge.

"The champagne's not cold," my mum said, glaring at him for bringing Liebfraumilch out in front of a Morrison. My dad ignored her and gave me the first glass once it was open.

"Are you sure, Gloria?" he'd said. "Is this the man for you?"

I nodded, beaming. I was twenty-four and I'd had three boyfriends in my entire life. Duggie, one of the trolley boys from my Saturday job at the Co-op who took me rabbit-shooting and made me touch them, and Stig who drew a love heart on my pencil case.

TWENTY-ONE

Lynne banged on my car window.

"What are you grinning about?" she said, when I opened the door. "You look like love's young dream."

"Believe it or not, my husband," I said.

Lynne snorted and took my bag out of my hands so I could clamber out and lock the car door. "It's nice that you're so happily divorced," she said. "I saw Duggie yesterday, as it happens."

"Oh?" I was opening up the office and hurrying in to get the heating on as quick as possible. We had someone coming to register a birth and this old building, after a closed day in winter, was no place for a new baby.

"Out for lunch in Designs with his new squeeze, I think she was," said Lynne.

"Straightened hair, suede suite, posh nails?" I said.

"Big bum, bad dye job, I was going to say."

"Zöe," I said. "She's actually very nice." And I felt the same sinking feeling I'd had yesterday when she was sitting on his desk. She was nicer than me. She was even nice *to* me.

"Except for her terrible taste in men," said Lynne. She had a lot of divorced friends and she was automatically nasty about the ex-husbands. I went along with it, never admitted I would take him back in a heart-beat if he asked me, to be a happy family again. "Cup of tea?" she went on. "I've got éclairs."

She would only be gone a few minutes, so I had to decide who to look for, and that was easy. The Scarlets and the Irving girls — the weather girls, Wee J had called them — might have disappeared in a string of marriages, names gone forever. But there was one boy left. Jo-jo Jameson would have stayed Jo-jo Jameson from his cradle to however near he had got to his grave. I keyed in JAMESON, J—, a rough birth date of 1972, and the county DUMFRIES. If he had lived in Moniaive his whole life, I might be lucky.

Luckier than Jo-jo Jameson, as it turned out. I stared at the screen trying to take it all in and jumped when Lynne came back.

"So," she said, plumping down and blowing a raspberry at the stack of filing she should be doing, "have you heard the goss?"

I bit into my éclair and waited for her to tell me. I never heard gossip before her. Lynne loved that about me.

"Death," she said. "It happened in Glasgow, but it's connected to here."

"How's that then?" I said.

"Remember the Tarrants? They tried to buy the station yards and they ran the country store for a bit and then that mad school out in the sticks where they had the tragedy, then they took on a hotel? You must know them. She dresses like a drag act and he dresses like a villain and they've got two sons must be near your age."

"I think I was at school with one of them," I said. "Is one of them dead?"

"One of them did it!" said Lynne. "The victim's a woman but the guy that killed her is one of the Tarrant boys."

"That's terrible," I said. "I wonder if it was the one I knew."

"I don't know which one's which," said Lynne. "But he killed this girl. Well, woman. She was forty, but she had everything to live for. She was going into business with a friend. Reiki and aromatherapy and all that, those ear candles. Had a business loan and a premises lined up. Everything to live for, and then this guy just loomed up out of the past and slashed her to ribbons."

Before I could answer, the door opened, letting in the thin, high-pitched keening of an eight-day old baby who'd rather be at home getting cuddles than in his buggy in my office getting a name.

Lynne swept up the cake plates and pushed them into the slot under the counter. It was fine to be drinking a cuppa on a cold morning, but registering is serious business and messy cream cakes give the wrong impression. I left my desk and came around the front.

"So who have we got here then?" I said, peering in under the hood of the buggy. He was kicking his blanket and waving mittened fists in the air, screaming hard, his eyes squeezed shut and his mouth wide open, the little white milk stripe down his tongue looking bright in his purple face. "Can I?" I asked.

The dad, harried and dazed, nodded straightaway but then checked with his wife. She was just as dazed but dreamy with it, still looking soft and undone from the birth, bags under her eyes and her hair tousled. She gave the baby a look and then nodded too.

"Oh, little man!" I said, working one hand

under his head and one under his bottom and lifting him, letting the blanket fall away. I brought him up to my shoulder and let his head rest there. I patted his bottom rhythmically and bounced up and down. First he said, "Hoowoo-hoowoo," then he grunted, then with a quivering sigh he shut up completely and the room was silent except for the snuffling of his breaths and the clanking of the old radiator. I smiled at the young mum and then turned to Lynne. She wasn't in her seat. She was standing with her hands on the back of my chair looking at my computer screen.

"I suppose you get a lot of practice," said the mum, grabbing my attention again.

I tried to read Lynne's face, failed, and turned away. "New ones are easy," I said. "Once he's worked out who his mummy is, no one else'll do. So make the most of it while you can."

That pleased the woman, and she smiled again.

"But now I'll pass him over to Daddy," I said, "and let's get started. Have you got the card from the hospital? That's grand." I sat down again and regarded the screen. I could have opened another one. In busy offices they have half a dozen registrations going on at once sometimes, loads of windows

open while people are looking for documents or arguing over names. But this was
a sacred moment. I didn't want to register
this little scrap on a computer where Jo-jo
Jameson's death record was open — a death
I had no business looking at. I'm not usually superstitious, but that was a bad omen
if ever I saw one.

"And any other documents for me?" I
said. I glanced at her left hand but she had
gloves on.

"Marriage lines," said the dad, putting his
hand into his back jeans pocket and taking
out an envelope.

"Perfect," I said. "Righty-ho. I've just got
a few entries to make, but I'm dying to ask
you: What's the name?"

"Mario," said the girl. "Mario Tobias Carson."

"That's lovely!" I said. It was one of the
first things I learned in basic training.
"Mario Carson. That's really lovely, the way
it rolls of the tongue."

"Unless . . ." said the dad. "Is there any
way to check — I mean, can you look up in
that thing and see if there's been any Marios
already? Round here?"

"Gloria can look up all sorts of things,"
Lynne murmured. "She should be able to
manage that for you."

"I don't need to," I said. "I can tell you that there hasn't been a single Mario. Not in this office or in the local region. You've done the impossible for your little boy: a lovely name that everyone can spell that nobody else has thought of. Well done."

They beamed and I guessed that their families — the Carsons and whatever clan she came from with her red hair and freckles — had had plenty to say.

Ten minutes later they were gone. I waved them away and turned to face Lynne.

"Mario," I said. "That's worth entering."

Registrars take their duties seriously, of course we do, but we have to have a bit of fun sometimes. And "Mario" was in with a shout for the weekly sweepstakes in the southwest region. We had had no winners from our office for four years, not since we took the weekly sweep, the monthly national round, *and* got to silver placing in the annual championship with a pair of twins called Tancred and Ulrika. And the sweep's an exception; most of the games we played were just between Lynne and me, like The Hand Of Woman, where we tried to tell whether a toddler had been dressed by its dad when the mum was still on her back from the birth.

"She laid that outfit by," Lynne had said

one day, full of scorn, when a young man brought in a child, chittering and blue-lipped in a matching sundress and sandals during a sudden cold snap. "That's the hand of woman," she said, and the phrase had stuck.

But Lynne wasn't up for games today, wasn't to be distracted.

"What are you up to, Gloria?" she said. "Who was John Jameson?"

I didn't answer. Where would I start? John Jameson was a boy called Jo-jo who had gone to school in the woods with twelve others, and like every one of them I'd found so far, except Stig and Duggie, he was dead now. He had died in 2005, in France, falling off a bridge into a ravine at a place called Herault. And his cause of death, amended after toxicology and a full investigation, was accidental drowning.

I brought up Google and typed in *Herault.* It was a town in the Languedoc, a region with good beaches and popular with tourists. But the main claim to fame of Herault itself was *Le Pont du Diable.* The Devil's Bridge.

"Glo?" said Lynne. "Is everything okay?"

"Almost nothing," I said. "Listen, you didn't finish telling me about the murder."

"What?" said Lynne. Wondering what I

was up to had driven gossip out of her brain. "Oh! Yes, I did. There's nothing more to tell really."

"He loomed up out of her past, you said? So . . . he was her ex?"

"My mum didn't think so. She's got a pretty good memory for all that sort of thing. And she didn't think so." Lynne was trying not to look at the computer as she spoke; if she tried any harder, in fact, she might snap a tendon in her neck.

"Do you want me to check?"

"My mum asked that and I said, 'no way because Gloria's a real stickler', and you never do that, do you? Look up old boy-friends and whatnot. You never do."

"How did your mum find out about the business loan?"

"From her friend Maureen that works at Enterprise Scotland."

I closed Google and opened up our own system again. "Here's the deal," I said. "I do this for you and you just forget that you saw me looking up a record before?"

"No idea what you're on about, Gloria," said Lynne. "What record? Before when?" She winked at me, and I turned and rested my fingers on the keyboard.

"April Cowan," said Lynne. "And Tarrant. No idea about the first name."

"Let's try Stephen," I said. "It was Stephen Tarrant who was the same age as me and I think his brother was younger, so if she was forty it's probably him. If it's either."

I entered the search and waited, aware that my mouth had turned dry and my palms were prickling with sweat.

"No matches." I let my breath go in a rush that clouded the monitor, it was still that cold in here.

"Huh," said Lynne. "Course she might have been April somebody else when she married him. Check on Tarrant alone."

But under TARRANT, STEPHEN, dob 1972, CASTLE DOUGLAS there was only a marriage to Carol née Watson, and a divorce from the same two years previously.

"So it's not a domestic," said Lynne, finally getting her éclair out from the ledge below the desk. "Unless they were just shacked up. But if he was married until two years ago and she's been on her new life kick since then — training and all that — it's hard to see how they know each other. I wonder what the connection is then."

"It might have been the other brother," I said. "Maybe he likes older women."

Lynne wiggled her eyebrows at me. "Like your Duggie," she said. "His new bit must be fifty."

"Never," I said. Then I tried for a very casual tone. "Maybe April and Stephen were at school together. Not primary. And I'm sure April Cowan didn't go through CD High School with me or I'd remember her, but it was what you said about the Tarrants' school in the woods. Maybe they knew each other from there."

Lynne was dabbing up crumbs with a wetted finger. She licked it, wiped it on her jeans, and took her phone from her body-warmer pocket.

"Mum?" she said, after a pause. "Are you busy? Gloria's just had a brainwave. That April Cowan that the Tarrant lad bumped off? Do you think she was at the school they had up there in the hills for a bit?" She listened, nodding distractedly for a while, and then she sat up straight with her eyes wide. "Thanks," she said. "Look, I've got to go." She snapped the phone shut, then turned those wide staring eyes on me.

"What?" I said.

"She can't think of a Cowan," said Lynne. "But one of the Tarrant kids was definitely there and the wee Best kid too — he was the one that died. An accident in the woods when they were camping, Mum said. And some hippies from the Borgue called River and Leaf. But then she said — get this — your Duggie was there too. Said quite a lot about that, actually. The Morrisons had a storage warehouse at the station yards, and Mum reckons Duggie's dad swapped it for school fees."

"I never knew Duggie was at Eden," I said.

I didn't see the mistake I had made. But Lynne spotted it.

"That's right," she said, looking at me archly. "That's what it was called. *Eden.* My mum just reminded me."

We regarded each other for a long moment.

"Well, no wonder your eyes were out on stops," I said.

"Oh, that wasn't the big surprise," said Lynne. "The big surprise was the other name my mum remembered." She turned and looked very definitely at the computer. It had gone on stand-by and her face was reflected in it. "Jameson," she said. "John Jameson from Moniaive. Gloria, what's going on here? What do you know?"

TWENTY-TWO

Moniaive is one of those places you only get in Galloway. It's seventy miles from Glasgow — only twenty miles from a town with a Marks and Spencer, an ice rink, and a cinema — and yet it's as isolated as any clutch of highland crofts. It's partly the bad roads, and they're partly the fault of the poor land. And the approach from the west, from Dalry, is the worst of all. But I'd have walked there barefoot that day, once I had Lynne's blessing.

"I can't tell you what's going on," I said. "But on my life, on Nicky's life, you can trust me."

"Of course I can," Lynne said. "You're the honestest person I've ever met. I just want to help you."

"You can't tell your mum."

"I don't tell my mum anything," she assured me. "I didn't tell my mum I was pregnant until after the scan. I didn't tell her when Malcolm got done for speeding. But she found out anyway because she knows all the cops."

"But if I promise you that, once it's all over, I'll tell you every last detail and your mum'll be begging you to dish it, will you help me now?"

"What have I just finished saying?"

"Okay," I said. "I need to try to track down the hippie girls and then there's two more. I want to use the FER, like I did for Jo-jo Jameson."

"Jo-jo?" she said, her eyes growing wide again. "Glo, did you know him?"

"I can't explain," I said. "I've never met him, as far as I know."

Lynne spent a minute taking it all in and then, with a sniff, she took over. "Moniaive. You could be there in half an hour. Nobody here'll know that you're not off to do a wedding somewhere. We've nothing booked and it would do the buggers good to be shown you're not a drop-in service anyway. Meantime, I'll look up the records. If you give me the names."

So I wrote down the Scarlets and the weather girls, warned her to hide them if anyone came in, anyone at all, and set off into the hills to Jo-jo Jameson's one-time home. I tried not to think of the Barrwherry trip. At least today I already knew there would be no good news waiting for me. Jo-jo died when he was thirty-three; there's no way to make that a happy ending.

The Jameson house was more what I expected from a family who stumped up for boarding school. A solid, whitewashed block of good Galloway stone, red sandstone round the windows, and red tiles on the roof. It was bare-looking, like everywhere this late in the year, but orderly and bare, not ravaged and bare like Rough House. Looking at the pruned apple trees sitting in circles of dark earth in the front lawn with all the dead leaves swept away, and the bare stems of the climbing roses that sprawled over the front of the house, tied into proper tensioned wires with proper tree-ties in figures of eight, all of a sudden I could see why my place bothered Stig. It wasn't just cabin fever; it really *was* a pity to let a house just sink into the hillside while I came and went, did my job, and sat with Nicky. When all of this was over, I told myself, I would go round with a clipboard, try to work out what needed to be done. Everything from the slipped slates that made damp patches on the upstairs ceilings to the dandelions and daisies where the grass should be.

Here at the Jamesons', the grass was like

velvet, flat and smooth, with edges as crisp as a starched cuff. The windows were glittering too, clean right into the corners, and even though they were the same wood-framed Victorian as mine, they weren't thick with a dozen layers of paint slapped one on top of the other, and the panes weren't loose from slipping where the putty had dried up and dropped away.

In fact, everything about this place intimidated me. The people who lived here wouldn't invite a Bible thumper in or share malicious gossip. I was out of my depth and I knew it. *I'm as good as anyone else,* I remember my mother saying when the Duchess of Gloucester came to open the new primary school. *I don't see why I should wait to be spoken to, or curtsey either. She's no better than me.* But she was. I knew that as soon as I saw her, kindly and beautiful and sort of shining with light from the golden hair and the silk coat — I had never seen someone wearing a coat made of yellow silk before; silk in Castle Douglas was something that only blouses were made of, teamed with a good plain skirt of tweed or serge. Coats were dark and plain so you could wear them all winter long and they'd not get dirty on the buses. So I looked at the duchess, with her golden hair, golden coat, and shining smile, and thought she *was* better than my mother; she was lovely. And later, when I learned to sew, I made myself a yellow coat just the same, bias-cut and contrast-lined, shaped like a tulip and closed with hidden hooks and my mother scoffed all the time I was sewing and laughed out loud at me when it was finished and I tried it on.

Somehow the memory of the duchess in her golden coat gave me the courage to pull the iron handle and ring the bell.

"Coming!" a voice called, and a minute later the big heavy outside door was swept open and a woman stood there, a look of polite enquiry on her face. She had one hand in the collar of a black Labrador who looked about as old as Walter Scott and she was so short, a neat little elf of a person, that she hardly had to stoop at all to reach it.

"Mrs. Jameson?" I said. She looked about fifty, but I'm not good with ages and she had that thick creamy skin that lasts well, so she could have been his mother at a pinch.

"Sally Jameson," she said. "Doctor."

"I'm . . . an old friend of Jo-jo's," I said. "I wonder if I could have a word."

"Jo-jo?" she said. "Johnny-oh? Is my mother expecting you?"

I did a swift recalculation. Dr. Jameson was his sister, then, not a well-preserved child-bride.

"She's not," I said. "I stopped by on the off-chance."

"It's not great timing, actually," Dr. Jameson said. "She only just finished her chemo the day before yesterday and it's hit her hard this time. That's why I'm staying. If you left it another week she'd be much more up for visitors. And she does love to talk about Johnny-oh."

"I see," I said. "Well, I certainly don't want to barge in. I'll . . ." I gestured behind myself at my car, half-offering to take myself off.

"Where do you know him from?" said Dr. Jameson. "You weren't at the funeral, were you?"

"No," I said. "No. I didn't make it to his funeral."

"My God!" she said. She let go of the dog's collar and it bounded away from her and set off across the lawn, sniffing and marking the apple trees. Dr. Jameson took a step towards me and peered up into my face. "You're not Fronia, are you?"

"Fronia?" I said. "No. My name's — Who's Fronia?"

"Sorry," she said. "*Where* do you know

Johnny from?"

"School."

"Oh! What a pity. That would have been marvellous."

"If I was Fronia?" I said. "Who is she?"

The little woman looked past me at the dog, then sighed out a great big puff of air that bloomed in the cold that was creeping in as the sun moved behind the hill. "He needs a walk," she said. "Adder! Come here, you daft dog. Come and get your lead on." She put her head back inside the house and shouted. "Linda? Are you there? I'm going to walk Adder. Be back in ten. Tell Mummy if she wakes, will you?"

Then she unhooked a raincoat that was hanging up behind the door and put a leather dog's lead round her neck like a scarf. "I won't need bags," she said. "We're only going up the lane and I can kick it into the undergrowth. So long as you don't tell on me."

Adder knew exactly what it meant that his mistress was wearing a coat and walking down the path, and he shot off through the gate like a greyhound.

"How old is he?" I asked.

She laughed. "Yes, his looks have gone, but he's fit as a fiddle," she said. "My mother jokes about it. She doesn't look a day over sixty, but it's her lungs now. It was her breasts last time. I've been checked, and so has Linda and we're both gee-ing ourselves up to get all four whacked off if need be. It's not a popular plan with the menfolk, mind you."

She reminded me of Miss Drumm, that brusque way of talking, stripped of any sentiment, and I'd had enough practice with Miss Drumm to know better than to offer sympathy.

"Mine's fifteen, arthritic, with a heart that sounds like a dishwasher," I said, mimicking her. "His breath would make you weep too, but he's a good sort."

She smiled and accepted me — or, the me I had invented to match her.

"Fronia was Johnny's wife," she said. We were falling into a good rhythm, tramping along at the side of the lane. "Well, his bride, I suppose you'd say. He died on his honeymoon."

"Eeh," I said. Then I thought about it for a minute. "But you thought I was her . . . Does that mean you weren't at the wedding?"

"None of us were. It wasn't a wedding as such. They sent postcards from Dover before they got on the ferry. 'Am married. See you in two weeks. F sends love.' And that was the last we heard from him. The next time we *saw* him was when they shipped him back. He's up there now." She pointed east. "In the churchyard. My father never recovered from it, and he's up there too now. Poor Johnny-oh."

"Poor all of you," I said.

"Oh, it was a mess," she agreed. "My father steamed in — he spoke wonderful French — and more or less plucked Johnny away before the poor girl had time to decide which way was up. He hadn't taken to her at all when Johnny brought her here to meet the family. Thought she was too 'worldly,' whatever that means. Johnny was hardly a curly-haired boy."

"What did you think of her?" I said.

"Wasn't here," she said, shortly. "I was on call at Ninewells and couldn't get away, and Linda was living in Colorado of all places with the loathsome Chris. She's dumped *him* now, at any rate. I do always wonder whether, if Linda and I had been around, the visit might have gone better and Johnny might have capitulated in the matter of a big family wedding, and then who knows."

"He wouldn't have been in Herault that day," I said.

"Exactly," she said. Then she looked up at me sharply. "You know how he died then."

"Another friend told me."

"Such a stupid way to go," she said. "Not even skiing or hunting or anything you would expect to have dangers. Just walking over a stupid bridge that people walk over all day every day."

"How did he come to fall off?" I said.

"God knows. Larking about, I expect. Johnny broke more bones in a year than Linda and I broke our entire childhoods. That was what made me want to be a doctor, sitting in Casualty with him, watching him get patched up." She walked a few steps in silence. "I think it was the sheer senselessness of it that made my father so angry. He blamed Fronia completely. Got it into his head that she was a gold-digger and set out to get the marriage annulled."

"Good grief," I said. "That's a bit . . ."

"Mean?" said Dr. Jameson. "Nasty? Bitter? We all said all those things to him, believe me. Of course, he didn't manage it, but he did succeed in driving her away."

"Absolutely away?" I said. "All these years?"

"I've got a theory about that," she said. "I reckon she was pregnant. Maybe that's why they got married so quickly. And my father put her back up so badly over moving the body and the funeral and everything that she vowed to keep the baby from us."

"I hope not," I said. "Or maybe I hope *so*. I mean, maybe one day the doorbell will ring and it'll be your niece or nephew."

"Well, I hope he or she gets a bloody move on, for Mummy's sake," said Dr. Jameson. "God, it's freezing. Let's turn back, eh? Adder? Come on, dozy dog. Come get a Boneo!"

The rustling ahead of us in the undergrowth stopped. There was a pause and then a streak of black shot past in the other direction, heading for home.

"So what memories of Johnny can you share?" she said, when we were underway again. "You were at school together, you say?"

"Briefly," I said. "At Eden."

"Oh." There was a world of meaning in that one syllable that I wished I could decipher. "Well, that was Johnny all over. Mummy and my father were thrashing it out — Glenalmond, St. Leonard's, one of the Edinburgh schools — and then he appeared with a leaflet for that ludicrous enterprise. Sorry, that was rude. You might have loved it there."

"It was so short-lived," I said. "It's all a bit of a blur."

"Well, Johnny loved it," she said. "He was

281

wild about Linda and me going to join him there. I told him to forget it. I wanted to be a doctor. No way I was going to some hand-knitted hippy school where the science consisted of going out to lie on your back in the woods and look at the stars. And Linda couldn't have been prised away from her hair-dryer with a crowbar in the eighties, so that was a no-go."

"Well, I do remember one of the girls was pretty welded to her crimping irons," I said. "April. But I see what you mean. Anyway, it ended with a bit of a thump."

"And Johnny went to Glenalmond after all. And only just managed not to get expelled, despite some trying. So, you see, it didn't even put him off. The longest suspension he got at Glenalmond was for some rather nasty teasing one Halloween."

I thought that over to see if her meaning would reveal itself, but eventually I had to speak again. "I'm not sure I'm with you," I said. "What didn't put him off?"

"You know," she said. "Well, if you were there that last night, you do. It sounded ghastly to me then, and it still does now."

"I wasn't actually there for all of the last night," I said. "I was indisposed. We had cooked our own sausages —"

"Oh God! I remember that," she said.

"Johnny was as sick as a dog the next day. He was sick in the car coming back and he said to me if I wanted to be a doctor I had better clean it up and bring him some Lucozade. I told him that was nursing, not doctoring, and if he wanted doctoring then he had to let me examine him. Then Mummy explained to me that he was in shock and I had to be very kind. Shock! You couldn't shock that boy with a taser. God knows what it was like when you were all together there."

Lord of the Flies," I said, and again she gave that shout of laughter.

"So I imagine. I bet your kids didn't go anywhere like it. Mine are local comp and all the better."

"My son has special needs," I said. "PKAN." I can never resist talking about it to someone who'll understand.

She sucked her breath in over her teeth. "That's rough. Infantile or adult-onset? There's a kid over near Dalry with late-stage infantile PKAN."

"Adult onset," I lied. "In Edinburgh. So he wouldn't be camping and cooking his own sausages even if he wanted to."

"Silver lining," she said, callously. I concentrated on saying nothing, telling myself she didn't know it was as bad as it was because I'd told her the wrong kind. "And that nasty trick," she went on after a pause. "It sounded like some sort of mad shunning from a sect or something."

"What's that?"

"Eh?" she said. "Didn't you know? The children who were sleeping out in the woods picked one to go and spend the night alone in some haunted little chapel place. Sent him off in the dark, dared him to spend the hour over midnight all on his own."

"Moped," I said softly.

"That rings a faint bell," she said. "Something like that. What was his real name?"

"Mitchell," I said. "The boy who died."

"That must be right then. The child who was out on his own *was* the one who died. Johnny insisted it was nothing like the way it sounds, though. He said the boy was full of bravado and taking bets that he would do it. He said he was sneering at all the other kids who were too scared. Johnny wanted to be the one who went, he told me, but this other boy shouted him down and told him to wait his turn."

"I missed all of this," I said. *Stig had missed all of this,* I was thinking.

"Anyway, thank God — Mitchell, was it? — did shout him down. It was bad enough him dying in his thirties. If he'd drowned at twelve —" She stopped walking, frowning and staring straight ahead. "That's a bit horrid, actually, isn't it?" she said. "When you get right down to it, the way the child died in the woods that night and the way Johnny died on his honeymoon in Herault are not a million miles apart. That's rather nasty."

I nodded but said nothing. *Nasty* wasn't the word for it when you added April Cowan dead in the same huttie where Moped went to win his bet, and his brother dead in a churchyard, hanged against a sculpture of Adam and Eve. And Edmund McAllister drowned at another ravine with a huttie of its own.

We were back at the garden gate now and as we turned in we saw a woman — another tiny elfin woman, dressed in the same black jeans and dark, chunky jersey as her sister.

"She's asking for you," this new woman called to us. "She's a bit brighter, but she wants another painkiller and won't take no for an answer from me."

Dr. Jameson sped up until she was almost trotting.

"Sorry," she called over her shoulder. "I'll have to go. Thanks for listening. Above and beyond." Then she hurried away.

I got into my car and started the engine,

waiting for some warmth. My feet in my work shoes were almost numb from the icy ground, but not quite numb enough not to hurt. I cranked the heater up and turned the blowers downwards.

Mrs. Jameson was too ill to have been out in the woods on Monday night and then driving to Glasgow on Tuesday to avenge her son. And if Dr. Sally Jameson knew anything about it, she was the best actress ever born and wasted on medicine.

The noise of the fan was so loud that I jumped when the knock came the window. It was the sister.

"Cryptic message from Sally," she said. "And I quote: 'It wasn't Moped. It was Van.' Don't ask me why she's talking like Charlie Chan because I can't tell you."

"Thank you," I said. "Tell her thank you."

"Does it make sense to you?"

"I wouldn't go that far," I said. "But I know what she means anyway."

TWENTY-THREE

Deirdre was in her place on the bench by the front door, swinging her little pipe-cleaner legs to and fro.

"Well, this is a day of surprises and no mistake," Donna said as she buzzed me in. "What's going on?" She had a point. I'd been coming to the home at the same time every day for at least eight years. Then last night I was late and tonight I was early.

I wanted to . . . I didn't want to finish the thought because the only ending was to say *get it out of the way,* which wasn't true. What I really wanted was to be able to go home, cover the kitchen table with sheets of paper and write down everything I knew and everything Stig had found out in another day on the Internet and try to make it make sense. I couldn't face another night where I filled Stig in quickly and then went out again, came back tired, and tried to pick it up where I'd left off, with Nicky and Miss

287

Drumm distracting me in between times.

"I'm not feeling well," I said. "I need to get home and get settled."

"You shouldn't be here if you're ill," Donna said. She didn't exactly bar the way, but she certainly didn't stand aside for me.

"It's just a heavy period," I told her. "Nothing catching."

"I'm glad to be past all that," she said. "I didn't know you were troubled with your monthlies, Gloria. You've never said."

"I've never been troubled until now," I told her. I was shocked at the lies spilling out of me. To poor Mrs. Best, to Sally Jameson, and now to Donna who'd always been so kind to Nicky, so good to me. "I think it must be the start of the change."

Donna nodded sagely. "Sounds like it, though you're young," she said. "In my day they'd have you in for a D&C, and if that didn't work they'd whip the lot out. These days, you can be that anemic a vampire wouldn't bother with you and they just tell you to eat a bit of spinach and do some Pilates." She pronounced it *pie-laits,* but thankfully, when I laughed, she just thought she had cheered me up and wasn't hurt.

"So it's just a coincidence?" she said.

"What is?" I asked her.

She wiggled her eyebrows. "You'll see."

■ ■ ■ ■

I heard it before I saw it. When I was halfway down the corridor, Duggie's voice rang out, confident and loud, set to carry across the golf-club-house bar when he was buying a round or claiming the floor at a Rotary meeting.

"You'd think they'd bring a cup of coffee," he said. "Bloody place costs enough. It wouldn't kill them."

I sped silently the rest of the way, and the first he knew was when I blatted the door wide open with my fist and made for him.

"Don't you dare swear in front of him," I said. "And don't you dare find fault with these people who've cared for him his whole life. And don't you *dare* talk about the cost of it when you don't pay a sou."

"*A sou,*" said Duggie. He reached a hand out as if showing me off like a object of curiosity, as though he was a tourist guide pointing out a funny little statue somewhere. "Gloria, where do you get your patter? And what makes you think Nick would prefer you slamming around and screeching like a fishwife?"

At long last I turned to the other side of the bed to where he was gesturing at Zöe

289

sitting there. She was wearing another one of her moleskin suits, sage green this time, and had one of her hands over one of Nicky's. She took it away when she saw my eyes flash, put it up to her neck and fiddled with her scarf.

"Gloria, I'm so sorry," she said. "I wanted to meet him. We thought we'd be here and gone before you got here. I wouldn't have had this happen for the world."

I had been winding up to unleash a good mouthful, but she took the breath out of me.

"You wanted to meet Nicky?" I looked between her and Duggie, but my eyes came back to her.

"I pestered Dougall," she said. "Blame me."

"I can't blame you for him not setting foot here in ten years," I said, my anger rising again. "Did he tell you that?"

"Men," she said. "They're not like us. Even the best of them."

I turned again to see what Duggie would make of being criticised this way. He had two spots of colour high up on his cheeks and his mouth was working as if he was gathering saliva for a spit, but he said nothing.

"Mine was just the same," Zöe said. "And

I learned too late. Mind you, if I'd been less of a battle-axe to him and we'd made it, I wouldn't have met this piece of work here." She winked at Duggie and got up to go around and tousle his hair. She even dropped a kiss on his head.

I sat down in her chair and took hold of the hand she had let go.

"I'm not a battle-axe," I said. "I'm just a mother."

"Oh, I know," said Zöe. Duggie made a snorting sound and rolled his eyes. "Behave, you," she told him, tweaking his ear and shaking her head at me. "*I* was, though. When our little one was taken, my husband couldn't do right for doing wrong."

"Your —" I said.

Even Duggie turned to her with a curious look on his face. "You never told me that," he said.

"Stillbirth," said Zöe. "It's not the sort of thing you say on a date, and then the moment passed. But don't worry, Dougall, I'm reformed. Life is short and you've got to see what you've got and hang on hard, I say." She squeezed him with one arm, a really friendly sort of hug, no clinging, no nuzzling, not the sort of hug Duggie used to wriggle out of when I was married to him and craved a bit of contact. "Now, I'm going to go and get you two some tea. You should just sit here, the three of you."

We didn't speak for quite a while after she left. Duggie was staring at the floor. I was staring at him. It pains me to say it but, for the first time ever in that room, I wasn't looking at Nicky. And I wasn't thinking about him. I was thinking, miserably, about myself. Hankering and hoping and making Duggie feel trapped and angry, instead of tousling his hair and teasing him.

"You've won the jackpot there," I said at last. "And I don't think you even paid for a ticket."

"What are you on about now?" Duggie said.

"Zöe," I told him. "She's great. She's really lovely." Then I had to go and spoil it, adding, "and she doesn't seem to mind that you're not."

"I'm not looking to get sucked into anything."

"Well, you're an idiot then. Because women like that don't come along every day."

"You branching out, Glo?" he said, and thinking of something so crude put him in a good mood again. He smirked at me.

"I've got a question for you," I said. I gave Nicky a wary glance but decided to press

292

on anyway. "It's about the night Mitchell Best died when you were at Eden." His smile snapped off as if he'd flicked a switch. "Was it you who took the dare to go and sleep all alone in the hallowed place?"

"Hallowed place?" said Duggie, sneering again. "You sound like that old bag Naismith. *Hallowed place, bridge of souls.*"

"You know what I mean," I said. "It *was* you, wasn't it? You weren't there sleeping with the rest of the kids. Did you tell the police that?"

"What are you on about, Gloria?" said Duggie. "Who have you been talking to?"

I considered the question. I'd have to tell him something or he might guess that I was in touch with Stig. "Jo-jo Jameson's sister told me," I said. "I know her, and it came up because of the news about April Cowan and Stig Tarrant. She told me what Jo-jo said about that night. That you were showing off, blustering on about not being scared."

"God, Jo-jo Jameson!" Duggie said. "How's he these days? Bungee jumping in Oz? Climbing Kilimanjaro? He was a complete nutter when I knew him. Unless that posh school turned him into a ponce. Probably, eh?"

"He's dead," I said. "He died crossing

another 'bridge of souls.' Devil's Bridge, I think it was called, actually. You never volunteered to do that, did you? Just to spend an hour in the safest place for miles around."

"Safe?" said Duggie. "For God's sake, Gloria, you sound as if you believe it. *Wooo-woooo.*" He waved his hands like a ghost, mocking me. "The rest of them were giving themselves cheapies going on about it, so I thought somebody should show them what it meant to have a pair."

"You are so unremittingly crude, Duggie," I said. "And cruel too. You went to a sanctuary and left the rest of them out where the devil could get them."

He was staring at me. "Have you any idea how completely doolally you sound? You should get checked out before you end up in here with his lot." He pointed at Nicky as he spoke, gestured to him with one hand, the way you would show which lobster you wanted out of a tank, or the way you would tell someone where the rat was they'd come to kill for you.

I stumbled to my feet. "Why do you do that?" I said "Why pretend to be such a monster? Nobody could really think the things you say."

"Here we go," said Zöe's voice and she

backed into the room, pushing the door open with her bottom and turning to show us a tea tray. She looked from one to the other, took it in in a second. "Oh," she said. "You having words? Gloria, I'm sorry. I've pushed this too far too fast. Look, we'll shoot off now and let you have your time with him. I'm really sorry you're upset." Then she glanced at the bed and her face softened. "But I'm not sorry we came." She put the tray down went over and kissed his head, brushing his hair back just the way I do. Then she stood in front of me for a moment. She didn't hug me or even take my hands. She just stood there and smiled at me as if she was trying to will me to understand her.

I found myself smiling back. I even reached out and brushed her sleeve with my knuckles.

"It's a start," she said. "I'll see you soon, eh?"

I didn't notice Duggie leaving. I was so sideswiped by the whole thing. He'd had a visitor who wasn't me. He'd been kissed by someone who wanted to meet him and she'd held his hand. Maybe he was going to have a stepmother. Maybe there was going to be someone else who cared about him that I could talk to. Not Duggie, in my daydream of our happy little family re-formed, but Duggie's new wife in a new, messy, modern family. Could I let go of the daydream and hope for that instead now?

"Gloria!" Miss Drumm shouted weakly. "I heard all of that and I've got to talk to you."

"Back soon, darling," I said, kissing Nicky's eyes. "It's the railway carriage poem coming up! I won't be long."

Miss Drumm was in bed again, lying down flatter than she'd been the evening before.

"Are you okay?" I asked, but she shushed me, waving her arm like a policeman direct-ing traffic. "Are you not feeling well?" I whispered to her.

"I'm listening," she said.

I listened too, but there was nothing to hear. Just Nicky's ventilator, faintly audible through the half-open connecting door, and the sounds of the kitchen away along the offshoot. Different sounds from usual — clattering and clinking as they got ready for dinner, instead of the whoosh of the dish-washer and Tracey singing along to her iPhone as she washed down the floor.

"They've gone," said Miss Drumm even-tually. "Voices are my faces, Gloria, as you know. I never forget one. So I knew who that was right away, in Nicholas's room. But why now? After all these years?"

"New beginnings, Miss Drumm," I said.

She nodded. "And endings. I'm so tired."

"I'll leave you."

"No!" she shouted. Then she dropped her voice and whispered urgently. "I have to speak to you."

"Don't upset yourself."

"I let him out, you see. Fool that I am. Stupid woman."

"Miss Drumm, don't," I said, trying to soothe her. "I'm sure that's not true."

"You know nothing of it," she shot back. "Nothing at all. I should have known better — *did* know better, because I knew what happened the first time. Listen and see if you don't agree.

"It was 1785," she said, and I had to hold my breath to stop myself from groaning. "It was Midsummer's Eve. And it so happened that a band of merrymakers decided to spend the night in the woods. A night of revelry — dancing and drinking and what my mother used to call rousing the devil. I didn't know how literally she meant that until I was a grown woman and she explained it to me."

I could imagine. Even the words she was using sounded like a fairy tale: merrymakers and revelry. I could easily imagine Mrs. Drumm regaling her daughter with it and the little girl, her eyes like saucers, drinking it in. But I had other things on my mind and other calls on my time.

"This was before Rough House was built, of course. The stone was still in a clearing in the wood. And the merrymakers lit a fire and danced around it, all in their garlands, and unbeknownst to any of them, they roused him from his slumbers. He heard their music and came to join them, leaving the place he'd been for a hundred years."

"He left the stone?"

"And as soon as he found himself back in our realm he remembered the debt, still unpaid, and he flew through the woods to his bridge to claim the soul he had been owed for all that time. And the merrymakers, seeing him, stopped their revelry and fled. Three to the hills and three to the dales, three to the trees and three to the meadows. But the last one, all alone, fled to seek sanctuary in the castle beyond the stream." She paused. "It *was* a castle then, Gloria," she said in her ordinary voice, and then she continued in the sing-song she had heard at her mother's knee.

"And the devil chased her — oh, yes he did — roaring and gnashing his teeth, sure that tonight he would win the promised soul. But because she looked back at him, she stumbled and fell. One should always turn one's face away from evil, you see, Gloria, but she looked back and was done for. Her foot was caught in a vine and the more she struggled, the faster she was held. And the devil, seeing that she could not free herself and knowing that she would not cross his bridge, flew into rage. He could hear the shouts of the villagers, dogs barking and horns blowing; soon they would recapture him again. And so he devoured her, there in the woods. He ate up every scrap and left not so much as a buckle or a bow for her parents to mourn."

I was speechless. I don't think I was even breathing because Miss Drumm said, "Gloria?" in a querulous voice, as if to check that I was still sitting there.

"How old were you when your mother told you this story?"

"It's not a story, and I was old enough to wander the woods," she said. "I knew from when I was big enough to reach the handle that the hallowed place was where to go if anyone chased me."

"Why didn't the merrymakers go there?" I said, in spite of myself. I couldn't resist a fairy story when I didn't know the ending.

"Ah," said Miss Drumm. "Because it wasn't there. It was built with the stone from the bridge. After that night the bridge was put asunder and the stones used to build the hallowed place to honour the child devoured."

I shuddered. "But then your father built another bridge?"

"Exactly!" said Miss Drumm. "He said it was a wooden bridge and not the least bit dangerous, but then look what happened. Those poor children. That poor boy. If I'd had the sense to demolish the footbridge before those fools opened the school, then there wouldn't have been a tragedy. But it was dilapidated. It wasn't usable."

"They mended it," I told her. "As part of their woodwork classes."

"And how was I to know they'd let thirteen children sleep in the woods? Light a fire and sing and dance, just when I was away from home and the stone was still? Who could have guessed that anyone would be so reckless with children's lives?"

"Thirteen?" I said. And I repeated what she'd told me in that sing-song voice. "Three to the hills and three to the dales, three to the meadows and three to the trees. And one left to run to the castle."

"Yes," said Miss Drumm. "Like I told you."

"Moped and Bezzo," I whispered, counting on my fingers. "Ned and Nod. Stig and April. Duggie and Jo-jo. Two Scarlets and three Irving girls."

"Thirteen," said Miss Drumm. "And one died."

"But they weren't all there," I said. "One of them left because he wasn't feeling well." I wasn't making any sense, but I couldn't stop arguing. Anything to keep this crazy nonsense out of my head. I had known this woman for ten years. I knew she was a bit peculiar about the rocking stone, but this made her sound dangerous. Badly unhinged.

"Well, someone must have joined the other twelve then," she said. I said nothing, thinking about the car. "That teacher was supposed to have gone out and checked on them, isn't that so?"

"But she didn't."

"Oh, don't I know it," said Miss Drumm. "She lost her job over it and the school was closed."

"I think that was for the best," I said. "It was a very strange setup all round, if you ask me."

Miss Drumm nodded, her lips pushed out

in that way that makes the hairs on her lip bristle. "I always thought so," she said. "I always did wonder why that man — Tarrant — wanted to open a school. He wasn't the type. Not the type at all. One did wonder. But they were much more innocent days, even thirty years ago. One didn't hear the stories one hears now. Priests and Scoutmasters and the like. Now it would ring the most tremendous alarm bells, obviously."

"Big Jacky Tarrant?" I said. "But he only put the money up, didn't he? He wasn't involved day to day."

"Oh, wasn't he?" said Miss Drumm. "He was there more than I could understand, and he never went in the front way. I challenged him more than once when he came roaring along the lane in front of Rough House, frightening the cats and Rabbie, in that ridiculous car of his."

I remembered it well. I remembered Stig getting into it at the school gate, and once I had seen Angie Tarrant clambering out of it on Castle Douglas High Street, looking like a beetle trying to right itself in her tight skirt and stilettos. She had slammed the door loud enough to make the other shoppers turn around and stare, then stalked off without a backwards glance at her husband. It struck me hard. Even my parents observed the niceties of a peck on the cheek and a wave as they parted, a peck on the cheek again when one returned. I had only felt sorry for Stig at the time, imagining living in a house where people slammed car doors and didn't say goodbye. Now though, sitting by Miss Drumm, I found myself wondering what a man would have to do, what kind of man he would have to be, to turn his wife so bitter.

"It's a serious accusation, Miss Drumm," I said, thinking that just a rumour of it could get a man hounded to his death. But who better to start the rumor that wrecked Alan Best's life than someone in the know? Someone who could make the details authentic from experience? A small moan escaped me.

"You sound worn out, Gloria," said Miss Drumm. "And Lord knows I am. My sleeve is unravelled beyond all knitting." Her voice was growing slow and slurred now, as she talked herself into rest. "When I was a child I couldn't imagine going gently, you know. And now, I wish it would just hurry up and . . ." She took a great breath in and then was silent. I watched her, my heart beginning to bang so hard in my chest I could see my dress moving.

No, no, no, I told her, willing my thoughts

silently into her head. *Nicky first, and then you, and then Walter. And no one just now until this nightmare is over. No one tonight. No.*

"Miss Drumm?" I said, too loud and too sharp. She was so still I was sure she was gone.

"Wha—" she said, jerking awake.

"Good night," I said. I stood and kissed her thin white hair, feeling the warmth of her pink scalp under my lips. "I'll see you tomorrow."

I was halfway home before I realised I'd forgotten to go back and read to Nicky.

Twenty-Four

"Jesus, Glo," said Stig when I got in. I lowered myself into a chair and let my head drop back. "What the hell happened to you? Can we make a deal that, as long as I'm here, you'll let me know if you're going to be late?"

"Sorry," I said. "Not used to anyone waiting for me."

"So, what's new?"

I told him: Jo-jo and the Pont du Diable, Duggie in the hallowed place, Duggie in Nicky's room tonight. I told him about Miss Drumm's crazy stories and how the worst part of them was that they rang so true. There was only one thing I didn't tell him. BJ was his father and I couldn't say it. I could ask, though.

"Stig?" I said, still with my eyes shut. Still with my head back, my hand gripping the whisky glass he had handed me. "Do you really want to get to the bottom of this?"

"What?" he said. "Are you kidding? How could I not?"

"No matter what the truth is?" I said. "No matter what we uncover if we lift the rock?"

"Is it Duggie?" he asked me. "Are you scared of what you might find out about him?"

I lifted my head and opened my eyes then, squinting even the light was low. "Me?" I said. "I was thinking about you, actually. Are you protecting someone?"

His eyes flared. "Who the hell would I be protecting?" he said. "I haven't seen any of them since I left high school. Haven't seen most of them since I left Eden that morning. God knows if any of them are left for me to see anyway."

"Oh God, that's right!" I said, hauling myself to my feet and going over to the telephone. "Lynne was going to try to track down the girls. I need to ring her before it's too late."

Stig was staring at me. Gaping, really. "Who the hell's Lynne?"

"Admin assistant at work," I said, too tired to be defensive; too tired to care what he made of it. Which was plenty.

"You told your assistant?" His voice was loud enough that Walter stirred.

"She put it together. She doesn't know

about you."

Lynne's number was ringing, and I held up a finger to quiet him.

"Have you got a bit paper and a pen?" she said. "Okay. Scarlet McFarlane, born 1973, Glasgow. She registered a birth in 1989, a daughter. The address was in Perth. I'll give it to you."

"1989?" I said.

"Yeah, I know. What are the chances she'll still be there?"

"That too," I said, "but in 1989, Scarlet McFarlane was sixteen."

"Should have called her Chastity," said Lynne. "So that's not very hopeful, and there was nothing at all about the other one — Scarlet McInnes. Not a dickybird. But the Irving girls are a different story. You know how they lived at the Borgue? Well, they're still there. Two of them anyway." There was a pause. "Cloud died two years ago. Suicide. Rain and Sun registered it."

"How do you mean?" I said. "Only one person can register a death."

"Yeah, but it was at Dumfries," said Lynne, "and the Dumfries office put their names in the sweepstake."

I sucked in a breath. "That's not right. That's births only. We never have a laugh with a death reg."

"I know," said Lynne. "It got disqualified, of course it did. But Terrence at Dumfries put it in. I thought the names seemed familiar when you said them today, and when I found the death reg and Terrence's name as the registrar, I remembered. I looked at the email, Gloria. I can forward it to you."

"No, there's no need," I said. "Thanks, Lynne. And now, just forget all about this. Just pretend today didn't happen, right? See you Friday."

"Who's dead?" said Stig as soon as I'd hung up the phone.

"Cloud Irving killed herself," I said. "I'm going to go and visit her sisters tomorrow."

I was almost too scared to go to sleep, tired as I was, in fear of the dreams that might come to haunt me. But as soon as I closed my eyes, I was in heaven. It had been a while since I'd found myself there. It had been years since I'd tried to work out what sent me there and tried to make it happen, with cheese and meditation and drops of his shampoo on a hanky clutched in my hand. Long ago, I decided there was no rhyme or reason. I couldn't court it; I could only enjoy it when I came.

He was wearing a filthy football strip, mud caked all up one side of him where he had slid into a tackle. He stopped in the back lobby — it was the house that Duggie and I had moved into when I was pregnant with him — stopped in the lobby, kicked off his boots, and shucked off his clothes until he stood in just his underpants, shivering.

"Mu-um!" he shouted. I was right there in the kitchen, but for some reason he bellowed at me. "Goan turn the shower on. Goan bring my dressing gown."

"What did your last slave die of?" I said. "Put your dad's sweatshirt on. Look, on the coat hook there. It's due for a wash anyway. I'm not washing your dressing gown in this rain. I'll never get it dry."

But in my dream I did go and turn the shower on, and laid out a fluffy towel and a new catheter tube and feeding tube, and then I closed the door between Nicky's room and Miss Drumm's room so he could shower in peace and went back to the kitchen.

"Has that wee toe rag nicked my sweatshirt?" Stig said, coming in the back door with an armload of herbs, enough herbs to fill a sack, more than anyone could ever use, and the smell of them was overpowering, a choking stench of cheap carpet and underlay and the sweet plastic smell of vinyl flooring.

"What are you making?" I said.

"Alibis," said Stig, and he poured the herbs onto the kitchen floor and kicked them until they covered the stone slab there. "She'll start to smell soon."

"Mum," said Nicky. "Can I ask you something?" He was lying in his high hospital bed through the door from the kitchen where our little dining room should be. But he was propped up on his elbows with his legs bent, his feet flat on the sheet underneath him.

"What is it?" I said. "I'm cooking your tea. I'm busy."

"Why are shadows wicked?"

"I'm sorry, Nicky."

"Must we to bed indeed?"

"I'm sorry, Nicky."

"Why did he go to the Land of Nod?"

I woke up, sweaty and tangled in my bedclothes with William and Dorothy on my legs, and lay there panting. There was a soft knock at the door.

"Glo?" said Stig. "You were shouting."

"Nightmare," I said. "But a good one."

"That's different," said Stig. "Are you okay?"

I thought about it. *Was* I okay? What was bothering me? It was just an anxiety dream — April in the hole, Stig and the garden, mixed with one of the wonderful dreams where Nicky is awake and full of mischief. And dreaming about the three poems called "North-West Passage" was nothing new. I always did when we were getting around to that bit of the book. So what was troubling me?

"Glo? Tell me you're okay or I'm coming in." His voice was shaking, and so I answered him.

"I'm fine," I said. "But there's something . . . Look, come in if you want. It's too cold to stand out in the passage."

"It's too cold to live," said Stig, hurrying in. "If this was my house, I'd be in a sleeping bag down in the kitchen. Beside Walter."

"Get in at the other end, if you like," I suggested. "Keep warm while I try to work this out."

I could see his dim outline in the light from my radio alarm and I saw him hesitate for a second before I felt the tug of him untucking the covers at the foot end and then felt the mattress drop out from under me on that side as his weight was added to it.

"Shift, cat," he said, and Dorothy Words-worth rolled away as he tugged the blanket out from under her. She righted herself and curled up again on his lap. I passed a pillow down and heard him settling it behind him. Then he took a huge breath in and let it out again.

"Shoot," he said.

"It's the book I read to Nicky," I said. "I told you about it. *A Child's Garden of Verses?*"

"By the guy who wrote Frankenstein, yeah," said Stig. I didn't correct him.

"There's these three poems, called 'North-West Passage'," I said. "Like a trilogy. And I always have bad dreams when they're coming round again. They're about a little kid going to bed and . . . I don't know. I used to think they were sweet, but there's things in them about how he's scared of the dark and the shadows in the passageway and he's scampering to his bedroom through the haunted house. Anyway. I was reading the middle one — 'Shadow March' — the last time Nicky . . ."

"What?" said Stig, when the silence had gone on too long. "Spoke? The last time he laughed?"

"Oh my God," I said. "If you only knew.

"It was the last time he did anything. Mr. Wishart the consultant had finally persuaded me about full sedation. It was four years ago. And I was reading to him while they did his drugs, and he groaned. Sort of moaned. Whimpered, I suppose you'd say. I was reading 'Shadow March,' the bit that goes: 'All the wicked shadows coming tramp, tramp tramp, and the black night overhead.' And he whimpered. I've never been able to get it out of my head that the very last thing he was aware of before the dark closed in forever was his stupid bloody mother reading a horrible scary poem to him."

"But he *wasn't* aware," said Stig, once I had explained it. "Of course he wasn't. I've looked up PKAN, Glo, these last few days, and that groan can't have been Nicky feeling frightened. He was just relaxing. Just his throat unclenching. You know that, really."

"Yeah," I said. "Course I do. But every time we're coming round to those poems again, I dream about Nicky asking me, 'Why are shadows wicked?' and 'Must we to bed indeed? Well then. Let us arise and go like men. And face with an undaunted tread the long black passage up to bed.' "

"Fucking Nora," said Stig. "What the hell are you reading that to him for when you

313

could be reading him *The Beano* or . . . Christ, I don't know. How old is he? Fifteen? Okay, well, something with some tits and ass in it? Or Stephen King?"

"Stephen King has plenty of . . . that in it, actually," I said. "Lots of books do. But listen. A question he just asked me tonight in my dream wasn't one of the usual ones."

"Okay," said Stig. "I'm listening."

"The last poem ends up 'See me lying warm and fast, in the Land of Nod at last.' And tonight in my dream, Nicky asked me, 'Why did he go to the Land of Nod?' He's never asked me that before. Usually he asks me, 'Where's the land of Nod, Mum?' Or 'What's the land of Nod, Mum?' But tonight he said, 'Why did he go to the Land of Nod?' and I think it's a clue."

"Nicky is giving you clues in your dream," said Stig. It wasn't a question. It was more as if he was repeating it to test how mad it sounded. Like me with Miss Drumm.

"I think he was talking about Nod — Nathan — McAllister," I said. "I think what he was really saying was, why did Nathan kill himself in a car park at Stirling University?"

"He's a chip off the old block then," Stig said. "Because that's a good question. Why *did* Nod kill himself there? He didn't live there, didn't go to college there. He went to Robert Gordon. And it wasn't an isolated spot or one of those classic suicide spots like Beachy Head or Dartmoor. Why there?"

"Maybe he set off from his house and drove until he'd made up his mind, and that's just where he was when the moment came."

"Could be," said Stig. "Still."

"Yeah," I said. Our discussion was at its end, it looked like. And here we were in bed together. Sort of. Head to tail, and a cat in between us.

"Right then," Stig said. "I'll get back along to my room. Unless I go downstairs and get hot water bottles first. Want one?"

I considered it very carefully before I spoke.

"Or you could just stay here. I mean, just to sleep, just for warmth. And comfort. Not for . . ."

"Down this end?" said Stig.

"That's a bit weird," I said. "Isn't it?"

"Up to you," said Stig. "D'you want my feet or my breath?"

I giggled, almost in spite of myself. He was so crude, but somehow it didn't bother me the way Duggie did.

"Swivel round," I said. "But seriously, just for warmth. And company."

It took him a long time to get settled, a lot of punching his pillow and tugging at his clothes before he subsided.

"Night-night," he said.

"Sleep tight," I answered.

"Don't let the bed posts bite," he said, already beginning to sound groggy. I listened to his breathing and found mine lapsing into time with it, then my eyelids were fluttering, and then I was gone. No dreams this time, just sweet oblivion.

TWENTY-FIVE

Friday

When I opened my eyes again, a thin, cold light was seeping in around the edges of the curtains. I knew what that meant: it had snowed in the night. I groaned and slumped onto my back to stare up at the ceiling. But where the bed should have been behind me, cold and blank, there was a warm bulk stopping me from rolling all the way. I turned. Stig was propped up on one elbow watching me.

"Morning."

"What time is it?" I asked him.

"Half seven," he said. "I'll go and get some coffee now. I didn't want to wake you by thrashing about like a walrus getting off a rock."

He eased himself out without lifting the covers or making any drafts, and then shuffled off across the room and out into the corridor. The cats leapt down and followed him with their tails high and waving at the ends.

"You shouldn't do that," I called after him. "You're always putting yourself down."

"I know," he called back. "Oprah would have me across her knee for a good thrashing. I've written to her and asked, more than once."

"She's old enough to be your mother!" I shouted to him.

"So she's old enough to spank me then."

Walter had heard him and started barking, and Stig switched his attention forward to the closed kitchen door. I lay back and smiled. It was the last easy laughter between us, the last morning when we'd wake up finding comfort in our togetherness in spite of all the trouble we were in and the dangers we were facing. When Stig came back with two cups of his rolling-pin coffee, opened the curtains on the snowy garden, and got back into bed beside me with a long groan like an old man, it was the happiest moment I'd had in a lot of years and happier, in a way, than any moment I'd ever have again.

He took one sip of his coffee and then stopped dead as though he'd been turned to stone.

"What?" I asked him. He set the cup down

on the bedside table, swung his legs out and got up again — leapt up, no old-man moving noises this time. He went back to the window and peered around the edge of the net curtain.

"What?" I said again, jumping out of bed and going to stand beside him, ignoring the cold of the floor under my bare feet. Outside, the garden lay under a good fall of snow, at least for Galloway. The longer tussocks of grass were poking through, but all the flat places and the paths, the steps, and the tops of the hedges were blanked out. Stig pointed, and I followed his finger, then gasped. Footprints. Footprints leading to the rocking stone and away from it, and a jumble of footprints all around it. Stig swept out of the room and downstairs with me following him.

"I'll go," I said grabbing his arm in the porch. "In case someone's still there. They mustn't see you." So I slipped on my Wellingtons and put a coat on over my nightie and opened the front door. The snow was crisp under my boots, as though the temperature had dropped since it fell, freezing it to a crust. I took care climbing the steps to where the stone sat, scared that my trembling legs would betray me and I would slip and crack some part of myself on these chunks of cold red sandstone. But I made it and stepped onto the rough grass where the daffodils grow. I stopped a few feet from the nearest print, then took one more careful step forward and bent to examine it. Like the virgin snow all around, it had frozen in the hours since it was made.

"You can come out," I called back down to Stig. "They're long gone."

He took no care at all, bounding up the steps and skidding a little, but, like me, he stopped well away from the prints and studied them.

"Not cloven anyway," he said. "That's something."

I tried to laugh, but he shushed me.

"I'm not kidding, Glo," he said. "When I saw them I thought, *That's it then. There's the proof.* Steps leading away and steps coming back again. It took me until just now to realise it could be the other way. Someone came and then they left."

"But where did they go?" I said. I walked over to the front gate and studied the footprints disappearing along the drive to the lane. "They must have parked quite a way off for us not to hear them."

"Dunno," said Stig. "I'm quite a deep sleeper. How about you?"

"Not usually," I admitted, and I thought I

could feel my cheeks warming.

Stig gave a small half smile. "Yeah," he said. "First night we've both felt safe to fall asleep completely. Bloody typical, eh?"

His words had started off another worry. I sprinted around the stone and peered across the garden to the locked byre where his car was hidden, but the snow was as smooth as a counterpane. Whoever had been here hadn't gone snooping. I looked back at the front of the house and felt my shoulders drop with relief.

"Your bedroom curtains aren't shut," I said.

"I never shut my curtains," said Stig. "Why? What's the problem?"

"No, that's good. It means whoever was here wouldn't think there was anyone else in the house but me."

"Whoever was here," echoed Stig, and he turned to the footprints in front of us again. He put one of his own feet down beside the nearest one. "I'm size nine," he said. "This looks like a ten to me. It's not quite a walking boot, but it's not just a shoe. What do you think, Glo? A rocking-stone enthusiast with the worst timing in the history of the world?"

"Not at night," I said. I thought for a minute. "You know who's a size ten? Dug-

321

gie. And we were talking about this place — or the huttie anyway — at the home last night."

"Gloria, plenty of men have got size-ten feet."

"But how many of them were at Eden with you?" I said.

"My brother's a ten," said Stig.

"And your brother knows that I'm involved," I said. "It wouldn't be too hard for him to find out where I live."

"I didn't mean that. I meant my brother, *for instance.* My dad's a ten too."

I swung round and gave him a hard look. "What are you saying? You think your dad's involved?"

"I'm saying," he said, in a loud, slow voice, "that ten is a really common shoe size."

"Stig," I said, nearly as slow but not so loud, "we need to talk about your family sometime. They owned the school where this happened and nobody understands why. Why they opened it."

"They didn't open it. It was my dad. Just him on his own. Nothing to do with my mum. She hated the idea from the start, and she's never shut up about it since." He started to say something else, but bit it off. "Anyway, why would my dad or my brother be here in the middle of the night looking at the stone? Why would *Duggie* be out here looking at the stone, for God's sake?"

"Because he's the only other boy from Eden who's still alive." I walked around the stone, peering at its base.

"That makes no sense," Stig said, following me. "Mind you, at least Duggie or whoever it was didn't come out here to rock it thirteen times and release Armageddon. There's no break in the snow at the base."

"So what was the point?" I said.

"To frighten you," said Stig. "A woman alone with all of this going on."

"But who knows that any of this is going on?" I said. "And knows that I know? It must be Duggie, or who else?"

"But he doesn't know everything," Stig said, putting an arm around me. I was shivering badly and he felt warm even though he was only in a sweatshirt. "Come in and I'll make some fresh coffee. Duggie can stuff himself, trying to frighten you, because you're not alone, are you?"

The Irvings' place wasn't so very different from Rough House, or any other of the endless Galloway farmhouses made on the same design, like a child's drawing of a house with two windows either side of the front door and three windows in a row above. It even had the same bumpy track with tussocks of dock and dandelion growing up the middle. The frozen stalks scraped the underneath of my car as I trundled along. The view was different though. Where I had the rolling hills outside my back windows and the solid bulk of the Milharay wood outside my front windows, Low Borgue farmhouse sat in the middle of endless blank fields, cruelly exposed, not so much as a hawthorn bush to protect it from the biting wind coming at it off the sea. Maybe in the summertime that arc of sky with the sun rolling gently across it all day and the stars scattered like spilled jewels all night would be a blessing, but now, in the winter, the house seemed naked and tiny, huddled in the inadequate shelter of its low garden walls and showing the stress of standing against the battering wind in its lopsided chimneys and leaning gateposts. Even the very stone it was built from was starting to crumble from the wind and rain, the smooth facing slipping off in flakes, leaving soft pockmarks, exposed to let the rain seep in and begin the work of killing the house from the inside too.

I couldn't help my spirits sinking as I climbed out of the car, shouldered open the gate (tied with twine where the hinges should be), and trampled over the few feet of dead weeds and slushy gravel to the front door.

There was no bell or knocker, so I just rapped on the blistered wood and waited.

Before long there came a scuffling inside and a rough voice, dark and guttural: "Who is it?"

I had considered a couple of different plans on the drive over. The Church of God again, a true crime article in the making, even the truth. But by the time I had got to the Dumfries bypass and the big Tesco, my nerve failed me; all I could think was that I had been to Mrs. Best's door, to Mrs. Jameson's, to Glasgow where that shopkeeper had clocked me, and up to Barrwherry asking questions of an obvious nosey parker. And I couldn't stop remembering the neighbour in the physio's uniform, looking at me and saying, *Don't I know you? Didn't you live here? You look exactly the same.* Could I really go to another family touched by Eden and ask my questions again? What if the police were putting it together and doing the same? They'd soon have an APB out for someone who looked like me. They'd have their prime suspect and a great description of her: hairdo, wardrobe, and all.

Only if they suspected that a woman could do these things, I told myself, and women don't do these things, except in books. Mrs. Danvers and Rebecca, Snow White's stepmother, Lady Macbeth and her unwashable hands.

Right then I almost thought of something; I saw it whisking away round the corner as I turned towards it, but when I tried to follow it, it was gone.

Better be on the safe side, I decided, so I pulled into Tesco's car park and went shopping. It was remarkably easy, and not even all that expensive. I chose high, wedge-heeled boots in plum-coloured suede and black trousers that skimmed the top of them. They were made of some kind of very sturdy elasticated fabric I had never come across before. I pulled it in every direction, wondering what it must be like to sew seams into, then I put the trousers over my arm and went looking for tops too. Standing in the changing room, I looked at myself in the pink and black leopard-print chiffon blouse and the black fake-leather jacket; in the sturdy trousers, balanced on the not-quite-sturdy-enough wedge heels. I clipped on the earrings I had chosen and then set to unwinding my hair. It was longer than I thought. I don't look in mirrors much and the small one in the bathroom that I use to make sure my parting is straight only shows me from my scalp to my chin. I had no idea that my hair would cover me to the elbows.

After I had wrenched off the price-tags to go through the checkout, I walked carefully back to the accessories stand and chose a big clip like a monster's jaw. I scraped some hair back, let some fall out, pulled some into tendrils and, even though I felt as if I'd been dragged through a hedge, I looked similar to how some other women look, and that was all I wanted. I helped myself to some testers of rouge and lip-gloss and then went to pay for what I was wearing and get a bag for my dress and mackintosh, my warm tights and flat shoes.

It was a marvellous disguise, but it didn't help me come up with a story. Even when I was standing on the doorstep at Low Borgue and that harsh voice behind the shut door demanded to know who I was, I had no answer.

"Rain? Sun?" I said. "I want to talk to you about Cloud."

"Are you one of *them*?" the voice shot back.

I considered whether a yes or a no would be more likely to open the door, but before

I had decided, she went on. (I was sure it was a she now; the more she spoke the reedier she sounded, although there was still a gruffness that made me wonder if she was ill.)

"Look, you'll have to come round the back anyway," she said. "This key doesn't work."

Walking round the house gave me a bit more time to come up with something, but then seeing what was round there put it out of my mind. The yard at Rough House is no beauty spot, but the yard at Low Borgue was in another league.

There were two cars, one with flat tyres and one with no tyres at all, and at some point the Irvings had given up dragging their wheeliebin to the road-end. There were black bin bags, some ripped open with their contents strewn around, piled up half-under an open hayshed. The green tinge on the lower bags told me that this mountain had been underway since summer at least.

Making my way to the back door I passed a television set, one of the big old heavy ones, and a Hoover, one of the new grey and purple ones, and right by the back door there was a burnt-out frying pan sitting on the step, the congealed fat showing where birds or rodents had pecked out scraps. I knocked softly on the back door, but it was already moving, already opening.

"Hi," I said.

The woman who stood there told a story that matched the tale of the farmyard in every particular. I could believe she was my age, but her life had been harder than mine. She was rail thin, her bony chest poking out in the middle, her chicken-bone legs looking too frail to support her. Only her swollen fingers and the bags under her eyes — both purple — weren't wizened. Her face — a once-beautiful face, I thought, with enormous dark eyes, chiseled cheekbones, and an arching jaw — was blotched and yet also sallow. She took a deep drag of her cigarette, and the way her cheeks hollowed told me that she had lost at least some of her teeth. She coughed richly, covering her mouth with the crook of her arm, and stood back to let me enter.

"Sue's not up," she said. "Coffee?"

I looked around the farmhouse kitchen, so similar to my own, and wondered if I could swallow a cup of coffee made there. The smell was worse than the bin bags outside could be on the hottest day: a mixture of cooking oil, mouldy cloths, rancid food, and — I was sure of it — urine. The sink was piled with dishes, but not this morning's dishes and not yesterday's. These were weeks old, maybe months old, dried out and crusted, discs of brown in the glasses and humps of moss in the bowls and on the plates. Then at some point the sisters had given up on dishes altogether, because on the worktop nearest the kettle and microwave there were plastic packs of paper plates and polystyrene cups, and on the floor underneath there was a bin bag full of used ones.

"Lovely," I said. "Black, no sugar," thinking that boiled water and a polystyrene cup couldn't do me much harm.

"Sit down," the woman told me, turning away. She filled the kettle, edging it expertly under the dishes in the sink, which must have been nudged to either side purely to let the kettle fit there. I looked around. There was a table against the far wall, away from the fireplace, and a chair at either end of it. But one chair was covered in newspapers and the other had a pile of washing over the back of it, dried stiff there, sour smelling and black in its folds. That left the couch by the stove. There were two spaces on it; two small, bottom-shaped holes between the piles of magazines and ashtrays, the half-emptied carry-out trays and the wine bottles filled with a sludge of wet cigarette ends. Both ends of the couch were stained dark in the seat area, but I chose the one without the bright crusted stain on the back rest.

"There's no biccies," said the woman, who must be Rain Irving, handing me a polystyrene cup and sitting down. "Sue eats everything that doesn't move when she's like she is. Can't keep a meal in the larder."

"How is she?" I said. "Sue."

She nodded. "Thank you. It *is* Sue these days. And Rena. And she's as dry as a nun's crack." Between the laugh and the hot coffee, she set off on a bout of coughing that left her red and spluttering. "Christ," she said, taking another drag, "I need to pack these up. That's what I need to do."

"Not easy," I said, nodding as if I would know. I'd never had so much as a puff in my life.

"Not the right time," said Rain/Rena Irving. "Sue's good and off the 'done. Now she's off the booze too. Next I need to get off the booze, and then when we're both straightened out, we'll see what we can see about the fags."

" 'Done," I said. "Methadone?"

"We're absolutely bloody brilliant at getting off it," said Rain. "And absolutely bloody hopeless at *staying* off it."

"You're very cheerful," I said.

331

She gave me an odd look then. "Who did you say you were?"

I wasn't proud of it, but I thought this woman, with the life she was living, wasn't going to put my cover story under the microscope and find it wanting.

"I'm a friend of Cloud's," I said. "I only just heard that she'd passed away, and I wanted to come and give you my condolences."

"A friend from where?" said Rain. "Not from the Bridge if you call her Cloud." I blinked and said nothing. "Germany? London?"

"London," I said, thinking that was safest. "What bridge did you mean?"

"The Bridge To Wellness in town there," said Rain. "So you're a pal from London days. I don't remember you. What happened to you?" She gave me an up-and-down look as she asked.

"Happened to me how?" I said, trying not to bristle.

"You've piled on a bit of lard there," she said. "Or weren't you one of the girls?"

"A prostitute?"

Rain cackled with laughter again and the cough that followed sounded like a thunder clap. Then she raised her eyes as a creak sounded overhead. "Ah, Christ, I've woken

Sue," she said. "No, not a proz, a model."
She shook another cigarette out of a packet
that was lying amongst the papers and tissues on the couch and then offered the
packet to me. I shook my head.

"I wasn't a model," I told her. "I was a
neighbour." She squinted through the
smoke at me as she lit her fag.

"At the Battersea flat?" she said. "Why
don't I remember you?"

"I don't know," I said. "I don't think we
met. I don't remember you either."

She pulled in a long drag of smoke and
then let it go in a thin stream. Towards the
end she made biting motions with her jaw
as if she was trying to form smoke rings,
but the stream just carried on.

"You wouldn't know, from seeing me
now," she said. She leapt to her feet and
went over to the window. Under the windowsill was a deep shelf, and she pulled a
file out from it. "See," she said, handing it
to me. It was made of black velour–covered
card and was tied shut with a black ribbon.
I undid the ribbon and let the file fall open.

"Wow," I said. "You were — I mean, that's
a lovely photograph." The girl in the picture
was wearing nothing at all except a length
of draped chiffon. She was lying along the
back of an ornate velvet settee with her neck

333

twisted so that her face was full-on to the camera. There were the enormous eyes, the cheekbones made even more extreme by careful shading, and the full pouting mouth from before lost teeth and too many cigarettes had turned it mean and sunken.

"You look beautiful," I said, turning it over and moving on to the next one. It was a close-up, a headshot. Her hair was pulled straight back and her face looked bare of make-up, although surely it couldn't be. "Absolutely beautiful."

"That's Claudie," she said, in a cold voice. "Who the hell are you?"

TWENTY-SIX

I could hear the footsteps coming along the passageway to the kitchen door, and just for a minute I considered running. Then, coughing and clearing her throat as though she'd just swallowed a fly, the third Irving sister, Sun — Sue, now — arrived.

She was very different from Rain. The dark hair was the same and the dark eyes, but hers looked as small as currants in her face, and her cheekbones and jaw line were long gone in a thick padding of pale, doughy flesh. She plodded across the kitchen — I could feel the floor jouncing under my feet with her steps — and stared dully at me.

"Who's this?"

"Good question, Siouxie Sue," said her sister, passing over her half-smoked cigarette. "She was making out she was an old friend of Claudie's, but I busted her."

"I'm going to level with you," I said. "I'm not an old friend of Cloud's."

Sun interrupted to say, "No shit," but I ignored her.

"I'm an old friend of Stephen Tarrant. Stig Tarrant. He was at Eden with you."

Both sisters drew their breath in so sharply that it hissed over their bottom teeth.

"We don't talk about that place," said Sun.

"We don't *think* about that place," said Rain. She went over to where the table was and tipped the dried-out clump of washing onto the floor, then brought the chair back over to the stove and sat in it, back to front, like in *Cabaret.*

"I understand," I said. "But I need to talk to you about it. I know Cloud — Claudie — killed herself."

"She didn't kill herself," said Sun. Her sister had handed her a polystyrene cup only half full of coffee, but her hand was shaking so much that it spilled onto her arm, soaking into the cuff of her dressing gown. She raised the cigarette to her lips and sucked on it as if it was oxygen and she was drowning.

"Claudie muddled her drugs," said Rain. "She was on a heavy script. Stupid doctors. The addiction clinic gave her one thing and her thyroid clinic gave her something else. Then her GP wrote her up for sleeping tablets. We could have sued them."

I wasn't supposed to know better, so I said nothing. If it made things easier for her sisters, why would I argue?

"Did she die here?" I asked. The sisters glanced at each other, and again it was Rain who answered. I wasn't sure if she was the elder of the two, or the natural leader, or if she was just in better shape.

"She died at home, yes. It was a rough time for all of us, and she died."

I nodded. I thought I understood her. She didn't mean that Cloud dying made it a rough time. If I was interpreting the glances and the stilted words right, what the sisters weren't saying was that Cloud had died and the other two were too far out of their heads to notice for a while. I wished I could tell her that I wasn't judging, that I'd never judge anyone for not coping very well. Then I decided the best way to show them what I thought was to trust them and show them they could trust me.

"Do you remember April Cowan?" I said. "She died on Monday. I'm surprised the cops haven't been to ask if you've got an alibi."

Rain coughed. "We were here together," she said. "Bloody useless alibi, but not as useless as our cars. If we wanted to commit a murder, we'd have to do it with a taxi metre running."

"And April's not the only one," I said. "Jo-jo Jameson. Alan Best, Nathan and Edmund McAllister. They've all gone. None from natural causes."

Both sisters stared at me, their family resemblance stronger than ever with their eyes wide open that way. I glanced down at the file still on my lap and the face of the third Irving sister staring up at me.

Again Rain spoke first.

"And Mitchell," she said. "He was first, all those years ago."

"Don't, Rena," moaned her sister. "I can't stand it."

"I'd be really grateful if you'd tell me what happened that night," I said. "It maybe sounds crazy, but I think it's connected."

"Of course it's not crazy," said Rain. "Of course it's connected. How could it not be?"

"I can't stand it," said Sue again, getting to her feet. "I'm going back to bed. I'll take a couple of bye-byes and get some sleep. I can't be here when you're talking about it. I've got to go." She blundered off, kicking over her coffee cup on her way. Rain looked at the stain spreading on the lino, seeping into the scores and scratches. She fished a newspaper out of the pile on the couch and dropped it over the puddle, stamping it down with her heel.

"It wasn't a good night," she said. "Bad energy from before we even got out there. That whole place had bad energy. The old bat in the farmhouse with her Baskerville hound, that useless bloody teacher that cared more about the trees than the kids. Making us hack up old pews full of nails to fix a bridge instead of just buying some planks. She made this one kid, Van the Man Morrison, go and apologise to a tree for tying a Tarzan rope to it and rubbing a bit of its bark off."

"She sounds like a nutter," I said.

"Anyway," said Rain. "We went camping in the woods. It was the midsummer Solstice, I think."

"May Day," I said, and she clicked her fingers at me.

"That's right," she said, "May Day. The Beltane. Quite a dodgy night for spirits and no way we should have been out there on our own."

"And Miss Naismith didn't come to check on you, did she?" I said.

"Naismith!" said Rain. "That's her. What a cunt she was. Making out she was so worried about us and all that." I tried to keep my face neutral, but I'm sure my cheeks coloured. "She was jealous of us, of course."

Rain nodded at the file on my knee. "Keep looking through it. We're all in there. Claudie's on the top because we've been looking at her. But all three of us got our portfolios. Look and see."

So, as she spoke, I leafed through the pictures in the folder. They were beautiful, all three of them. Rain had always been the slightest — like a pixie — and Sun had always been the largest of them — a Valkyrie — and Cloud was the Goldilocks sister, the one not too big and not too small, who was just right. Her face, her body naked, her body in clothes — every picture of her was perfection.

"So what was the story again?" Rain was saying. "Oh, yeah. That's right. Naismith was supposed to come and check on us and we were going to ask if we could go inside. But she didn't come, and so we were stuck there. No torches and no moonlight to see by because of the clouds. That's right, I remember now. But she locked the gate. She wasn't completely useless, because at least she locked the gate and we were safe inside the grounds, right?"

"And what happened?" I said, prompting her. "You all snuggled down and went to sleep?"

"One kid left because his guts were bad,"

said Rain. "That was quite early on. And then Jo-Jo and Moped started daring Van to go and sleep all alone in the haunted chapel. But that was after."

"After what?" I said.

Her eyes misted over and she took two long puffs on her cigarette and stubbed it out before she answered. "After we had finished telling ghost stories and we'd eaten our supper and got in our sleeping bags," she said. "Jo-jo and Moped started in on Van. They were always at him."

"Bullying him, you mean?" I felt a flash of sympathy.

"Taking the piss," said Rain. "Bursting his bubble. Daring him to go to this place we all thought was haunted. Van — I wish I could remember his real name — anyway, he was a complete prick. A real arsehole. You wouldn't believe him unless you knew. He dressed like something from a golf club even when he was a kid, and he talked like a bloody bank manager. Honestly, he was just such a complete wanker that it used to drive Jo-jo and Moped nuts. They were good kids — a good laugh, good pals, no harm in them — but nobody could be in the same room as Van Morrison and not want to kick him."

I felt as if I had had a bucket of cold water

thrown over me. I thought about Duggie, when I first met him, about how he dressed so smartly and how mature he seemed, serving on committees and playing golf. I thought about how lucky I felt to be chosen by him; Gloria Harkness, plain as pudding as my mother used to say. And suddenly twenty years of nonsense just sloughed off me and my eyes opened.

I had thought he was popular because he bought drinks for people and loaned his van and always stood laughing at the bar. But the truth was that no one could stand him. He *had* to buy drinks and lend vans to get anyone to put up with him, and he stood at the bar because no one ever wanted to share his table.

My mum and my sister fell for it, but not my dad. He didn't give his permission for Duggie to marry me, and he tried to get me to say I didn't want to. And I hadn't said I *did* want to. I had never said yes until we were standing in the church and people had travelled and paid for hotel rooms and new outfits and it was too late.

But why did he want me? All of a sudden I knew that too.

I was easy. He didn't have to try with me. I was so grateful and loyal and stupid, I suited him down to the ground.

Until we made Nicky. I almost gasped from the pain of it. After Nicky, I wasn't easy anymore. Nothing was easy. Duggie hadn't left us because his grief was unbearable; he had left us because there was absolutely no reason for him to stay.

At last I looked up. Rain Irving was watching me with a curious look on her face.

"So Van took the bait," I said.

"Off he marched, bouncing on the balls of his feet." She was right. He did! "And we were just glad to be shot of him for a while. Glad not to have to listen to him. We were just about sleeping, Cloud, Sun, and me — all zipped into two sleeping bags made up together like a double bed. Then we heard someone moving and giggling. It was Moped. He said he was going to give Van a fright, pretend to haunt him. He wanted Jo-jo to go, but Jo-jo was too tired and cold. We should have gone back when we had the chance, you know? It might have been May, but it was bloody freezing."

"So Moped went to the little . . . chapel, you said. Where Van was?"

"And that's the last anyone ever heard of him. I tried to stay awake for him coming back, but obviously I failed because the next thing I knew, Van was there, shouting. Saying Moped had disappeared."

"Disappeared from where?" I asked. "From where Van was? From the chapel?"

"No," said Rain. "He never made it that far. Van hadn't seen him at all. He just came back, saw that Moped was missing, and woke us all up to go and find him."

"So you're saying Moped fell off the bank when he was trying to find his way to the huttie?"

"Yeah," said Rain. "Only that doesn't really make any sense, because the huttie — that's what we called it! The huttie. It was much closer to where we were camping than where the bridge and the Tarzan swing were. And if Moped got close enough to hear the waterfall, he'd know he had missed the huttie and he'd turn back. I don't see how he can have got close enough to fall in."

"Unless he was running. If he was panting, he might not have heard the water. He might not have had time to stop."

"Why would he be running?" Rain said. "He'd be creeping along trying to be quiet so Van didn't hear him."

"What if he was frightened? What if he'd heard something that scared him?"

"Mope didn't believe all that," she said. "That's how come he didn't mind creeping about the woods all on his own in the first

344

place. He didn't believe in ghosts and monsters."

"I wasn't thinking of ghosts," I said. "Or monsters either. I was thinking about someone who was there and shouldn't have been. Someone who might have come in a car."

Rain frowned at me, trying to dredge up memories that were buried deep under years of sorrow.

"That's right," she said. "One of the kids said there was a car. I never heard it. Or maybe I heard it and then we decided . . . I can't remember the story. Wait! I never heard it and the gate was locked, so it wasn't true, right?" She lit another cigarette and rubbed a hand roughly across her eyes as if to wipe tears, although I couldn't see why that — out of all things we'd been speaking about — would upset her.

"No car?" I asked.

"I don't want to talk about it anymore."

"So tell me about London," I said. "You were all models?"

"In the eighties," she said. "London was the place to be. It was Claudie that got discovered."

"What? Walking along Oxford Street like you read in magazines?"

"Walking along Castle Douglas High Street," said Rain. She hugged herself,

345

wrapping her arms right round her skinny body. "It was May Day then too, and Claudie and Sue had been back to Eden to put flowers in the water for Moped. Claudie had cried mascara all down her face, and she was just trailing along the street, weeping. And this guy came up and put a business card in her hand and said she had a very interesting look and he could always get work for her. God knows what a talent scout was doing in Castle Douglas, by the way. And God knows why a sixteen-year-old kid all blotched and snotty from crying would ring his bells, but she did. Claudie used to say she had started heroin chic, right there outside the baker's shop. Never mind *Trainspotting*. Never mind Kate Moss. Claudie reckoned it was her. Or Cloud Irving and JCM Modelling between the two of them."

"And it was legitimate?" I said. "The scout was for real?"

"We asked our mum," she said. "We're not idiots. And we weren't allowed to go, but we could send pictures and see what happened. So we sent a load of snaps we took out there in the garden with Sue's little automatic and thought no more of it. Next thing, the agency sent our train fares — first-class tickets and hotel rooms. *I* was eighteen by this time, so Mum said fair enough and off we went."

"Sounds like an adventure."

"It was," she said. She had slipped down into her seat on the sofa with her legs stretched out in front of her. "It was like something from a movie. There was champagne and flowers in the suite when we got there, a car came for us, we had our hair done and our faces done, got waxed from head to toe — we didn't even know what waxing was! Castle Douglas in the eighties, who did? We got taken to a studio and styled and dressed and got started on our portfolio. Those pictures you've got there. We did all those on the same day and then went to a big party at night."

"And did you stay in London working or did you travel around?" I asked her. "I always think of models being off and on planes all the time."

"We didn't work," she said. "We got sent out. Claudie most and me next and Sue sometimes too, but we just didn't get the jobs. The phone would ring and it would be his secretary — can't remember her name — and she'd give us auditions to go to. But we just weren't lucky."

"Whose secretary?" I asked.

"Oh, yeah. JC," said Rain. She waved her

new cigarette at the folder. "Turn one over."
On the back of the picture was stamped
Property and copyright JCM Agency and a
London phone number.

"So eventually there was a big meeting.
We weren't at it, but we heard about it, and
the upshot was that we were all wrong.
None of us was thin enough for couture,
even though Claudie and me were tall. Sue
was the only one curvy enough for glamour
work, but she didn't have the right look,
and I was too thin for catalogues because
they like a size ten. A six for catwalks and a
ten for catalogues, and I was stuck at eight.
Like Claudie. No shifting it."

"But you were beautiful," I said. "All of
you. Why couldn't you just be face models,
in magazines? Perfume and make-up and
things."

"Because there's not enough work to go
around," said Rain. "Anyway. We went to a
party and we told this friend of ours, who
was at the same agency. And she . . . helped
us out."

I knew where it was going now. It wasn't
too difficult to work out when where it had
ended was sitting right there in front of me.

"Drugs," I said.

"It was 1989 and it was London," said
Rain. "I'm not talking *Midnight Express*. Just

a leg up to get the fat shifted and start us on our way. Just one of us and then she'd help out the others."

"What went wrong?"

"We got busted," said Rain. "Stupidest thing. We never found out who said what or which one us was silly at a party — Claudie was a bit of a chatterbox when she was speeding — but anyway, we got busted. Search warrant for the flat. The works. And to this day I don't understand how it happened, but there was more coke and speed in that flat than all three of us had used in our lives. So when we got done, we got done for dealing. It wasn't mine, I swear to God, and Sue swore an oath to me when we were both standing in the chapel of rest right beside Claudie's coffin. She swore it wasn't hers either. So it must have been Claudie's. Anyway."

"Did you go to jail?"

"No," said Rain with a laugh. "You've led a sheltered life, haven't you? We went to rehab. Or Claudie did and I did. Sue didn't need to. She got a fine and community service. Sloshing a mop around in a hostel in Hammersmith. Rehab would have been less depressing. Christ, *jail* would have been less depressing. And the agency dumped us like hot turds."

"And rehab didn't work?" I said, hoping it sounded sympathetic and not nasty, because it wasn't meant to be.

"It worked on me," said Rain. "Sue had a harder time. But the last thing fucking JCM Modelling did for us — by way of an apology, I suppose, for not taking better care — anyway, the last thing they did was put us on to a therapist. A rebirther. Total nutjob. She worked out of her house away up in Grantham and she sent Claudie right over the edge. Took five years, but it broke her in the end. It was when she fell off the wagon again after the fucking therapy that she went to prison."

"Why jail that time then?" This was a different world to me.

"She lifted scripts," said Rain, "And bingo! Eleven months in Cornton Vale."

"Scripts?" I said, thinking of the modelling agency and acting jobs.

"A pad of blank prescriptions. She hadn't touched heroin before she went into the Vale, but she came out the biggest junkie ever born. Never had another straight day in her life."

"I'm so sorry," I said. "I can't even imagine."

"We're all right most of the time," Rain said. "The parents left us okay for money

350

and the thing about heroin is, it's not actually all that bad for you. Coke'll kill you and speed'll kill you even faster — ha-ha — but if your supply is clean and you eat right, there's no reason heroin will ever do you much harm."

"That's an unusual point of view."

"I don't beat myself up anymore," Rain said. "I look after Sue and I look after me and I've let Claudie go. I can't change it, and I can't spend the rest of my life feeling bad about it."

I nodded. She must have had some therapy of her own. No one spoke like that who hadn't been trained to.

"It took me long enough, though," she said. "When Claudie was in Cornton Vale, I went to track down JCM, give JC a piece of my mind. But it had closed. The agency was gone, no sign of it, no listing in the yellow pages, no way of getting hold of him. When she died, I tried again. I got a detective this time. Sent scanned copies of our old agency contracts, the lot. I just wanted to be in the same room as the motherfucker that told Claudie she needed to lose some weight and spit in his lousy face, just once."

"Did you find him?"

"The detective agency couldn't turn up so much as a whisker," she said. "Searched old business listings, all the industry contacts. It was like JCM had never existed. Mark — that was the detective — even started asking me if I was sure any of it had actually happened. As if London and the hotels and parties and our flat in Lurline Gardens was some kind of drug dream. I paid him off and tried to forget about it."

It sounded like the end of the story, but something about her held breath, her tense pose, suggested she had more to say.

"Can't really blame him," she let out at last. "Bits of it have never made sense. Where the stash came from that Claudie got done for. The agency paying for that bloody therapist in Grantham. Maybe it *was* some creep in his spare room playing an elaborate trick on us. Only . . . what was the punch line?"

It took me a minute to understand her.

"You mean, you never went to the offices while you were on the agency's books?"

"Never went there, never met JC. Just spoke to his secretary on the phone and saw his signature on papers. We used to laugh about it. Charlie's Angels, like. It seemed normal. All the other girls — the ones we met at parties — just got picked up in cars to go to jobs and had their contracts couriered to their flats. What did we know?"

"Do you mind if I make some notes?" I asked her. "Can I sit here and jot things down and ask you if I need reminders of anything?"

"I'll make you another coffee," she said. "Want something to eat? Toast or a yoghurt?"

"Some toast would be lovely."

"April, Jo-jo, the Best boys, Ned and Nod, and Stig all dead, eh?" she said.

"Stig's not dead," I told her. "But he's missing."

"What about the Scarlets?" she asked. "Are they okay?"

"I haven't tracked them down yet."

"And Morrison?" she said. "What about him?"

"He's still in Castle Douglas," I said. "He works in his dad's carpet shop and he still plays golf."

"I bet he does," she said. "Tell me he's single, at least. Tell me he's sad and lonely."

"He's divorced," I said. I didn't mention Zöe. It troubled me to think of someone so kind and happy being taken in by him. Or maybe she was more than able to look after herself. She seemed so.

"Good," said Rain. "He reeled one in, but she got away. Maybe I should go and spit in *his* face, eh? If he hadn't been such a tosser,

Moped and Jo-jo wouldn't have egged him on to spend the night in the huttie, and then Moped wouldn't have followed and wouldn't have died and Claudie wouldn't have been walking along the high street with her make-up in streaks, and JC's scout wouldn't have seen her. No London, no bust, no prison, no rebirthing therapy. We'd all be married to farmers and swapping scone recipes."

This time when she stopped talking, it was really as if she had nothing left to say. I bent my head and started writing.

"Can I do anything for you?" I asked once my notes were done. I had tried to stick to the facts and not scrawl down all the theories that I couldn't help building, up and up, into the airy reaches of complete fantasy.

"Likes of what?" said Rain. She looked around that filthy kitchen as if she couldn't imagine what I might think she needed.

"Go and bring you some shopping back or something," I said.

"You'd do us more good carrying on with that," she said, nodding at my notes. "Something doesn't make sense. It never has. I'm too tired to think it through now, but you can do it for me. And for Sue. And Claudie."

TWENTY-SEVEN

There wasn't much to go on. Twenty-four years ago Scarlet McFarlane had lived on Methven Street in Perth and had registered a birth from there. The chances that she'd still be at the same address all these years later were slim to nil. But what else did I have? And when else would I get the chance to drive all the way to Perth and see? I was working the next day, and I had a wedding on Sunday.

I topped up with petrol at Kirkcudbright and got myself a pie and a pint of milk to keep me going — the instant coffee was fizzing inside me and the adrenalin wasn't helping it any — then I turned north and put my foot down.

It wasn't until nearly two hours later when I saw the sign for Stirling University that the idea occurred to me, but I swung over into the inside lane, indicated, and shot up the slip road before I could reconsider. It was a maze, like every college or hospital always is, and I looped around for nearly ten minutes, until I was beginning to feel stupid and telling myself my schedule was tight enough without wasting time on this wild goose chase. Then I saw a sign for the Sports Centre and took the narrow winding road to what must be its car park. It was *a* car park, anyway, and there was the stadium right over my left shoulder. I pulled into an empty space, ignoring the sign — A PERMITS ONLY, NO GUEST PARKING — and looked around.

At nothing. Behind me was the stadium, in front was the athletics track. To either side were more buildings with parking and clumps of those bushes that always get planted around car parks, the red ones with the thorns and the shiny ones with yellow splashed leaves. Stig would know what they were. I got out of the car and stood up, looking beyond the sports grounds. The land sloped away in front of me to a row of scrubby trees — hard to tell what they were at this time of year with their bare branches. Behind them, across a valley, were more boxy buildings that must be another part of the university. I locked the car and started walking around the edge of the car park. I was looking for a memorial, I suppose. A man had died here, and maybe there would be a plaque or a little sculpture or something. *In memory of Nathan McAllister, who died here on May Day 1995, in the place that . . .*

But I couldn't guess what it would say.

I walked all the way round, finding nothing, and only noticed the man when I was almost back at my car. He was bending over the bonnet as if looking in the window.

"Hey!" I shouted, starting to jog towards him. "What are you doing?"

"Looking for your permit and not having any luck," he said, standing up and glaring at me. He was dressed in a grey uniform with a crest on his top pocket and he was holding a pad of forms and a biro with its lid off.

"Oh," I said. "Parking? I was just here for a minute."

"There's five-minute drop-off parking over by the Alpha Centre."

"It was the sports centre I was after," I said. I was studying him as I spoke. He looked to be in his sixties, and that amount of personal affront at a parking misdemeanour was the sort of attitude that came from long association with a place. "Well," I added, "the sports centre car park anyway. Because this is where that boy died, isn't it?

357

Years ago?"

His eyes flashed, but at least he put his pad of forms away. "You a relative?" he said.

"Cousin," I said. "But I live in Australia and this is the first time I've been back since it happened. I wanted to find the spot and maybe say a wee prayer."

"Aye, well," said the man. "You're nowhere near it. Here, follow me."

He led me to the far corner, to the last space, looking out between the trees across the valley.

"It's the longest walk to the buildings from here and the spaces fill up from the other end, so it was gone ten before somebody pulled in alongside and saw what had happened."

"Poor Nathan," I said. "No one ever found out why he did it, you know. My auntie's never been the same since. I saw her a couple of days back and she's a shell, so she is. Just a shell."

"Aye, well," said the man. It seemed to be his favourite comment. "There's copers and there's quitters. If he had thought on his poor mother before he did it, she'd be a happier woman today. But then, she brought him up and made him what he was."

Even to me, a stranger, this sounded like the most cold-hearted, smug-faced drivel anyone could think up if they were paid to try. If I really had been Nod's cousin, it would have been unforgivable. To compose my face and get my voice under control, I turned away.

"And as to why he picked here," the man went on, speaking to the back of my head, not caring if I was praying apparently, "nobody had a single clue. He had no association with Stirling. He had no reason to be here upsetting staff and giving us grief. But that's the same thing again, isn't it? Selfish. Like them that throw themselves under trains and never think about the drivers."

"What's that over there?" I said, pointing at the distant buildings, more to shut him up than because I cared.

"That!" he said. "That's nothing to do with the university. That blot on the landscape's not part of the campus at all. That's the hen house." He gave an unpleasant laugh.

"A chicken farm?" I said, turning back to him.

He laughed ever harder then. "Good one," he said. "Naw, that's the women's prison, love. That's Cornton Vale."

I thanked him. I was so happy finally to have

made a connection that I really did feel grateful. He took it as no more than his due and waved me on my way.

Cornton Vale, I repeated to myself. The prison where Cloud Irving was sent for her drug offences. Nathan McAllister died looking right at it. Moped died at the Devil's Bridge, Jo-jo at another, Edmund died near a second huttie, Alan by a sculpture of Adam and Eve. And Nathan McAllister died right here looking at the place where Cloud Irving's troubled life finally tipped and went off the rails forever. I had them all connected at last.

The only problem was that none of it made sense. There were no motives, no reasons, no suspects, no way to make one whole story. I turned my mind resolutely away from what Miss Drumm had told me — there was no place for devils and curses here with so many lost and so many still alive but hurting. There had to be a rational explanation. There was the car, for one thing. The car that Stig and April had heard that first night and Rain hadn't. And the question of why BJ Tarrant had opened a school. There was the fact that Stig knew or suspected something he couldn't even bring himself to say. There was a story emerging; I hoped it wouldn't be the true one.

I shook the thought away and tried to focus my mind on what I might discover at the other end of this journey. Of course, Scarlet McFarlane might be dead. If she had married in England and changed her name, then died afterwards, Lynne wouldn't have found her. But maybe she was alive, and maybe the Perth address from the time her baby was born was her parents' place, and maybe they'd tell me where she was, or at least take my number and get her to ring me. And maybe — this was a stretch, but I couldn't help it — everyone talked about The Scarlets as if they were a pair, and Rain/Rena Irving had said they were curled up together sharing a sleeping bag the night that Moped died — so maybe they were best friends. Best Friends Forever, like youngsters say now. And maybe in their case it had really meant something, and when I found one I would have found the other. I didn't hold out much hope, but I pressed on anyway.

The tenement on Methven Street, when I found it, looked much more like somewhere a girl would have digs while she waited for her baby than somewhere her parents would make their home for all their married life. It was two streets back from the main shopping precinct, with businesses below and flats above and, although some of the stairs looked trim enough, this one with its scuffed paint and lopsided rush-blinds was definitely bedsits, or at least private lets. Great for transients but pretty hopeless for me. I opened the front door, went upstairs anyway to 4C as Lynne had told me, and knocked.

It took a long time for it to be opened, but one good thing about a bedsit is that there's a good chance whoever lives there doesn't have a job and doesn't get up very early either, so I wasn't surprised when eventually I heard slow footsteps approaching, a pause while the person inside looked through the peephole, and the clink of the chain being taken off.

It wasn't who I was expecting. The woman who stood there was neatly dressed in a soft cream fleece and stretchy leggings with crocs on her feet. Her hair was brushed smooth and her face was made up with blue eye shadow and pale lip gloss. She was enormously pregnant, impossibly pregnant, carrying her belly in front of her like a snail carried it shell on its back, the rest of her looking insignificant behind that massive billow.

"I'm sorry to disturb you," I said. She smiled and shook her head. "I'm looking for someone who used to live here." She shrugged and shook her head again. "Scarlet," I said. "It was a long time ago, but I just wondered . . . Can you understand me?"

"No English," she said. "Thank you."

"Oh," I replied. "I see. Well, good luck with the baby," I said, pointing. She ran her hands over the expanse of soft cream fleece stretched across her front and smiled. Then she shut the door and I heard her footsteps retreating again, their slowness making sense now. I imagined her waddling back to her seat and easing herself back down from where she had struggled up and was sorry I had disturbed her.

Maybe a neighbour, I thought, turning round and looking across the landing at the opposite door. I thought I heard a noise inside when I first knocked, but no one came, not even to look through the peephole. Maybe they only ever had trouble, never good news, knocking at the door.

I looked up the stairwell. There was one more storey above, two more flats in all, and I had come this far, two hours driving and two hours back again. It would be silly not to be thorough. So I grasped the banister and started to climb the stairs.

I knew I had hit the jackpot as soon as I turned onto the top landing. One of the flats was the same as the two down below — dulled paint on the door and the glue from old stickers partly peeled off again, but the opposite door was exactly what I was looking for. Its plastic mat, its wrought-iron trough on spindly legs with the plastic begonias, its polished brass name plate — *Thomas* — and the brass lock plate, knocker and handle all glittering to match it; even the fanlight above with its arch of ruffled net and its small bowl of dried flowers picked to fill the space the arch left bare — everything proclaimed that here lived a resident of many years' standing, one who could not possibly fail to have a view of the neighbours whose housekeeping lagged so far behind her own. I rang the doorbell, resisting the urge to pull my cuff down and polish the button after my finger had touched it. This time the footsteps sounded right away, the soft thump of slippers. The pause as their wearer peered through the peephole was a short one, but this time the door opened a crack with the catch still on.

"I'm not buying anything and I'm not changing my gas and electric," said a reedy but firm old voice. I could see one eye behind the lens of a pair of spectacles and below it a very firm mouth, pursed so that the flick of pink lipstick it wore looked fluted around the edges.

"I'm not from a company," I said. "I wanted to ask you about one of your neighbours."

The door banged shut. She took the chain off and then threw it wide.

"Are you from the letting agency?" she said. "Because I don't know where to start. That lot over there come and go at all hours and the minute they're in the door they've got the music on. Downstairs is as bad — *tromp tromp* in their work boots and they've no need to be wearing them because none of them work. None of them are up before noon and then the telly's on till the small hours. I don't even know what they can find to watch. And as for her!" The little woman jabbed a finger down and across the landing.

"She seemed nice," I said. "As far as you can tell when she doesn't —"

"She doesn't!" said the woman. "Not a word. The good Lord alone knows where she's from, but she doesn't understand a single word I say to her. And that man of hers is not much better. *Please* and *thank you* and *good morning* and *good night*, but that's it. And he's out twelve hours a day. It'll be worse when there's a new baby screaming the place down and kicking up mud in the back green."

"It's not actually any of current neighbours I wanted to ask about, to be honest, Mrs. Thomas," I said. "But it was a young girl with a baby, right enough."

"Another one of these whatever they are?" she said. I had to bite my lip on the retort. What they were — more than likely — was citizens of an EU member state, and it sounded as if the husband of the girl in the soft cream fleece worked long hours every day and had a courteous word for his neighbour when they passed on the stairs.

"No, she was Scottish," I said. "This was a while back, mind you."

"Aye, it would have been," said Mrs. Thomas. "You've to hunt to find a Scot getting given these flats these days. So what was her name then and when was she here?" I opened my mouth to speak, but before I had the chance, she changed her mind. "Look, away you come in," she said. "Come and sit and I'll get the kettle on. There's no use standing here letting the dust blow in on my good carpets. For they're no better at closing the front door than they are at sweeping the stair." This last was delivered in ringing tones, in hopes, no doubt, that the deadbeat neighbours would hear it and be chastened. Then she drew me in with a hand on my arm, shut the door behind me, locked it, and applied the chain.

The sitting room, at the front with the big bay window, was stuffed with furniture. Good ugly post-war furniture, skinny chairs with wooden armrests and a gate-leg table with a matching sideboard. Mrs. Thomas settled me and went through to the small kitchen, shouting over her shoulder as she fussed about, making tea.

"What was the name, dear?" she said.

"Scarlet McFarlane," I said. "But it was twenty-odd years ago."

"Twenty years is nothing when you get up as far as I am," she said. "Of course I remember. It's not every day you have two Scarlet women living underneath you. Ho! But, mind you, there was never a lad coming or going in the time they were here. Just the two girls and then the baby. And then the trouble and they were all gone."

"Trouble?" I said, with a cold, sinking feeling inside me.

"Post-natal depression they'd call it these days," said Mrs. Thomas. She was back already, as if the kettle was kept constantly on the boil and the tray set. I hadn't seen those brown smoked-glass teacups since I volunteered at the charity shop ten years ago, and even then we used to get stuck with them. "Baby blues it was when I was a young mother," Mrs. Thomas went on. "Not that we had the time. Slopping around in a housecoat and letting the baby scream. When I had mine, I was up, curlers out, along the street with the baby in the pram for an airing. Cooked breakfast, lunch, and dinner for Mr. Thomas and knitted every stitch they wore. I couldn't stand to live that laxadaisy way these girls go on now."

"So the trouble was depression?" I said. I took a cup of tea and a biscuit, balancing it in my saucer.

"And if somebody had nipped in quick and had the kiddy away to a good home, it might have worked out just fine in the long run," said Mrs. Thomas. The cold feeling was spreading through me. "But three times she left that poor mite lying and came home without it, until finally one day it was gone for good."

"What do you mean?"

"Oh, it was all over the papers here," Mrs. Thomas said. "I've probably still got the clippings from the *Courier* but goodness knows where, because I've been meaning to turn out that big cupboard since I put the tree away last Christmas and devil if I've got round to it."

"But can you remember the gist of what

happened?"

"She took the baby out in its pram, must only have been a month old the first time. Then she came back screaming and wailing saying someone had stolen it. Stolen the pram with the baby in it. There was police, neighbours out searching, the works. And then it turned out the poor soul was right outside the shop where she'd left it. She'd walked away without it and then caused all that stink to try and cover up after herself. You wouldn't credit it, would you?"

"Well, sleepless nights can leave you quite . . ." I said, before Mrs. Thomas withered me with a look.

"So you can well imagine that the second time it happened, we were a bit more thingwy about it all. Oh, the police came back, but there were no neighbours out scouring the streets, and that time she got taken to the station and given a talking to. Got a social worker, if you don't mind, who — wait till you hear this — had the cheek to come knocking on *my* door."

"What for?"

"Assessing," Mrs. Thomas said. "Assessing the environs. Seeing if we were good enough for that piece to live beside or if she needed a shift."

"I can see why that would be offensive," I

said, wondering how badly she was garbling what the social worker had actually said.

"The third time she left the kiddy out lying somewhere, she kept quiet, but there was letters stuffed down the folds of the pram hood, and the woman that found it lying there abandoned — away up the back of the swing park where it might have been hours before someone passed — anyway, she saw the address and brought it back again. Young Scarlet hadn't come back from her jaunt and it landed to me. She was a very nice woman, well-dressed and neat — a lot like yourself dear — and she knew it was safe to leave the baby with me."

"What did you do?" I asked.

"What could I do?" said Mrs. Thomas. "I phoned the police, of course. And the lot of them — all three — were gone within the week. The baby to Social Services and the two girls, I don't know and I don't care."

"Heavens," I said. "What a sad story."

"I never saw hide nor hair of either of them again for twenty-two years," she went on.

"Twenty-two?" I said. "Then what?"

"Then two years back I was in DE Shoes, just browsing," said Mrs. Thomas. "And there she was. I knew I knew her, but I couldn't just place her at first. Then she saw me and *I* haven't changed much. Her eyes flashed and her face turned as white as a sheet, and it was then that I knew who I was looking at. There she was, bold as brass, helping a kiddy try on winter boots."

"DE Shoes in Perth?" I said. "Two years ago?"

"It'll be two years come Christmas."

"Thank you for the tea," I said. "I'm going to have to rush off, but you've been very helpful."

"Here's your hat, where's your hurry," said Mrs. Thomas behind me. "You're as bad as the rest, madam, with those manners!"

She was still clucking and fussing after me as I pulled her front door shut behind me and trotted downstairs to the street, holding on to the banister, trying not to turn my ankle on my wedge heels, praying that it wasn't too good to be true.

TWENTY-EIGHT

There was a DE Shoes on every High Street in the country. Cheap trainers, vinyl boots, novelty slippers. When I was a child I'd have died for a pair of anything but brown Clark's sandals in the summer and black Clark's lace-ups in the winter. I was glad of them now, proud of my straight toes and high arches, although Lynne always said nice feet were wasted on women who earned them. She wore strappy stilettos all summer long and for winter parties, and her bunions made it look as if her feet were chewing gumballs. That made me think of Zöe and her pink and white toenails. She might wear pretty shoes now, but she must have been Clark's all the way when she was young to get that even row of little piggies.

I found the shoe shop sitting in between a Greggs and a Samuels, took a deep breath, and went in.

There was a woman in her sixties, with

glasses hanging on a gold chain over the bust of her hand-knitted jersey, and a boy of twenty with that ugly, brushed-forward-and-gelled-to-death hairstyle that always seems to go along with very bad skin, as if the glop is creeping down from the scalp and blocking all the pores. But, as well as those two, there was a woman who could easily be forty and who had a well of sadness inside her deeper than any I had ever seen.

"Scarlet?" I said.

She nodded, squinting as if to work out where she knew me from, and my heart soared inside me. *Scarlet McFarlane.* I had found the last of them! One of the last of them anyway.

"I don't suppose you're due a break, are you?" I said. "Can I buy you a cup of coffee and have a word?"

"Do I know you?" she said.

"Friend of a friend," I said, "from the old days."

"Is it about Rosie?" she said. I thought about it for less than half a minute. I'm a registrar. I see fashions come and go, and I can guess a person's age from their name, like a party trick. The Lynnes and the Laurens and the Emmas in order. And the Rosies too.

"Your daughter Rosie?" I asked. Her eyes seemed to grow until they were half as big again and she leaned forward, searching my face for clues.

"Di?" she shouted, without looking away from me. "I'm going on my break. I'll work through later."

She didn't say another word until we were sitting at the smoking tables outside a Caffé Nero.

"What can I get you?" I asked her. "The millionaire shortbread is really lovel—"

"Are you her mum?" she asked me. "How did you find me?"

"I went to ask your old neighbour round on Methven Street," I said. "I got your old address from her birth certificate."

"You're her mum, aren't you?" she said "Is she with you?"

"Scarlet, I don't understand," I said. "I'm an old friend of a friend of yours from Eden."

"Scar's friend?" she said. She lit a cigarette and sat back, considering me. "Huh," she said. "I haven't thought about that place for twenty years and then it pops up twice in a week."

"Oh?"

"It was on the news, in the papers. Someone who went there died again. April

Cowan. And they're looking for one of the other kids to 'help with their enquiries'."

"Stig Tarrant," I said. "What do you mean 'died again'?"

"I mean another one. There was Alan Best. Do you know who that is? And Scar, of course."

"Scarlet's dead?" I said. "The other Scarlet?" I felt my face prickling, and I knew I had paled. I put both hands on the table to steady myself.

"Hey," said this Scarlet, putting a hand out and covering mine. "Sorry. I thought you would know. If you know Rosie. 'My daughter Rosie'." She smiled again. "It's nice of you to say that. But she's certainly not my daughter now."

"How did Scarlet die?" I asked. "When?" I really had no idea when, but I thought I could guess how.

"She killed herself," came the answer, just as I'd been expecting. "Jumped off the bloody bridge into the Dee when the baby got taken away."

"I heard about that from your neighb—"

"If you heard from old Mother Thomas, then you heard a load of crap," said Scarlet.

"I'll bet," I said. "So. Your baby got taken away and Scarlet's dead. I'm really sorry. I know it was a while ago, but I'm sorry for your loss. Losses."

She nodded a thank you.

"But why is there no record of her death?" I said. "I looked and there's nothing under Scarlet McInnes. Did she change it?"

"Ohhhh," Scarlet said, sitting back. "I thought you were being kind saying 'your daughter,' but really you're just mixed up. *I'm* Scarlet McInnes. And there's no records on me because I never did anything to record. Scar had Rosie and we all changed our names after."

"You *all* did?"

"Yeah," Scarlet said. "Rosie *was* our baby, but it was Scar who had her. Scarlet *McFarlane.* And when she was found unfit, I might as well have been . . . what's the expression?"

"Chopped liver," I said. "You and Scarlet were a couple?"

She nodded, narrowing her eyes, waiting to see what I'd say next.

"And you had a baby at sixteen?" She relaxed a bit. "Deliberately?" Now she was almost smiling. "Sorry," I said. "I shouldn't judge you. I waited until I was twenty-five and then married a complete wanker who left me and our disabled son."

I spoke as if these truths had been lodged in my head for years, growing roots; not at all as if they had been sprung on me that morning in Rena Irving's kitchen.

"Rosie was a surprise, actually," Scarlet said, "but a welcome one."

I wanted to ask a hundred questions, but they were intrusive and probably offensive, so I left it. "About what Mrs. Thomas told me," I said instead, wondering how to ask what I needed to ask.

"Nobody believed Scar except me," Scarlet said. "She wasn't depressed and she wasn't confused. And she would *never* have done anything to harm Rosie. The truth is someone kidnapped Rosie. Three times." She saw my look. "The first time was easy. Everyone left their prams outside wee shops back then. Not like today. And the second time was because Scar was trying not to overreact to the first time."

"I can't imagine how you must have felt."

"We were going out of our heads and the police wouldn't even ask around. They made up their minds Scar was lying, and after that they never followed up on anything. They never even asked that stupid old cow Thomas for a description of the woman who snatched Rosie and said she'd found her in the park. We were nowhere *near* the park. We were in the supermarket — I'd gone back to get something we'd forgotten in the fruit and veg, and Scar turned her back for a second — a split second. We were still searching the shop when that woman brought her back and knocked on our door. And it was nothing like the two hours she'd said. It was ten minutes at most. Only no one believed us."

"I believe you," I said. I believed that Scarlet McFarlane wasn't a neglectful mother, just like I believed that Alan Best wasn't a paeodophile and I believed that Cloud Irving couldn't be a drug dealer without her sisters knowing. This wasn't the devil's work, but it was just as evil.

"Thank you," Scarlet said.

"And I'm sorry, because this must be very upsetting, but I'm going to have to ask you some questions." She nodded for me to go ahead. "First, and please don't jump up and storm off, but I need to ask you where you were on Monday night. And Tuesday too."

Her eyes narrowed again, but she nodded and answered. "That's easy," she said. "I've got a bar job at nights. I was serving behind the bar at the Brig O'Dee. A hundred witnesses. I couldn't get down to Glasgow on Tuesday. What happened on Monday?"

"Someone was chasing April Cowan all over the countryside down by Eden," I said. She swallowed hard and looked away from me. "I don't like thinking about it," she said. "It was a bad place. It was a bad place even before Mitchell died. It . . . It didn't make sense."

"Why did your parents send you there?"

"My dad had some kind of business dealings with Jacky Tarrant that owned it," Scarlet said. "I think he got a good deal."

"And Scar?" I asked. "Was that the same?"

"No, she was connected to the teacher," said Scarlet. "She was some kind of second cousin or something. That's right: Scar was Miss Naismith's cousin's daughter. Not a close connection, but Naismith must have put the word out that they could get discounted fees." She stopped talking and stared into the distance, her eyes following the shoppers who were passing on the street. "Maybe Naismith thought she'd have an ally, her cousin's kid and all that. And Scar *was* kinder to her than the rest of us. Well, Scar was kind to everyone, always. But she didn't hold out at the end. When the hm-hm hit the fan."

"What are you talking about?"

"That boy — Douglas, was it? Douglas Martin?"

"Duggie Morrison?" I said, and my heart was thumping the way it always did whenever the talk turned to him.

"He persuaded us to . . . what's the expression? Drop Naismith in it. She nearly blew a gasket. I really thought she was going to give herself a stroke."

"Scarlet, I have no idea what you're talking about," I said.

She quirked an eyebrow at me. "I thought you knew what happened that night."

"So did I," I said.

We had been getting filthy looks through the window from the Caffé Nero baristas, because we'd been sitting there for ages and hadn't bought a thing, so I left her lighting another cigarette and went to order. Two lattes and two pieces of the millionaire shortbread, whether she wanted one or not. She was strung out with all these painful memories and the sugar would be good for her.

"So," I said, sitting down. "April the thirtieth to May the first, 1985. What really happened?"

"We cooked sausages," Scarlet began. "They were really disgusting, and one of the kids — it was Stig, I think — had to make a run for the bogs but the rest of us just bedded down. All the weather girls, that's these three —"

"I know," I said. "I spoke to Rain and Sun this morning."

"Okay, well, they were all zipped into the same sleeping bag and Scar and me were too, and we were teasing the boys about being too macho to cuddle in together and keep warm. It was bloody freezing for a spring night, that I do remember. Then, about eleven o'clock, Naismith came and asked us all if we wanted to go back in and sleep in our beds."

"What?" I said. "She *did* come?"

Scarlet looked into her coffee cup and swirled it around for a while before answering. "Yeah, she came. Once, though, not twice like she said. We lied, but she lied too."

"Why?"

"It was Duggie Morrison's idea. When we realised that Moped had drowned, he said we would be blamed for it and that wasn't fair because it wasn't our fault. He said Naismith had left the gate open — we'd all heard a car — and then she'd gone and locked it. Covering up after herself. So we needed to make sure she was punished. So we all said she had left us out there. And she got done for it."

"Wait!" I said. "Scarlet, wait! You're saying Duggie Morrison put together this whole story when you realised Moped was drowned? When you saw Moped's body on the way back to the school in the morning?"

"No," she said. "When he fell in. It was about four o'clock, just getting light. We all woke up when we heard the car and then Duggie came back and told us that Moped was dead, in the water."

My head was reeling. This was nothing like what Stig had told me.

"Why did you wait?" I said "Why didn't you go back to the school right then and raise the alarm?"

"We didn't want to get into trouble," she said. "We knew it was too late for Mope. Alan Best was terrified. He thought his dad would kill him. We all thought if they knew Duggie was traipsing about the place and Moped was mucking about, we'd get blamed. So we decided to say we'd all been asleep, like little angels, and we didn't know when Moped left or why. And we said nothing about the car because we didn't think the cops would believe us. How can a car drive through a locked gate, you know?"

"But how did you know the gate was locked?"

"Duggie told us at four o'clock when he came back."

"How did *he* know?"

Scarlet shrugged. "We were just getting our story all straight when Stig Tarrant came back from the bogs. So we all shut up and kept quiet and when it was a bit later, Duggie woke him up and tried the story out on him. He bought it hook, line, and sinker."

"But why did you not trust Stig?" I said, starting to feel sick again.

"Because his dad owned the school," said Scarlet, "and we thought he'd shop us."

"So you said the teacher failed in her duty, when she didn't?"

"But she *did*," said Scarlet. "She did. She let someone drive out and locked the gate behind them. And she said she came back out after the first time when she didn't. All *we* did was change the story of what she did wrong. So the cops would believe us."

I couldn't help shaking my head as I listened to her, and her eyes filled with tears.

"You ruined a lot of lives," I said. "People couldn't live with the guilt."

"I know," she said. Now the tears were falling. "Scar was one of them. When Rosie kept disappearing, she went kind of nuts. She started talking about the curse and about not taking care of Moped and how she was being punished for it. She even tried to get in touch with her cousin to say sorry. Can you imagine how that would have blown up?"

"Couldn't she find her?"

Scarlet shook her head. "If only she'd

been as hard to get in touch with when we were twelve as she was when we were seventeen," she said. "Just think. Scar was from London. If it wasn't for Eden, she would have stayed in London, and she'd still be alive."

"But Rosie wouldn't exist."

"There's no pain in not existing," Scarlet said. "I've lost her anyway."

"And where would you be?" I said. "If there'd been no Eden."

"Well, not working in a shoe shop and a pub in this tinpot town."

"Why do you stay?"

"I stayed until Rosie's eighteenth birthday in case she came looking for her mum. I thought it was better to be near. And then the last few years . . . I've got a girlfriend here and her kids are settled in their schools." She gave me another smile. "I'm okay. I'm a damn sight better off than Mrs. Best."

"What do you mean?" I said. "Sure, Alan Best killed himself, but he wasn't the only one. Why did you pick *his* mother?"

"Don't you know?" said Scarlet. "He's Rosie's biological father. He's on the birth certificate. You should see your face!" She was laughing at me, but it was so good to see laughter in her eyes that I didn't care. I couldn't believe Lynne, with her love of gossip, had missed it.

"Alan Best," I said. "How did that happen?"

"Party," said Scarlet. "We were young and daft. It could have been either one of us that got knocked up, actually." She laughed even harder, and I couldn't blame her; goodness knows what my face looked like as I took *that* in.

"You know what happened to him, right? The rumours?"

"Yes. It was one of the few times I've been glad Scar was dead."

"It wasn't true," I told her. "No one who knew him believes it."

"Of course not," she agreed.

"The only person who even half believes it is his mum, and that's only because she's so miserable. I don't think she knows about Rosie. I'm sure she doesn't. I don't suppose you've got pictures, have you?"

"Only baby pictures," said Scarlet. "Better than nothing, though, eh?"

I said goodbye soon after that and walked away. I hardly knew where I was going, dizzied by the thoughts whirling around in me. They had made up stories, hidden the truth — hidden a lot of what the police needed to know to find out what really happened that night. And then what?

Did one of them finally realise the power they held? If one of them threatened to change their story, they could have black-mailed everyone else into —

I brought myself up short. One of them *had* started changing her story. April had finally told Stig she'd heard the car. When everyone else had been hurt beyond the reach of more pain — when Jo-jo and Alan and Nathan and Edmund and Scar were gone, when Sun and Rain had lost their beloved sister, and Scarlet had lost her first love and their baby — April had turned to Stig to back her up before she confronted . . . I had to face it.

Before she confronted Duggie.

Duggie, who knew what the other kids thought of him. Duggie, who masterminded the story of poor frightened children out in the dark and put all the focus on the teacher and the school. Duggie, who had managed to make the others say he was in his sleeping bag, when in fact he was somewhere in the woods when Moped died (and he knew about that first too, with plenty of time to make up a story). Duggie, my husband, who had fooled me into thinking I was lucky. Duggie, who was so far from the great guy he pretended to be that a son like Nicky was just a dent in his pride, not a blessing.

I was back at my car. I got in and sat staring out through the windscreen.

But Duggie had an alibi for Tuesday night when April Cowan was moved. He had been with Zöe. *Could I trust that?* I asked myself, and decided that I could. A wife might lie for her husband, but a new girlfriend wouldn't tell a lie like that for a man she'd just met and hardly knew. Only she did seem to have fallen for him. And it hadn't taken him long to get his hooks into me all those years ago. I lowered my head and rested it against the steering wheel. It pounded right behind my eyes when I leaned forward and deep in towards the back when I sat up again. I couldn't do this on my own. I needed Stig to help me.

TWENTY-NINE

How I got home without driving off the road I'll never know. It was dark before I was bumping down the track to Rough House, and when I tried to get out of the car and stand up, I found myself bent over like a crone, my arms set stiff from gripping the wheel so hard and my clutch foot cramping. I hobbled towards the back door as Stig opened it.

He took a step back, his eyes flaring with fear.

"What's wrong?" I said.

"Gloria?" he said, stepping forward again. "I didn't recognise you."

I put my hand up and brushed my hair away from where it was hanging over my face. I was so exhausted I'd forgotten.

"What else is wrong?" I said.

"Oh, Glo," he said. "I don't know how to tell you . . . it's Walter."

I shouldered past him into the kitchen,

dropped my bag at my feet, and rushed over. Walter was lying stretched out in his basket in front of the stove. In the low light I couldn't tell if he was breathing.

"Is he gone?" I said.

"No," said Stig. "But he's been really bad since lunchtime. He was having fits, but the vet came and gave him a jag to stop them."

"You phoned the *vet*?" I said. "Stig, you're supposed to be hiding!"

"But if you'd seen him," said Stig. "Nobody could have sat and watched. And anyway, it's nearly over, isn't it? We're getting to the end now."

I got down onto my knees, still stiff, beside Walter and laid my hand on his side. Now I could tell that he was breathing, shallow but laboured, and his fur felt hot.

"Didn't the vet ask who you were?" I said. "Was it Mandeep?"

"I said I was a friend," said Stig. "He was only worried about Walter, really."

"I've got to talk to you," I said. There was silence for a minute and then Stig spoke up, almost laughing.

"Me?" he said. "I thought you were talking to him. I think he's dying, Glo."

And yet I managed to turn my back on him and look at Stig. This was the thing I had been dreading, the second worst thing that could happen: Walter going before Miss Drumm.

"He's had a good life," I said. "And this is a pretty good death too. When my time comes it'll do me. Listen, Stig, I really need to lay this all out in front of you because I think I know who's behind it. And I think you know too. I think you've known all along."

"Yeah," said Stig. "But I couldn't face knowing, so I just . . . unknew. Does that make any sense?"

It makes more sense to me than it possibly could to anyone, I thought. I spent my life doing just that, just way he described it, all day every day. What didn't make any sense was why Stig would have any trouble facing the truth about Duggie. Unless because the shock of it or maybe the shame of it would floor me.

I made him tea, put a tot of whisky in it, and told him everything. How Moped followed Duggie that night, how Cloud Irving died, how Scar McFarlane died, how Duggie had tried the gate lock, how Miss Naismith *had* checked on the kids and Duggie had made up a story. He listened in silence until the end, but then he shook his head.

"She didn't check," he said. "I know she

didn't. I don't know why Scarlet said she did."

"Stig, Scarlet had no reason to lie to me about it," I said. "I trust her. Look, maybe Miss Naismith didn't come and bang on the latrine door, maybe she fell short by that much, but she did go out to check on the other kids. You wouldn't know. You weren't there."

He waited a while before he spoke again.

"I wasn't in the bog either," he said. "I'm sorry, Gloria. I lied to you."

"Why?" I said. Then all of a sudden I thought I knew. "Oh my God." The words fell out of me like clods of mud. "It was you, wasn't it? It's you." I scrambled to my feet and backed towards the door. "You got close to me to kill me, thinking you'd hurt Duggie that way, didn't you? You killed all of them, didn't you? Picked them all off one by one and now it's my turn."

"Gloria, you're disturbing Walter," he said.

"And you killed my dog!" I shouted. "What did you give him? What did you do?"

He stood up very slowly and snapped on the light above the stove. Keeping eye contact with me all the time, he put his hand into his pocket and pulled out a piece of paper. He reached forward and held it out to me. I reached forward too and snatched it, but I couldn't take my eyes away from his face to look and see what it was. He put his hands on his head and backed away to the far wall.

"You're safe," he said. "Read it."

I dropped my eyes and scanned the sheet as quickly as I could. Then I let all my breath go. It was a vet's bill, Mandeep Bhullar's signature along the bottom, with a note. *Looks like the end of the road, Gloria. You did well. Love, M.*

"So," said Stig. "Let's sit down, stop freaking out Walter, and face the facts. I've never wanted to be wrong about something more than I want to be wrong about this, but no more denial, eh? It's time to tell the true story."

"Once I'm changed," I said. "My feet are killing me and my head feels weird."

When we were settled and I was plaiting my hair, grips in my mouth and brush in my lap, he spoke again.

"I know Naismith didn't go out to check on the kids at eleven o'clock," he said, "because I was at her cabin hiding outside, trying to decide whether to go and talk to her. I got there about ten o'clock and sat there until I woke up at four. And she was inside, Glo. She was playing music and she had a bath. I heard her."

"Why?" I asked. "Why were you there? What did you want to talk to her about?"

"I really don't want to tell you," Stig said. "I can't tell you how much I don't want to tell you."

"Stig, if we're ever going to straighten this out, we're going to have to come clean about everything." I was amazed to see his eyes flash with anger.

"We?" he said. "*We've* got to come clean? What have you got to come clean about, Glo? You're golden, aren't you? You live here like a fucking saint. Looking after your son and your old lady, doing everyone's weddings and funerals. You're so bloody perfect your shit must smell like gravy."

"That's not fair!" I said. "And what happened to not disturbing Walter, by the way? That is *so* unfair. I've come back here and told you that my ex-husband, my son's father, is probably a murderer. Think I'll be 'golden' round here once that comes out? There's always someone ready to say, 'she must have known.' Another wife lying for her husband." As I said it, I knew my face changed, Stig's too.

"Duggie?" said Stig. "You thought I meant *Duggie*?"

"Are you talking about your dad?"

"You don't sound surprised."

"Look, I admit I don't know why your Dad opened a school," I began, "but it was Duggie who —"

And then the phone rang.

I answered, expecting a cold call, and almost dropped the receiver when I heard Duggie's voice on the end of the line.

"Gloria," he whispered. "I'm in trouble. You've got to help me."

"Where are you?" I asked him, mouthing *Duggie* to Stig.

"I'm at home," he whispered, "but Zöe's downstairs, and I don't want her to know I'm calling. I don't want her to see this."

"See what?"

"Please come," Duggie said, his voice taut enough to crack. "I don't know what to do. It's something to do with . . ."

"Eden," I said. "Duggie —"

But he had hung up.

"It's not your dad, Stig," I said, mumbling through lips that felt as cold and useless as when the dentist numbs them. "Duggie's trying to lure me to his house. He's pretending his girlfriend's there."

"That can't be right," said Stig. "I *know* it's BJ. I knew it was him right from the start."

"Unless it's both of them," I said. "Should

I go?" I glanced down at Walter. He was breathing easily, hadn't even stirred when the phone rang.

"We'll both go." He held up a hand as I started to protest. "Duggie and my dad against you and me? And us with the element of surprise? I'll take those odds."

"He's clever," I said. "Look what he's done already. You think he can't outwit the two of us and get you in jail? Or worse?"

"I'm past caring," said Stig. "I've got to get out of here before I go mad. I can't spend another day waiting for you to come back and tell me who's dead. Jesus! Cloud? She was so beautiful! And Scarlet McFarlet? Dead before she was twenty. I can't take any more. If I don't go with you, I'll go and stand by a bridge and wait for him to come and shove me over."

"Wait for who?" I said. "Duggie? Your dad? The devil?"

I hadn't been there since the day I moved out. I had packed up Nicky's room and put my clothes in suitcases, my books in boxes, then I had driven away, leaving behind every pot plant, every cushion cover, every wedding present, anything that he had touched. I had put Nicky's posters and toys in his new room at the home and bought cheap shelves for Rough House to get my books out again. They looked mean and wrong beside the heavy old furniture and if Miss Drumm could have seen them she'd be disgusted, but the thing about bookshelves is that, once they're filled, all you notice are the books and what's holding them doesn't matter.

Still it felt strange to be knocking at the door instead of using a key.

We heard footsteps inside immediately and saw a shadow through the tinted glass. Stig put me slightly behind him and I could see him squaring up, saw him clench his fists. The door opened and there was Zöe, looking startled, but smiling.

"Gloria!" she said and turned to smile at Stig. "Plus one."

"You must be Zöe," said Stig, frowning at her.

"Can we talk to Duggie?" I asked. "Is he in?"

"He's in his 'lair'," she said, rolling her eyes and laughing. "His man-cave. I'll shout up to him."

In our living room, the shelves we'd had made by a joiner were still there, full of golf trophies and silver-framed photographs of tournaments and nights out. There were some books here and there. Three on a shelf with a book-end made in the shape of a miniature whisky barrel. I looked at the spines. Andy McNab, Brad Thor. Good God in heaven, Dan Brown.

But she came back into the living room with a puzzled look on her face, a minute after we'd sat down.

"He says you have to go up," she told me. "Listen, you've obviously got some talking to do. I think I'll take off and leave you to it. Tell Duggie I'll be at home with wet nails so if he phones me, let it ring and I'll answer eventually." She gave me a smile and squeezed my arm; then, with a quick glance flicked at Stig, she made for the door.

"Zöe?" I said. "Before you go. Last Tuesday night, Duggie was with you, you said. That's right enough, is it?"

She stopped and looked from one of us to the other.

"Last Tuesday?" she said. "Why? I mean yes, he was."

"How about Monday?"

She nodded. "We went to the pub on Monday and then we had a quiet night in on the Tuesday, but why? Is everything okay?"

I gave her the best smile I could muster.

Duggie had had the smallest of the three bedrooms for a study since the day we moved in. We slept in the big front room, the second double was for the guests we never got, and the third — the one we called the nursery, smiling shyly at each other — was his until it was needed.

"Because I won't have time to use a study when I'm teaching my boys to ride their bikes and dodge an off-side trap, will I?"

But when Nicky moved out of our room, he needed the big double for his wheelchair, and by then Duggie wouldn't have wanted guests anyway.

I knocked on the door, wondering how he would look to me now that Rain Irving and Scarlet McInnes had opened my eyes. And Stig too. Surely Stig had something to do with me seeing so much so suddenly.

"Gloria, thank God," said Duggie when I went in. He looked different, right enough, but it wasn't my eyes. His face was painted with terror, eyes stark, cheeks pale, mouth trembling. He was sitting at his computer desk, and the blue light from his screen picked out every line on his face — some lines that surely hadn't been there when I'd last seen him two days ago. "Help me," he said.

"Van?" said Stig. "What's going on?"

Duggie turned to see who had spoken, but his face showed no recognition. He just repeated the words, even more desperate this time. "Help me, Gloria. This isn't right. This is nothing to do with me." He turned back to his computer and pointed a shaking finger. "I didn't — I don't understand — Help me."

I took a step towards him to see what he was pointing at, but Stig brought his arm down in front of me like a barrier.

"Don't, Glo," he said. "Van, shut it down."

"It's not mine," said Duggie.

"I know," said Stig. "Just close it down."

"How do you know? What are you doing here?" Recognition was slowly spreading over Duggie's face. "Stig?" he said and then glanced at me. "How do you know each other? And what do you know about this?"

"Close your computer down," Stig said. "Don't look at any more of it."

"Are you behind this?" Duggie said. He swung his monitor sharply towards me, showing me the screen. In the seconds before I squeezed my eyes shut, I took in a tree and a lawn and children. Three of them, chubby and rosy, rolling in the long grass with the sunlight dappling their skin. Then he clicked to the next screen, and I saw just a flash of it before I squeezed my eyes shut and turned away. *Happy hearts and happy faces, happy play in grassy places,* I found myself thinking, and I couldn't help a small moan escaping me.

"Shut it down, Van," said Stig. "For fuck's sake, man, you don't need to show us."

At last, Duggie hunched over the keyboard and started clicking.

"These days you don't have to start rumours," Stig said. "You just have to download a few files and wait for the laptop to go in for a fix-up. Have you checked your work machine?"

"This is —" said Duggie. "This is — It's my work email."

"Has the back office been left unattended?" Stig said.

"You don't need to get in to the actual office," I said. "You can do it remotely."

"Only if you know how," said Stig. "And he doesn't."

"Who doesn't?" said Duggie

Stig ignored him. "Answer me. Has there been anyone in there who shouldn't have been?"

"Zöe left the back door open a couple of weeks ago," Duggie said. "She was beside herself saying sorry. I told her it didn't matter. Jesus Christ, I told her it didn't matter!"

"Van," said Stig. "Just keep this off, and when you go into work in the morning, don't start up your system. Just say it's down. Make sure no one can see what's on there. We'll get it straightened out really soon, I promise you."

Then Stig took me by the hand and drew me out of the study and back down the stairs.

He said nothing all the way home again, through that clear bitter night. The ground was sparkling with frost and the stars looked ice-blue in the cold sky. The wind was whipping up leaves so dry they clattered as they bowled along the road in front of us and the twigs and branches on either side of us clashed with a sound like swords as the wind rattled them.

In the kitchen, William and Dorothy had both come to sit beside Walter Scott, pensive and watchful. I laid a hand on him again and then opened the oven door and let the warmth spill out over him. He gave one low grunt, and his tail twitched as he tried to thump it.

"Oh Walter," I said, bending to kiss him.

"How old is he?" said Stig.

"He's fifteen, same as Nicky." Tears filled my eyes and my breath was snatched away in a sob.

"It's a good age for a Lab," said Stig.

"Don't cry."

I shook my head and tried to explain. "I forgot to go and see him. First time in ten years. And Miss Drumm too."

"I'm sorry," said Stig. "When this is all over, I'll find a way to make it up to you. Or maybe when I get out of jail for keeping quiet so long."

"Tell me," I said. "What's the final version?"

He took his time, and I had a chance to have a good long look at him. I had thought he was showing wear and tear when he pitched up on my doorstep on Monday night, but this man sitting in front of me now looked ten years older again. There were long beard hairs in the fold of his neck, and I had never got round to buying him any Eumovate or Head & Shoulders. His skin looked sore instead of just dry, broken at the sides of his mouth like Nicky gets from the feeding tube. He'd lost weight too, in spite of the baking and not taking any exercise for days. Now his cheeks and the mounds under his sweatshirt, that had been buoyant and round only a few days ago, were pendulous. Except surely that couldn't be true. It must just be his exhaustion making him slump or my exhaustion making me think so, the memory of his father playing tricks on me.

"It was my dad's car," he said at last. "He was there that night. I heard it early on, recognised it. We hadn't bedded down and no one else noticed, but I knew the sound of that engine. No one else had a car like it. And so I said my guts were bad and went to look for him, find out what he was doing there.

"I found the car, hidden in the old stables. Really hidden, Glo, not just parked. It must have taken him ages to wiggle his way into the space and he might have scraped the precious paintwork, but he'd put it in there anyway.

"But I couldn't find *him.* He was nowhere to be seen. I didn't understand, so I went to tell Miss Naismith or ask her to help. I had no idea what was going on."

"But you do now?"

"She was in the bath," Stig said. "I could hear the water and the window was steamed up, so I waited. It was embarrassing to think of a teacher in the bath, you know? I kept checking my watch — I had one of those watches you push a button and it lights up? She was still in the bath at eleven o'clock. Like I told you. Not out checking the kids. And then I fell asleep.

"What woke me up was my dad's car leaving. Four o'clock, he took off like a bat out of hell."

"And he had a key to the gate!"

"Yeah," said Stig. "See? It all makes sense. Anyway, I went back to my sleeping bag. Never noticed who was there and who was missing. Just lay down and tried to sleep. Then it went like I told you.

"The next thing I knew Van was shaking me, telling me about Mope, and we all got up and went back and saw him in the river, and the girls started screaming and then my parents were there and Naismith was going mental saying she had been to check on us and we were all lying. But she didn't, Gloria. She was in her cabin, in the bath. And my dad was somewhere in the woods. And he killed Moped. Or he chased him and Moped ran away and fell in the river."

"But Stig," I began, "you're really jumping to conclusions."

"That's not all," he said, cutting in. "At first I didn't understand why my mum was so angry. She's quite an angry person anyway, but I'd never seen her like that before. She changed and she's never changed back."

I thought about the Angie Tarrant I had seen in the hotel, sharp and bitter; how scared I was of her even though I didn't know why.

"I overheard them arguing once, later," Stig said. "My dad saying that he was sick of living a lie and he was going to come clean, and my mum — she was hissing at him, Gloria, hissing like a snake, she sounded insane — saying she had stuck by him and covered for him and put up with him and he wasn't going to fling that back in her face and make a fool of her, let people look down their noses at her. That he had made his bed and now he had to lie on it. That she wasn't going to have Wee J's life ruined just so my dad could blab all his filthy secrets to the world."

"Wee J's life?" I said.

"Yeah," said Stig. "They're not so bothered about me because they think I know. Obviously they've thought for a while that I know. Or suspected it anyway."

"How do you work that out then?"

"Blackmail," said Stig. "Someone's been blackmailing Dad for years. And once when Mum was drunk she let slip that she's leaving everything to Weej because I've had mine."

"She thinks you're the blackmailer?"

"Yeah. My mum thinks she's so subtle, but it's not hard to piece things together from what she says. She snipes on and on about paying for his mistakes and how she shouldn't have to work herself ragged, about how much she resents — how does she put it? Scrubbing people's smelly feet and ripping their pubes out — but she'll die of old age servicing his debts."

"But 'his debts' might mean anything."

"He's got no legitimate debts," said Stig. "Not beyond what any business would have. I asked Wee J and he told me. What he does have is sweet Fanny Adams where most of the profits should be. He's been paying someone. I think he's been paying them since the very beginning and he's been trying to find out who. Picking them off one by one. He even went for me, and now he's gone for Duggie."

"So . . . like a vendetta?" I said. "Are you serious?"

"Scarlet, Cloud, Jo-jo, Alan," he began. "It wasn't the devil who killed them all for crossing his bridge, Glo."

I couldn't hold out against it much longer. Even Miss Drumm had said BJ Tarrant hung around too much and never came and went the front way. And *everyone* said it was odd the way he started a school, discounting fees to fill it with kids. My stomach was turning.

"And speaking of Alan," said Stig. "Who

the hell would think of doing that unless it was in their minds anyway? Kind of takes one to know one, yeah?"

"And your mum *knows*?" I said.

"They've been in separate bedrooms for years," Stig told me, and I remembered Angie Tarrant's voice saying *for worse and worse and worse again* and finally I believed him.

"It was his idea, you know," said Stig. "Miss Naismith told us. She said the owner of the school thought it was good idea for us to sleep outside on that special night. She smirked."

"Oh my God," I said. "You don't think *she* knew?"

"No," said Stig. "I think she really believed all the guff about the Beltane. I think she just thought it was funny for the likes of my dad to care about it. Christ, if only she'd thought about it for a minute, asked herself why a man would want a lot of little kids to sleep outside."

"Do you think your mum'll give him alibis?" I said.

Stig shook his head. "Once it's out, she'll drop him like a ton of bricks," he told me. "She's got no loyalty, not really. Only pride."

"And you've suspected this all along?" I said. "From when you got here?" He seesawed his head, screwing his mouth up. "But you let me go chasing around all over the place, tracking people down? I really thought I was helping you, Stig, and all the time you were holding out on me. What a fool I am."

"I've hated it every day when you go out," he said. "I was terrified for you. And it was your idea. I never asked you to do anything."

"You never told me what you knew either!"

"Yeah well, that's where you're wrong," said Stig. "I wrote it all down in the notes, but you ripped them up without reading them. While *you* were hiding the fact that Duggie was your husband, actually."

"You wrote it down?"

"I wrote that I recognised the sound of BJ's car. Then, when you didn't read the notes, it felt like I'd been let off the hook. It took me till tonight to face up to telling you again. Come on, Gloria, that's only two days. It takes time to face up to someone you love being a sick fuck."

I couldn't argue with that. "What are you going to do?" I asked.

"I'm going to go to the police," said Stig. "I just need to get everything straight, make a load of notes and then I'll go and turn myself in. They'll arrest me, I know that, but as long as they listen, in the end it'll be okay."

"They'll arrest Duggie too, won't they?"

"Probably," he said. "For a while anyway. Is that okay?"

"It's fine by me," I said. "He's up to his neck in this. Making up stories and hiding things. I still don't understand why he wasn't straight about what happened with Moped."

Stig thought for a while. "Me neither," he said. "Some people just aren't straight. Just not made that way."

Then we sat in silence waiting for the dawn, listening to Walter Scott's breathing get shallower and shallower and slower and slower until it was no more than a ragged gasp and the pauses in between the breaths were long enough to let us doze. By the time they stopped completely we were both asleep and, when we woke, his stillness was so perfect that even if I could have changed it and made it not true, I would have kept things how they were. I looked down at him and thought something I had never thought before: *Maybe I can do this. Maybe if it happens this way round, then by the third time I'll be ready.*

THIRTY

Saturday

"He never laid a finger on *me*, mind," Stig said. He had edged round the bathroom door and was watching me brushing my teeth.

"Of course not," I said. I damped my hands and pressed them over my hair. One good thing about my hairdo is that it never gets messy. No problem sitting up all night.

"Or Wee J," he went on. "I mean, not that I ever asked, but Weej brings the kids round to Mum and Dad's all the time and leaves them there overnight sometimes."

"When are you going to go to the police?" I said. "I could knock off about twelve and come with you."

He nodded. "I want to bury Walter anyway," he said. "I wouldn't have got through the last week without him. No offence."

"And I want to go and see Nicky," I said. "I still think it's weird that the home didn't

410

call me when I never showed up last night. They know I live alone. I could be lying at the bottom of the stairs with a broken neck for all they know."

"But if you've never not shown up before then you don't know what they do when someone doesn't show up, do you?" Stig said.

"Can't fault your logic," I said, smiling. Then we both remembered where Stig's logic had led us, and the smiles were gone.

Lynne was at work before me.

"Well?" she said. "Any developments?"

I closed my eyes and shook my head. Where would I begin? There was so much of it. For some reason, though, it was Duggie who was bothering me.

"Am I going to have something to hold over my mum's head for the rest of our lives?" Lynne said.

"Definitely. So was there any walk-in business on Thursday? It seems a bit too good to be true that I can just swan off from my job and nobody missed me."

"A birth," she said, "but I batted it back again."

I started up the computer and pulled my mail tray towards me. Duggie could wait; I owed him nothing. "What do you mean 'batted it back'?"

"Ocht, it was the dad on his own with the big brother. Mum and baby still in their goonies at home and he'd forgotten the marriage lines. So I told him he'd have to come back when he'd found them."

"That was a close call then," I said, wondering what would have happened to me if my bosses had found out I was AWOL.

"They're coming back today, first thing," said Lynne. "It was Leo McGill. I know fine and well him and Theresa are married because I was at their evening do, but he didn't argue. I think he was worn out from getting the wee boy up and dressed and out with his breakfast inside him. No Hand of Woman there, I'm telling you."

I laughed, but only briefly.

"What is it, Gloria?" said Lynne. "You suddenly got a really funny look on your face."

"Something," I said, vaguely. Then I shook my head. "I'm too soft for my own good, but I need to make a quick call."

Duggie was at the shop already. He always started early, a matter of pride to be in before his dad got there and long before the paid assistant-manager who ran the kitchen side.

"How are you doing?"

"What's happening?" His voice was ragged. "I'm going spare here, Gloria."

"It's BJ Tarrant," I said. "And we can prove it. Just sit tight."

"Easier said than done." Stig had had six days of this and Duggie was strung out already.

"Your computer's off, eh? And no one else can get into your email from the other stations?"

"My dad wouldn't know an email if it bit him."

"What about the other manager?"

"Zöe's called in sick."

I hadn't known she was a manager — I thought she was his assistant in the flooring side, from the way she was right there with him instead of in her own department along the street — but it made no difference.

"Probably just as well," I said, trying not to wonder what it was that was wrong with her and if she'd been incubating it when she went in to see Nicky. "I'll be in touch."

"Who was that?" said Lynne when I had hung up. "And what about BJ Tarrant? Glo, you really don't look too good, you know."

"I didn't get much sleep last night. We sat up with Walter."

"Who's this?" said Lynne.

"The dog, Walter Scott. He died in the

413

early hours. So, as well as everything else, I need to get ready to tell Miss Drumm about that when I see her."

"No, I mean who sat up?" said Lynne. I closed my mouth very firmly. I was so tired, my thoughts weren't making any sense and my mouth was running away with me.

"You know, it'll all be out by the end of the day anyway," I said. "I suppose there's no harm in telling you now."

But I didn't get the chance because the door opened and in came the McGills, all four of them today. Theresa, still slow and tired, was dressed in grey sweats like Stig, but the little boy — Adam, if I remembered right — was dressed in smart new blue corduroys and a wee checked shirt in blue and yellow with a yellow tee-shirt peeking out at the neck. The baby, a girl, was like a collection of marshmallows, palest pink and pure white, with swansdown round the hood of her hat.

"Aww, Tess, she's lovely," said Lynne, flashing her eyes at me. Hand of Woman, they were signalling. Again something flipped inside me as if I'd eaten a live fish.

"Congratulations, both of you," I managed to get out, but the young McGills and Lynne and the little boy and the baby disappeared, and I felt as if I was floating up out of my body and looking down. I could see the home and the woods, the bridge and the huttie, Rough House and the Rocking Stone, Stig in the garden and Walter covered with a sack, waiting until the hole was dug. I could see Mrs. Best and Duggie in town, both sitting alone and worrying; Angie and BJ in the hotel, locked together and hating each other; Rain and Sun Irving up at Borgue, locked together and loving each other still; Sally Jameson and her sister in the big white house in Moniaive tending to their mother; Scarlet in Perth, waiting for Rosie; those poor McAllisters wherever they were, and the car park overlooking the prison and the Hermitage up at Dunkeld; and April Cowan, who had started it all.

I could see all of them, except one. I had known all along someone was missing. But who was it? And where were they?

"Earth to Gloria," Lynne was saying.

I cleared my throat. "Sorry!" I said. "Miles away. What's the name?"

"Huh, well," said Theresa McGill. "Just as well this one forgot the forms yesterday because we changed our minds overnight. We were on Morgan yesterday, but then last night we started looking up meanings as well and we've settled on Zöe."

"What does Zöe mean, like?" asked Lynne.

"It's Greek," said Theresa. "It means Eve. So we've got Adam. And Eve!"

"We like the sound of it too," said Leo. "We wouldn't give her a minging name just because it matched."

"Eve," I repeated. Lynne gave me a careful look. The McGills couldn't see what I was doing from where they sat. No doubt they thought I was firing up the system to take their details, but really I was Googling. BABY NAME MEANING, I typed. And when I got to the site, I entered GIRL and then FRONIA and then stared at what it told me. There it was in dark pink letters on a pale pink screen and everything fell into place.

TEACHER, it said. An ugly name chosen for its meaning alone.

Somehow I registered little Zöe Morgan McGill and got the happy family out of the office again.

"Is there anything I can do to help?" said Lynne, as the door was closing behind them. I shook my head, dialling as I did so.

The phone rang out again and again until the answering machine kicked in.

"Stig?" I said.

"Who?" said Lynne.

"Pick up," I said. "It's Gloria. Oh my God, please God, tell me you haven't gone to the cops already." And then I heard the blessed sound of the handset being lifted and felt the tone change from the hissing tape to the warmth of a real connection.

"Glo?" he said. "Of course not. I'm still writing notes. I haven't even started with Walter. Why?"

"Well, rip them all up," I said. "And listen."

I told him, and Lynne because she was hovering. I told him how much I was kicking myself for not seeing it before. The hand of woman was everywhere, although the woman was missing. Jo-jo's wife Fronia who met the family only once and disappeared forever once he was dead, not leaving a single photograph behind her. The concerned stranger who brought Scarlet's baby home again after snatching the pram for the third time. The secretary who was the Irving girls' only contact with that wholly fictitious agency. Alan Best's girlfriend who supposedly let her daughter be groomed and then spoke out in gossip and rumour instead of police reports and legal action. The fake April Cowan sending Stig the texts, calling him Stephen. The business partner supposedly helping the real April set up in herbal therapies. And last but not least, Duggie's new girlfriend, so out of his league, so forgiving of all his failings, so willing to work late and use his computer, so happy to meet his son.

There, I lost control of my voice and had to breathe in and out for a minute or two, trying to swallow the bile rising in me. She had met Nicky. She had kissed him and touched his hair.

"And what about the McAllisters?" said Stig.

"We'll never know," I told him. "But we can be sure that she got her hooks in them, one and then the other. And she killed them. I bet she was put on remand. I bet she spent at least one night in Cornton Vale prison and that's why Nod died there."

"But how could Miss Naismith be Duggie's new girlfriend?" said Stig. "He'd recognise her. We all would."

"What?" I said. "Like you recognised me with different clothes and hair? You said she was a tie-dyed hippie. Hairy legs and no make-up. And it was nearly thirty years ago. A nose job, hair dye, different style. Think, Stig. Zöe — is it possible?"

"But she'd be too old."

"No," I said. "You're wrong. We always thought our teachers were old, but if she was just out of college twenty-eight years ago, she'd only be nudging fifty now. Zöe could be fifty any day."

"But how could she do it?" said Stig. "A flat in London and all the drugs and a honeymoon in France. Year after year. How could she . . ." He spoke slower and slower and then stopped talking completely.

"What is it?" I said. I could hear papers rustling on the other end of the line.

"I'm looking at the dates, Glo. I was setting it out for the cops when we thought that my dad — My God, if I'd gone to the cops and said that about my own father!"

"What *about* the dates?"

"They're spaced out," said Stig. "It starts with Scarlet's baby in 1989. That took care of both Scarlets, really. The weather girls' modelling-turned-drug-habits and Cloud's 'therapy' took up the early '90s. Nod was '95, Ned that same year. Bezzo's troubles started around 2000, but they dragged on. Jo-jo's whirlwind romance with Fronia was in 2005. I think you're right. They're spaced out like that because it's one person doing it. And she needed time for the campaigns. After Jo-jo she moved on to April, and through April she was going to start on me. I was supposed to be hauled in for April's murder."

"Except you threw a spanner in the works," I said. "She must have been seething about you going to ground. I can't believe she held it together when you showed up at Duggie's last night. I mean, she got out pretty quick, but she was calm."

"And finally Duggie," said Stig.

"I wonder why he was last."

"That's a really good question, Glo. Do you think she had something different planned for him before you started sticking your oar in? But then she had to fall back on a re-run of the Alan Best routine, because you were right there, getting in her way?"

"Me?" I said.

"You went to the shop the day after April was in the huttie," he said. "You asked her about it. Of course you were getting under her skin. I mean, for God's sake, Gloria. She came round to the house in the night and left those footprints around the stone, didn't she? She must have been wearing borrowed shoes — maybe Duggie's — but it was her."

"You think she's targeting *me*?" I said, and I knew my voice was tiny. I couldn't seem to get any breath behind it. "What would she do to hurt *me*?" The question hung between us until the silence was deafening.

"I'm on my way," said Stig and crashed down the phone.

THIRTY-ONE

"Glo?" said Lynne. "You've gone pure white."

I didn't answer. I was dialling again. Iveta answered.

"Hello," she said. "I'm sorry you're not well. Is it the stomach bug?"

"Who said I wasn't well?" I whispered. "Iveta, listen. It's about Duggie's girlfriend, Zöe. If she comes, you're not to let her in."

"Oh, Gloria," Iveta said. "Don't be like that."

"Iveta, listen to m—"

"Everyone likes her. Except for you-know-who. *She* seems to have a problem, but then she has a problem with everything in this world."

"Iveta!"

"But Zöe doesn't even mind Miss Drumm. She stayed for an hour last night and she's been here for an hour this morning alread—"

Nicky!

I was up out of my seat, out into the street, into the car and away, leaving Lynne spinning behind me. Never had the miles from work to the home seemed so long, the roads so humped and twisting, the corners so many and so very tight.

Nicky!

I rounded the last corner before the drive and slammed on the brakes to keep from running into Stig, who was pounding up the middle of the lane, his arms pumping and legs going like pistons. I screeched to a halt and flung open the passenger door, taking off again before he was fully inside.

"She's there," I said. "I phoned. She's there now."

I drove the car up as close as I could get to the home's door, hit the brakes, pulled the hand brake, and left it there, flying into the home with Stig behind me.

"Call the p—" I shouted, then saw Deirdre sitting there. I swallowed the shout and looked around. Donna was hurrying towards me along the passageway.

"Gloria?" she said. "I thought you were ill."

"Dial 999, Donna," I said, keeping my voice quiet but making it very firm. "The woman who's with Nicky is here to harm him."

Then I grabbed Stig's arm and dragged him along the corridor the other way, heading to Miss Drumm and Nicky and saying prayers under my breath that I hadn't said for years.

"She came with his dad!" Donna called after us. "He's on as next of kin after you!"

I ignored her.

The door to Nicky's room was locked, but Miss Drumm's was open and the connecting door stood open too. I glanced at her bed as I passed it and hoped against hope that it wasn't the way it looked, that it meant something else the way she was lying there with her eyes open and her mouth wide, not moving.

I stopped in the doorway and grabbed Stig to stop him too. Zöe was sitting in the chair beyond the bed, with one hand on Nicky's IV line and the other holding open the book.

"I wondered if you might be joining us," she said. "I half expected you last night. I had an hour last night, Gloria, once that old bag next door had finally shut up and gone to sleep. A whole hour, just me and Nicky. I could have done *anything*. Where *were* you?"

"Don't hurt him," I said. "Nicky, don't

worry, darling, Mummy's here."

Zöe rose and put her mouth very close to Nicky's ear and then she bellowed at the top of her voice. "Don't worry, Nicky! Mummy's here!" She shouted so loud that when she sat down again her face was red and she was panting. "I'm not sure he can hear you, Gloria," she said.

"You bitch," said Stig.

"But look on the bright side," she went on, as if he hadn't spoken, "I'm not sure I can hurt him."

Stig made a move but I kept hold of him, trying to make my arm as strong as steel.

"Please don't," I said. "If she rips out the line, the seizures will start in minutes. Seconds maybe."

"You wouldn't do that, Miss Naismith," said Stig. "Not with us here watching. You'd never get away."

"Stop it, Stig," I said. "Look behind you."

"Oh, yes," said Zöe. "Old Miss Shouty Face. I had to shut *her* up. And nobody's even been in to see her since I did."

I could feel tears beginning to form and fill my eyes and fall. "What did you do to her?" I said. "She's just an old blind lady who can't walk. Why did you hurt her?"

"But my God she can *talk,*" said Zöe. "She recognised me, you know. From years ago. I only came to scope things out, looking for a way to get to Dougall. But obviously I thought wrong. There was no point coming at him through his son when his son meant nothing to him, was there? And I'm glad I didn't now, because if I'd used this to hurt Dougall it wouldn't be here for me to use hurting you. Anyway, yes, I'm afraid the old girl got the pillow. And then we had some peace to read our lovely book, didn't we?" She spoke to Nicky in a stupid sing-song voice, as if he was a dog or a baby.

"We're almost finished, aren't we?" she said. Then she pressed the book open and started reading. " 'When the golden day is done, through the closing portal —' "

"No!" I wailed.

" 'Child and garden, flower and sun, vanish all things mortal.' "

"Please, I'm absolutely begging you," I said. "Why are you doing this? Why did you do this?"

"Come in and close the door then," she said. "Lock it behind you. We can have a nice chat, but not with that door open so people can come and disturb us." She was still using the sing-song voice and I wanted to scream from the sound of it.

"Come on, Glo," said Stig. "Do what she says."

And so we stepped fully into the room and closed the connecting door, pulling the bolt, shutting ourselves off from help, putting ourselves at her mercy. Even as we did it, I could hear footsteps behind me. The police already? It was too soon. And then voices, Donna and Iveta, talking and then shouting, running. They'd found Miss Drumm at last. At last, they'd get help. The police would come and they'd stop this. Somehow. With a megaphone or they'd talk to her through the closed door how they were trained to. They'd do it. They had to.

"You fucking children," Zöe said. "You lied about me. I was going to do so much for you all. Making the school lovely. Letting you do woodwork and art and dancing. I had it all planned, and you ruined it. You were shits. Every last one of you. Sleekit, evil little shits. Your lies lost me my clearance. I lost my job; I lost my reputation. I was arrested and put in a cell overnight because no one believed what I was saying and the police thought I was covering something up. For four fucking years I had to go and speak to a *social worker* and go to *classes* because of you."

"Probation," said Stig. "That's why nothing happened until you went after Scarlet in '89."

"Probation," she hissed. "I had done *nothing wrong.*"

"Yes, you had," said Stig. "You left us out in the woods. I know you did. I heard you in your cabin. You had a bath and you had music on."

"So I decided that if I was going to be *punished* for harming children, then I was fucking well going to have all the fun of harming them."

"Fun?" I said. "You're a monster."

"No," she said, suddenly loud. "I'm the victim here." She was beginning to sound agitated, and I couldn't drag my eyes away from her hand on the IV line.

"But I heard you!" said Stig. "You're lying."

I squeezed his arm, trying to signal that he should go easy, not upset her anymore. But his challenge made her smile and, if anything, she sat back a little. She let the book drop to the floor.

"Oh-ho! This is going to be good," she said, and then she really grinned at him, her mouth so wide that white lines formed like brackets around it. "No, you didn't hear me," she said. "That wasn't me. That was your father. He always had a bath to wash me off before he went back to that lipless bitch."

"My dad?" said Stig.

"Why do you think he opened a school?" she said. "It was a present for me. It was all for me, and when he ditched the bitch he was going to run it with me. We had it all planned, and I worked really hard to get it started, and then you spoiled little brats ruined it for me." I almost felt sorry for her just then; she had swallowed the biggest lie men ever tell. She had believed he was going to leave his wife. "So it didn't make sense," she said, "why he wouldn't back me up. Why he wouldn't say where he was that night and say I went traipsing out there to ask if the little shits were having enough precious fun."

"But it was your idea," I said, thinking it through. "You wanted them out of the way so that BJ would stay overnight. While Miss Drumm wasn't there to see him. Don't call them little shits for doing what they were told to."

She glared at me and her hand tightened on the line again. I might have been imagining it, but I think she even gave it a little tug.

"So I decided that if he wanted it that way, it would cost him."

"*You* blackmailed him!" said Stig.

"I was paid for my services. I took the

blame and so I took the rewards too."

"But he can't have been paying to stop you telling my mum," said Stig, frowning, "because my mum knows."

"Oh, that was delicious," she said, and she gave a little wriggle of pleasure that sickened me to see it. "That was years ago. He came clean to the bitch and announced to me that the bank was closed. Idiot. I put him straight about that. I reminded him he'd known the truth about the death of a child for ten years and not reported it. He had been there that night and he lied and told the cops he was at home. He knew I went out to check on them and he lied and let the cops believe I hadn't. And who knew better than me what happens to you if you lie about the night a child died? There was no way out of it for him then. Never mind after the rest of them. And you were going to be the grand finale, Stephen. When his own son was in danger, he'd have to tell the truth at last. Out it would all come. All the deaths, all the secrets, all the grubby little lies."

"You're joking," said Stig. "You think my dad would ruin his life for me? You picked the wrong son, love. You missed the mark there."

She didn't like that, not one little bit. Her face grew pinched again and her eyes narrowed. It was more to distract her than anything else that I spoke again.

"So you're saying Eden was a present to you from your lover, something to keep you sweet and somewhere for him to visit you? But he abandoned you after Moped died. So you blackmailed him for years. And you spent the money on a modelling agency, and a flat in London and drugs, and a honeymoon in France and —"

"Well, well, well," said Miss Naismith. "You've been busy, haven't you? Modelling agency! I gave some guy on Castle Douglas High Street twenty quid to hand a business card to that little trollop and tell her she was pretty. That's all the modelling agency ever cost me, and they did all the rest of the work themselves. And LetzGo was a budget operation too."

"What?" said Stig.

"The anti-paedo vigilante group," I told him. "You started that too?"

"And April the Cow's bloody reiki therapy crap," she said. "At least I've managed to off-load all that to some sucker on eBay and recoup my expenses. And Nathan and Edmund didn't cost me anything. Unless you count the nips and tucks so's they wouldn't recognise me."

"What did you do to them?" I asked.

"Don't," said Stig, miserably.

"Why, I'm glad you asked," she began.

I fired another question at her to stop her from telling us. Stig was right; it would be better never to know.

"Why did you save Duggie till last?" I said.

She was smiling again. "You really don't know? You were married how long and he didn't tell you?"

"I have no idea," I said. I guessed that would make her talk. She liked showing off, liked knowing best. I was right.

"Of all the evil little shits at that school, he was the worst of all," she said. "Playing the innocent the next day, getting them all to lie for him."

"What did he do?"

She took a deep breath as if to deliver a long speech.

But a hammering came at the door before she could say a word.

"Ms. Harkness? Are you all right in there? This is the police, ma'am. Speak up and tell us you're okay."

Zoë stood up and kicked the chair away from behind her.

"Go away," I shouted. "You're not helping."

"We need to hear that you're all right, ma'am," said the voice. "Who's in there with you?"

Zöe was fumbling with the window behind her, at full stretch between her hold on the IV and the latch she was trying to open.

"I'm coming over," I said to her. "I'll keep my hands on my head and only take them down to open the window for you."

"Ms. Harkness?" said the policeman outside. "We know you're upset. We know you're under a lot of strain. You're not in any trouble, ma'am."

"Jesus Christ," muttered Stig. "What did that nurse tell them?"

I was walking very slowly over to the window with Zöe's eyes on me. When I got there, I waited with my hands on my head until she stepped back as far away from me as she could get, far beyond my reach unless I lunged. Then I put one hand down and unscrewed the ball and cup lock on the old sash and opened it as wide as it would go.

"Ms. Harkness?" said the policeman again. "We need you to open this door. We only want to help you." Then he said in a softer voice. "Talk to her, sir." What I heard next turned my blood cold.

"What's up, Gloria?" said Duggie's voice. "Zöe called me."

"Its *her*, Duggie," I screamed. "It's not

Stig's dad. She's going to hurt him."

"Back across the room now," said Zöe.

"Your husband came to help you, Ms. Harkness," said the policeman again. But that didn't sound like Duggie to me.

"Back you go," Zöe said. And I stepped away slowly, still facing her.

"Duggie, for God's sake, tell them," I shouted. "I'm begging you."

"Tell us what, sir?" said a policeman.

"No idea," Duggie said. "She's been under a lot of strain."

Zöe gave me a gleeful look. "You weren't listening to me," she said, in a worse sing-song than ever. "Those kids said I harmed them, and so I harmed them. You've just said I'm going to hurt him." She grinned, yanked the IV, and then launched herself through the open window like a missile.

I sprang across the room as Stig hurled himself past me and scrambled out of the window after her.

It was still okay at the input end — the bag, the drip chamber, and the line all secure — but the port in his chest had been dislodged, the needle half out, a little blood beginning to seep along the edges of the dressing that held it against his skin. Outside the door they were shouting, the policeman and Duggie, and I could hear Donna's voice too.

"Break it down," I shouted, then I concentrated on what I had to do. I held the port hard against him, ignoring the crunch of it on his breastbone, and I pulled the needle out. Then, careful not to touch it or breathe on it, I held it up while I popped the seal on the extra port in his left arm, plugged it in swift and sure, grabbed his hand, and watched him, not even glancing at the door as it creaked and cracked from the policeman kicking it.

"Donna!" I shouted. "She yanked out his sedative. I've put it back in, but he needs to be checked. His chest port's weeping." Then I kissed his head, hoisted myself through the window, and ran.

THIRTY-TWO

I knew where they'd be going, and I knew the quickest way to get there too. I crashed through the woods, ignoring the roads, ignoring the paths, ignoring the thorns and twigs that scraped at me. I was almost at the bridge when I caught sight of them, just a flash of Stig's grey sweatshirt between the trees. I ran faster, ignoring the ragged burning that tore at my chest.

Now I could see both of them on the bridge and they were struggling, her hand clawing at his face and her leg hooking in around his, trying to unfoot him. He leaned back to get away from her nails, those pink and white nails, rimmed in red now as she gouged at him. He leaned further, she lunged, and then he was over the handrail and falling.

"Stiiiiig!" I screamed and leapt forward. She came full at me and could have tipped me over without even having to try, because

I was numb and stumbling. Instead she brushed past me, shoving me roughly with one shoulder, and then she was gone. "Stig!" I screamed again, bending over the bridge rail. I could see him far below, thrashing and wallowing in the water. I looked desperately to the steep banks at either end and took one step up onto the ledge to follow him, but then my mouth fell open and I blinked in amazement, looking down.

He had stood up, water coursing off him, his hair plastered down and his clothes dark. He had lost his glasses and his face looked naked as he stood there gazing up at me.

"How did Moped drown in this?" he called up. He waded under the bridge to the other side, and I crossed over it to see where he was going. "How did he drown in three feet of water?"

"They always say you can."

"Not Moped," said Stig.

"Maybe . . ." I said, but I couldn't finish it, because I didn't know. "You need to get out of there before you freeze to death." Stig nodded and began to wade, heavy-legged, to the edge and then pull himself up, holding on to tussocks of bracken and hauling his exhausted wet weight up the bank to stand beside me.

"How could anyone ever have believed Mope fell off that bridge and drowned?" he said.

"Because he was in there and he was dead," I told him. "And everyone else was tucked up in their sleeping bags, so it was the only story that made any sense."

"Only they weren't and it doesn't," he said.

I shrugged off my cardigan and draped it around his shoulders. "Come on," I said. "You're freezing."

But Stig turned away and began to fight through the brambles and bracken until he was twenty feet downstream from the bridge. He seemed to be searching for something.

"What is it?" I asked him.

He stood up with a round smooth pebble in his hand, looked up at the tree branch above him, shuffled a few steps along the bank, took aim and threw the pebble into the water. It made a deep, plunking noise, almost like a gulp, and disappeared, just the rings spreading out to show where it had been.

" 'See the rings pursue each other,' " I said. " 'All below grows black as night.' "

"I'm beginning to see what happened," Stig said, then he gave an enormous shudder. "I need to go and get dry clothes."

"I'm going back to see if Nicky's all right," I said. "I don't care where she is or where she goes. You're okay; that's the main thing. And I can't run anymore. I can hardly walk."

"Open your shed and get my car out," said Stig. "We're closer to Rough House than the home." And so we both turned for the path out of the woods, me limping and Stig squelching. We had got out onto the lane when an engine sounded behind us and a horn tooted. I turned round to see Duggie in his Volvo.

"They've got her," he said. "The backup car coming in from the other road-end intercepted her."

"How's Nicky?" I asked. "Is he okay?"

"He's sitting up in bed playing with his X-box and eating crisps," said Duggie. "For God's sake, Gloria, he's the same as ever. It would have taken about half an hour for the sedatives to wear off. If you hadn't been so hysterical she'd never even have got as far as she did."

"Don't speak to her like that," said Stig. He was shivering even harder now, not small movements like shivering usually is, but violent jerks that shook his whole body.

"Open up, Duggie," I said "And give us a

lift to the house."

He cast a look at Stig's dripping clothes and then one at his upholstery, and his face was twisted up with a wry smile as he popped the locks and let us in. We both slid into the back seat. I put my arms around Stig and draped one of my legs over him.

"Christ, Gloria," said Duggie.

"For the warmth," I said. "He fell off the bridge, like Moped did. He'll be lucky not to get hypothermia."

"Except Moped didn't," said Stig. His voice was shaking so much I almost didn't catch what he said, but Duggie heard it. I knew he did because the car swerved suddenly and then he braked too sharply before he righted it again.

"What are you on about?" he said.

"I didn't understand why she saved you till last," Stig said. "Even my dad's payback wasn't the grand finale. That was you."

"Why who saved me?"

"Christ, haven't you worked it out yet?"

"What's *that*?" I said, peering out of the side window. We were almost at Rough House now, past the last cattle grid, and I could see something that didn't make sense to me.

"Worked what out?" said Duggie, in that sneering voice of his. "Are you trying to get your dad off?"

"What *is* that?" I said, looking at a black haze in front of the house that shouldn't have been there.

"I think Naismitth was scared of you," said Stig, and the car jolted again. We were coming alongside the garden wall now, almost there.

"Oh God!" I cried out. "No! Duggie, stop the car. Walter!"

It was crows, a cloud of ravens and crows, swirling and cawing and endlessly pecking at the sack-covered hump that lay on the grass waiting for the hole that Stig never finished digging.

"Get away!" I yelled, bursting in through the gate and rushing at them, waving my arms. "Leave him alone." Almost lazily, the birds on the ground hopped back and then lifted off, and the whole cloud of them flapped away into the trees. "Oh, Walter," I said, feeling my legs go from under me, so that I was sitting down beside him. "Walter."

Stig came over and stood beside me, stroking my shoulder.

Even through my sobs, Duggie's footsteps sounded so peculiar that I turned away from the poor old dog, pulling the sack back over his pecked face and turned, watching Duggie strolling so casually towards us across the gravel and up the steps.

"Why would she be scared of me?" he said.

"Because she saw what you did," said Stig. "She said all along that she had come out to check on us at eleven. Then, when she got really hysterical, she said she'd come out twice. She'd come out again. In the early hours. I get it now. She was telling the truth, wasn't she?

"When my dad drove away she came out to check us again, but she didn't get any further than the bridge because she saw what you did there and she was terrified by you. That's why she was so blank and stilted when she heard the news. She already knew, didn't she, because she saw it."

"All very interesting," said Duggie. "But complete bollocks."

"In the morning, when we all came back with the news — except it wasn't news to her — she realised what a mistake she'd made not raising the alarm right away. When you all turned on her and started telling lies about her, she couldn't believe it. That's why she was so completely crazy. She covered for you, Duggie, and you dropped her in it."

"But she'll tell them now, won't she?" I said. "Zöe."

Duggie's face drained of all color.

"Of course she will," Stig said. He was almost laughing, or the shudders were making it sound that way. "The penny's just dropped this minute. He's not very bright."

"Did you throw Moped over the bank?" I said.

"No," said Stig. "That's not what happened. We all saw the clue to what happened when we were crossing the bridge in the morning to go back to the school. We all saw it and none of us realised what it meant."

"Zöe is Naismith?" said Duggie. He walked over to the Rocking Stone and leaned against it.

"What did you see?" I asked.

"The Tarzan swing," said Stig. "It was hanging down over the water instead of being hooked over the tree at the edge so we could use it. It was hanging straight down. He was on the Tarzan swing, wasn't he, Duggie?"

"I don't see what difference that makes," I said.

"And Duggie was there," said Stig. "How long did it take?"

"He came to try to scare me at eleven o'clock," Duggie said. "And I chased him. He went to the swing. I managed to snatch

443

his coat, just grab a handful, enough to slow him down."

"So he couldn't make it to the other side," said Stig. "And you broke the rule."

"What rule?" I asked.

"We had another rope," said Stig. "And if anyone did a bad swing and got stuck, the rule was you had to fling them the rope and pull them back in."

"He begged me," said Duggie. He rolled around until both his shoulders were against the stone, letting his head fall back. It almost looked like a relief to him to be telling it at last. "On and on for hours. Snivelling and begging and pleading. Everything *but* apologising, and that's all I asked him to do."

"Hours?" I said. "He was just a little boy, Duggie. How *many* hours?"

"It was his choice," Duggie said. "All he had to do was apologise, but he just hung there, swinging around and threatening me. God, who was he not going to tell? Then he went quiet, must have dozed off. And he just let go, slipped down, didn't make a sound. Didn't even make a sound when he hit the water. God knows how long it took, but it was just before the car engine, that I can tell you."

"Five hours," I said. "You stood there and

watched for five hours while a little boy clung onto a rope."

"All he had to do was say sorry."

Stig and I were silenced then.

"And I went in after him," Duggie said.

"You tried to save him?" I asked in a small voice.

"Of course."

"Bullshit," said Stig. "You were bone dry when you woke me."

"All right," said Duggie. "I took my clothes off first. So maybe it's fairer to say I went in to drag him under the bridge. Not really to save him exactly. What's the difference in the end? He was probably dead already."

He shrugged, then he took a deep breath and swung round to face us again and something about the series of movements . . . Well, I had been wondering since he first leaned against it. But that was only a few minutes at most, nothing like five hours, and he was a grown man, not a little boy. I heard the grating as the rock started to move and then a cry of panic, but I didn't see it. I had turned back to Walter, stroking his soft ears for the last time and holding one of his big velvety paws.

POSTSCRIPT

We left Scotland. Stig had lost his job already, and I lost mine too. They were sympathetic up to a point, but between the misuse of the computer records and the two times I skipped off that week, there was no way for them to carry on letting me be a registrar. It's a very responsible job. People have to trust you.

And it's not as though either the Tarrants or my family were enough of a tie to keep us there. We don't miss them, and Wee J comes to see us with his wife and the kids when he can. We've settled in North Yorkshire, by the sea. Plenty of tourists to eat Stig's food and plenty of long walks on the moors for us to work off some of what we eat ourselves. That's the idea anyway.

I like having the border between me and Duggie and Zöe — Janice Naismith, actually. She's back in Cornton Vale for a lot longer than an overnight stop this time, but he's still in Castle Douglas in the carpet shop.

The Rocking Stone didn't kill him, but at least for a minute he thought it was going to. And he didn't do time. He was twelve as well, after all, and failing to save someone isn't the same as killing them.

Mrs. Best has moved, maybe to get away from Duggie, but I like to think she's gone to Perth to wait with the other Scarlet in case her grandchild ever gets in touch.

Old Mrs. Jameson was too far gone to be told about Jo-jo, but the two remaining Irving girls took the news about Cloud quite well. They sold their story and used the money to straighten things out a bit. I only hope the money lasts and they stay that way.

The reason I know all this is that we didn't leave straight away. We stayed right there in Rough House for Nicky's last months. And I read him the whole of Harry Potter and The Hunger Games series, and Stig read him some things that he wouldn't tell me about and I didn't ask. Because he's probably right about lads of fifteen, and what harm could it do?

And of course I didn't have to find another home when Miss Drumm died and her heirs swooped in and sold up, because there was only one heir and it was me. So they all had plenty of time to find another place, Deirdre and Mr. Lawson and the rest of them. And after all that had happened, no one was sorry to go.

It never occurred to me to keep Milharay, or even Rough House, even though I'd been so happy there. Not that I believe the tales. Someone died in those woods once, hundreds of years ago, and the Drumms demolished the bridge and used the stone to build a sanctuary. Then Miss Drumm's father put in a footbridge and eventually, when it fell into disrepair, the children of Eden mended it. With old wood from breaking up the benches in the hallowed place. Not that I believe it, as I say. And I haven't heard from Lynne or Donna that the sky's come down from no one rocking the stone either.

So the whole Milharay estate is on the market and when it sells, if it sells, maybe it'll be a hotel or a conference centre or a retreat. Or maybe it'll *never* sell. It'll just sit there, the trees growing taller and undergrowth choking the paths. And the roof will cave, and the walls will fold, and brambles will cover the huttie, and the bridge will fall into the river, and on the river will flow.

ACKNOWLEDGMENTS

I would like to thank: Terri Bischoff, Nicole Nugent, Beth Hanson, Kevin Brown, Bill Krause, Mallory Hayes, and all at Midnight Ink; my agent, Lisa Moylett, once again; my family and friends, more than ever; Richard and Cathy Agnew for the ten years I spent living in Gloria's house; my late beloved step-grandmother-in-law, Laura McRoberts, who inspired Miss Drumm; Stuart Campbell, English teacher and RLS scholar; the real Mandeep Bhullar, vet extraordinaire; and Margaret Kenny, for help with the details about Scottish registrars.

FACTS AND FICTIONS

The towns, villages, and hamlets mentioned in this book are all real places. Close study of a map of the area between Dumfries and Castle Douglas will reveal Milharay Hill and Rough Hill, but the estate itself is fictional, as are the stone, the hallowed place, the devil's bridge, and all the characters depicted here.

ABOUT THE AUTHOR

Catriona McPherson was born in Scotland, where she lived until moving to California in 2010. She is the author of the award-winning Dandy Gilver historical mystery series and is a member of Mystery Writers of America and Sisters in Crime. *As She Left It* was her first modern standalone. You can visit Catriona online at www .catrionamcpherson.com.

The employees of Thorndike Press hope you have enjoyed this Large Print book. All our Thorndike, Wheeler, and Kennebec Large Print titles are designed for easy reading, and all our books are made to last. Other Thorndike Press Large Print books are available at your library, through selected bookstores, or directly from us.

For information about titles, please call:
   (800) 223-1244

or visit our Web site at:
   http://gale.cengage.com/thorndike

To share your comments, please write:
Publisher
Thorndike Press
10 Water St., Suite 310
Waterville, ME 04901

VAN READER RECORD-A

1	11	21	31	41	51	61	71	81	91	101	111	121	131	141	151	161	171	181	191
2	12	22	32	42	52	62	72	82	92	102	112	122	132	142	152	162	172	182	192
3	13	23	33	43	53	63	73	83	93	103	113	123	133	143	153	163	173	183	193
4	14	24	34	44	54	64	74	84	94	104	114	124	134	144	154	164	174	184	194
5	15	25	35	45	55	65	75	85	95	105	115	125	135	145	155	165	175	185	195
6	16	26	36	46	56	66	76	86	96	106	116	126	136	146	156	166	176	186	196
7	17	27	37	47	57	67	77	87	97	107	117	127	137	147	157	167	177	187	197
8	18	28	38	48	58	68	78	88	98	108	118	128	138	148	158	168	178	188	198
9	19	29	39	49	59	69	79	89	99	109	119	129	139	149	159	169	179	189	199
10	20	30	40	50	60	70	80	90	100	110	120	130	140	150	160	170	180	190	200

VAN READER RECORD-B

1	11	21	31	41	51	61	71	81	91	101	111	121	131	141	151	161	171	181	191
2	12	22	32	42	52	62	72	82	92	102	112	122	132	142	152	162	172	182	192
3	13	23	33	43	53	63	73	83	93	103	113	123	133	143	153	163	173	183	193
4	14	24	34	44	54	64	74	84	94	104	114	124	134	144	154	164	174	184	194
5	15	25	35	45	55	65	75	85	95	105	115	125	135	145	155	165	175	185	195
6	16	26	36	46	56	66	76	86	96	106	116	126	136	146	156	166	176	186	196
7	17	27	37	47	57	67	77	87	97	107	117	127	137	147	157	167	177	187	197
8	18	28	38	48	58	68	78	88	98	108	118	128	138	148	158	168	178	188	198
9	19	29	39	49	59	69	79	89	99	109	119	129	139	149	159	169	179	189	199
10	20	30	40	50	60	70	80	90	100	110	120	130	140	150	160	170	180	190	200